Beneath Cold Earth

A Yorkshire Murder Mystery

Tom Raven Book 2

M S MORRIS

ACKNOWLEDGEMENTS

With heartfelt thanks to Clare Stephens for her expert knowledge on the management of nursing and care homes. As well as being the best sister-in-law!

CHAPTER 1

The gaping, toothless hole in the ground that the locals called Old Man's Mouth poured out a steady gurgle of water into a stone trough below the roadside. It was a holy well, named after the mythical giant Wade. Old Man Wade and Bell, his Old Wife, had lent their names to many ancient features on the moors. The spring water mingled with other rivulets cascading down the valley, all heading for the river below.

Detective Chief Inspector Tom Raven emerged from the warm, dry interior of his BMW and set off on foot across the sodden landscape, his leather shoes squelching in the mud. He turned up the collar of his black overcoat against the relentless rain, wishing he'd had the foresight to bring his late father's old Wellington boots which he'd recently unearthed from the back of the understairs cupboard while hunting for a vacuum cleaner.

He ought to be grateful, he supposed. Today it was only raining steadily, a big improvement after a week of Biblical downpours which had caused flooding all across the county. Homes had been inundated, cars washed away, livestock drowned, businesses ruined.

The television news had been dominated night after night by stories of stranded residents in low-lying areas being heroically rescued from their bedrooms, even their rooftops, by the emergency services in inflatable dinghies. York had been especially badly hit, the River Ouse bursting its banks and surging through the medieval streets beneath Clifford's Tower. Elsewhere, intrepid news reporters in cagoules and waders had ventured to stricken towns and villages, thrusting their microphones into the faces of those who had been plucked from disaster, always on the hunt for the most heart-wrenching tales. Any story involving a family pet was always given prominence.

However, the reporters would soon have something else to take their minds off freak weather, insurance claims, and debates about whether global warming was to blame for the rising floodwaters. A new story was about to hit the news. One that could also be blamed on the heavy rainfall. A grim discovery, made in Forge Valley Woods the previous day by a team of conservationists checking the area for storm damage.

Raven made his way down the valley slope from the car park, struggling to keep his balance on the slippery path. A uniformed officer wearing a hi-vis jacket and appropriate footwear for the soggy conditions pointed the way across a wooden footbridge that spanned the River Derwent. Barely more than a quiet stream in the summer months, the waters now raged like a torrent, threatening to submerge the little bridge. Nodding his thanks, Raven crossed the river and trudged on through the woods, the bottom of his trousers now thoroughly soaked.

Ahead he could make out voices, one in particular. Holly Chang, the CSI team leader.

'Bloody hell, Scott, be careful! I nearly fell on my arse.'

Following the sound, Raven skirted a fallen tree trunk, pushed aside some overgrown brambles, and emerged at the site where the crime scene investigators were moving around in their mud-caked jumpsuits beneath a hastily-erected polythene canopy.

On a patch of ground that sloped down towards the river, the torrential rain of the last few days had caused a number of trees to topple, dislodging the soil and exposing tree roots – and something altogether more sinister. None of the CSI team paid Raven any attention, because they were all too busy, carefully scouring the disturbed ground.

As Raven watched, one of the investigators – Scott, presumably – handed Holly a white object caked in mud. She brushed the worst of the earth away before placing it on a table where the unmistakable outline of a human form was gradually taking shape.

Raven stepped closer for a better look.

Yes, once the reporters got wind of this, they'd soon tire of talking about flooded houses and rescued sheep.

An unearthed skeleton was a much more headline-grabbing story.

'Chief Inspector!' Holly had noticed his arrival and looked up to greet him. In her head-to-toe coveralls she was a stout and diminutive figure, at least a foot shorter than Raven. 'Good of you to venture out in this weather.'

Raven couldn't tell if she was being sarcastic. He feared that he may have got off on the wrong foot with Holly on his previous case, when he'd demanded that she and her team work late searching a victim's bedroom for evidence. But he couldn't really be held responsible for that. Unplanned overtime was the nature of the job when you worked in homicide.

She took in his soaked and muddied attire and her mouth curved into a sardonic grin. 'I can lend you some overalls if you like. And I know a good dry cleaner too.'

'I might take you up on that.' Raven's decision, just the previous month, to move back to Yorkshire after being away for over thirty years had been a sudden one – his estranged wife Lisa had called it rash – and he was still finding his way around.

The move had been brought on by his father's sudden death. Raven had travelled north to Scarborough to arrange the funeral and had decided to stay on. In a way it was the path of least resistance. London had lost its appeal, especially since Lisa had left him, and the pull of the old seaside town had been stronger than he'd anticipated. It was in his blood, he supposed. And blood ties ran deep.

'What have you found so far?' He nodded towards the table of bones.

'An adult skeleton, buried about four feet under,' said Holly. 'We're still searching, so we don't yet know how complete it is.'

'Male or female?'

Holly shrugged. 'You'll need to ask the expert.'

'I thought you were the expert around here,' said Raven, trying out some flattery to make up for any previous bad feeling.

Holly narrowed her eyes, obviously suspecting an ulterior motive behind his compliment. 'I arranged with Superintendent Ellis to bring in a forensic anthropologist to examine the bones. Dr Jones was here yesterday supervising the dig.' She indicated the excavation site which was carefully marked out with a grid of string and pegs.

'Oh?' Raven couldn't help feeling somewhat aggrieved that Holly had gone over his head and spoken to his boss without asking him, but he tried not to let his feelings show. Despite all his years' experience with the Met in London, he was still the newcomer here. He'd already ruffled a few feathers since taking up the job, and had vowed to take more care in future.

'Yes,' continued Holly. 'Dr Jones is due back again this morning.'

'Well, when he gets here, I'd like a word with him.'

Holly's mouth twisted into another grin. 'I'm sure Dr Jones will be only too happy to talk to you. In fact, here *she* is right now!'

Raven cringed. He'd made the classic blunder of assuming the gender of the scientific expert. He should have known better. After all, his boss was a woman, the head of the CSI team was a woman, and so too was his sergeant, DS Becca Shawcross. He was well used to dealing with female colleagues and didn't usually make such gross errors.

He turned around and saw a woman wearing a red parka standing behind him, her fur-trimmed hood pulled up around her face, a leather satchel in one hand. Raven judged her to be early to mid-thirties. Her skin was the colour of coffee, and her brown eyes met his with a confidence that told him she was well-respected in her field and quite used to dealing with buffoons like him.

She extended her free hand. 'I'm Dr Jones, from the University of York.' Her handshake was warm and firm. Friendly and professional.

Raven detected a strong southern accent in her voice. What Yorkshire folk would call "posh". It reminded him of all he'd left behind when moving north. In the short time he'd been back in Scarborough he'd already grown used to the flat northern vowels of his home town and suspected that he was beginning to fall back into the way he'd spoken as a teenager. An inflection that his years in London had softened but never eliminated.

'Pleased to meet you,' he said, somewhat self-consciously. 'I'm DCI Raven, SIO. Sorry, that's police jargon. Senior Investigating Officer.'

Dr Jones held his gaze steadily in hers. 'I suppose all professions use their own jargon. Forensic anthropologists certainly do. Even female ones.'

Raven flinched, aware that in his embarrassment he had now compounded his mistake by coming across as patronising. 'About that–'

Dr Jones moved past him and went to examine the skeleton. 'Ah yes, this is what I was hoping you might find.' She picked up a wide, flat bone from the table. 'The ilium.' She produced a metal implement from her bag and began measuring the bone. 'Adult male.'

'You're certain?' asked Raven, surprised that she had reached her conclusion so quickly. In his experience, experts were often reluctant to make such definite pronouncements. And to him, it looked like just another bone.

Dr Jones raised one eyebrow, as if he had cast doubt on her judgement. She held up her measuring tool for him to see. Raven braced himself for a lecture.

'This is called a caliper,' she told him. 'It's used for determining the dimensions of bones.' Next, she lifted the bone itself. 'The iliac crests of the male rise higher than the female's, while the anterior superior iliac spines are closer together. Also, the angle of the pubic arch is noticeably smaller. So, this is definitely the pelvis of an adult male. Women are curvier than men and adapted for childbirth, but they're also perfectly capable of practising forensic anthropology. Any more questions?'

'Look,' said Raven, 'I meant no offence. I'm not some unreconstructed dinosaur.'

A wry smile spread across her face, making her eyes twinkle. 'I'm sure you're not, DCI Raven. Even I don't deal with dinosaurs, although I do specialise in prehistoric remains.'

'Prehistoric?'

A thick lock of black hair escaped the confines of her hood and fell across her eyes before being snatched away by the wind. 'I usually work with much older skeletons. Part of my doctoral thesis involved carbon dating Gristhorpe Man.'

'Sorry, who?'

Her smile turned into open amusement at his ignorance. She had a clear, ringing laugh, but without any hint of mockery. 'Gristhorpe Man is one of Scarborough's most famous residents. He was a Bronze Age warrior discovered in the village of Gristhorpe during the nineteenth century. He's on display in the Rotunda Museum in Scarborough.'

'I shall have to go and take a look,' said Raven.

'I'd be happy to show you one day.'

Raven allowed himself a smile. He sensed that his tentative relationship with Dr Jones was moving onto safer ground after a slippery beginning.

Behind him, Holly cleared her throat. 'Chandice, you said that you usually deal with older remains. Meaning that you think this is modern?'

Once again Raven was wrongfooted. Chandice? How come Holly and the visiting expert were already on first-name terms? Then again, he had only just been introduced to her, and had hardly distinguished himself so far.

'It's difficult to estimate a date just from looking at the skeleton,' said Dr Jones. 'I can tell you that the body was probably buried at least ten years ago. There's no soft tissue remaining, and decomposition of the flesh is total. Beyond that, its age will be difficult to determine. But my hunch is that we're dealing with a modern find.'

'"Modern" meaning what, precisely?' asked Raven.

'Not prehistoric.'

'I see.' Raven was back on familiar territory, where experts stubbornly refused to tell him what he wanted to hear. 'So this man could have died ten years ago–'

'–or a hundred,' concluded Dr Jones. 'Sorry.'

'So what happens next?' he asked.

Before she could reply, there was a shout from the excavation site. 'Found something!' called Scott.

'What is it?' asked Holly.

Scott squelched his way over to them and proudly deposited a small, muddy object on the table.

Holly picked it up and carefully wiped away the grime to reveal a silver coin. She squinted at it. 'It's a sixpence. Looks pretty old to me. Whose portrait is that on the front?'

'It's George VI,' said Dr Jones. 'The current king's grandfather.'

'Is there a date on it?' asked Raven.

Holly turned the coin over. '1945.'

'Well that gives you an approximate timeframe,' said Dr Jones. 'If this was in the dead man's possession, then he must have been buried sometime after 1945, and probably before 1971 when the currency went decimal.'

A window of twenty-six years didn't narrow things down as much as Raven would have liked, but it was better than nothing. 'A historic crime. But within living memory.'

Dr Jones cocked her head to one side. 'You're certain this is a crime, then? A murder?'

Raven looked out across the cold, wet earth of the forest floor. It was a lonely spot, peaceful but isolated. Back when the body had been buried in its unmarked grave, there would have been no carefully-signposted woodland walk, no wooden bridges across the river and no conservation volunteers. Even the parking space where he had left his BMW might not have existed.

In short, it was the ideal location to hide a body.

His gaze returned to Dr Jones's face, drawn there by her dark chestnut eyes. 'Bodies don't bury themselves,' he said.

CHAPTER 2

Detective Sergeant Becca Shawcross parked her Honda Jazz beneath a tall yew and climbed out of the car. The rain of the previous week had abated, to be replaced now by a chilly frost that glittered and sparkled on the lawns and hedges. Becca didn't mind the cold. Freezing weather was part of the deal if you lived in Scarborough, and she was well prepared for it with her thick coat and warm scarf. But she was glad that the flooding had come to an end. Even though Scarborough itself had escaped, many areas of the county had been affected.

It was several days too since Raven had found his skeleton at Forge Valley Woods. Becca still thought of it as "Raven's skeleton" although of course he hadn't actually discovered it himself. The story had been released to the press and had featured briefly but prominently on the local news, and Becca's mum had plied her with questions about it. But Raven was being his usual uncommunicative self and so Becca knew nothing more than what had been reported on the telly. Now the news had moved on again.

Politics. War. Disasters from around the globe. The

usual, in other words.

Becca had little time for following the news herself. Family life and police work took up too much of her time.

Her breath misted in the crisp morning air as she walked along the drive to the entrance of Larkmead Nursing Home.

The nursing home was like a cross between a gothic country house and a Victorian asylum. Situated in the leafy southern part of Scarborough just off the Filey Road, Larkmead was a grand, three-storey redbrick building that boasted a porticoed entrance and a square tower crested by turrets. The windows were huge and looked onto extensive landscaped gardens dominated by gnarled oaks and laurel bushes. A gardener raking fallen leaves on the lawn glanced briefly in her direction before resuming his work.

The gardens were well cared for and Becca imagined it would be very pleasant here in the summer. But on a cold winter's morning, the watery sun cast long shadows across the grounds, shrouding the whole building in gloom. If Becca ever ended up in a care home, she would choose one with open sea views, just like her own bedroom that looked out across the ever-changing coast of the North Sea.

She knew that her own grandparents had a horror of ending up in a home like this. In their view, nursing homes were simply places where people went while they waited to die. It was just as well they were still able to manage in their house in Scalby by themselves, though Becca made a point of popping in to see them whenever she could.

She pushed open the heavy outer door of the home and stepped inside. The sense of a Victorian asylum was even more marked here. A tiled entrance hall hung with oil paintings emphasised the country house feel. A grand sweeping staircase led to the upper floors, although handrails and ramps provided the necessary support for frail and elderly residents and Becca spotted a lift next to the reception desk. The comforting smell of a cooked English breakfast was overlaid with the clinical scent of disinfectant. And compared to the icy temperature outside, coming inside felt like walking into an oven. Becca shrugged off her coat and loosened her scarf before she had taken more than a few steps.

'Can I help you?' A carer in a pale blue nursing tunic and navy trousers greeted her with a smile. The young woman wore her dark hair pinned back in a neat bun and spoke very precisely with a hint of an eastern European accent. Her name badge read *Natalia Kamińska*.

Polish, Becca supposed. She returned the nurse's smile. 'DS Becca Shawcross. I'm here to see Judith Holden.'

'Ah, yes. About Mr Swindlehurst.' A shadow passed across Natalia's face and just for a moment her lower lip trembled, betraying her emotions, but she soon composed herself. 'Judith is manager here. She is in her office. I take you to her. Sign in here, please.'

Becca signed her name in the visitors' book and then followed Natalia down a long corridor. The clink of cutlery and the murmur of voices could be heard from the dining room where breakfast was still being served. Becca, whose parents ran a guest house on North Marine Road, was no stranger to the delights of the full English breakfast. And no stranger to an expanding waistline as a result. Today, however, she'd persuaded her mum that she'd be fine with some cereal and a mug of tea. Now, the smell of fried bacon made her stomach rumble.

Natalia knocked on a panelled oak door and waited to be summoned inside.

'Come in.' Judith Holden looked up as Becca entered the office. She was seated behind her spacious desk, busy typing on her computer. Becca's first impression was of an efficient, well-groomed woman in her early fifties. She wore a green silk blouse, open at the neck, teamed with a gold pendant necklace. Presumably, as the manager, she wasn't actively involved in the day-to-day care of the residents and dressed as befitted her status as the person in charge. Becca could imagine her showing potential newcomers and their relatives around and selling the benefits of the home, like an upmarket estate agent.

'DS Becca Shawcross is here to see you,' said Natalia. She hovered in the background as if unsure whether to stay or go.

'Ah yes. Thank you for coming.' The manager rose to her feet, extending her right hand.

Becca noticed that she wore a gold wedding band on her left hand. 'No trouble, Mrs Holden.'

'Please, call me Judith. We're all on first name terms here. We try to make Larkmead feel like a real home as much as possible. After all, that's precisely what it is to our residents.' She smiled.

Definitely estate agent material. No doubt the care home manager had a sales patter all ready to go, if needed. And now there would be a vacancy for a new resident. Becca wondered if the room had already been allocated.

'Do take a seat.' Judith indicated an L-shaped sofa in the corner of the room. A vase of flowers was arranged on a low table next to it, together with a glossy brochure featuring a smiling elderly couple on its front cover. Becca took a seat and Judith sat down opposite her. Natalia continued to stand by the door, shifting her weight from one foot to the other.

'Judith,' began Becca, 'I understand that there's been a sudden death in the home. One that you think is not due to natural causes.'

Judith nodded, folding her hands neatly in her lap. 'Yes, as you might imagine, with so many of our residents in the twilight of their lives, we are quite used to death here. It is, sadly, very much a part of our routine. But in this case the circumstances are different. It would seem that tragically one of our residents decided to take his own life.'

'I see. What can you tell me about the deceased man?'

'Raymond Swindlehurst was ninety-six. He'd been with us for nearly ten years, ever since his wife sadly passed away. He was one of our longest standing residents.' Judith dropped her voice and leaned forwards confidentially.

'We're doing our best to keep this sad news as quiet as possible. We have no wish to upset our residents. Everyone here is elderly, as you can imagine, and many are quite frail. We need to proceed sensitively.'

'Of course,' said Becca. 'I do understand. Can you tell me how he died?'

Having established that Becca wasn't about to go charging about with all sirens blazing, Judith appeared to relax a little. 'An overdose of paracetamol, mixed with alcohol. He appears to have consumed several packets of tablets. We found the empty packets in his bedside locker, together with an empty bottle of brandy.'

Becca frowned. 'Where would he have got those from?' She was under the impression that medicines were tightly controlled in a nursing home.

Judith shrugged. 'Paracetamol isn't a controlled medication. And residents do enjoy quite a lot of freedom. This is a home, not a prison. We have a minibus that takes the more able-bodied into town or to the garden centre. Raymond could easily have bought paracetamol over the counter during one of those outings. Or someone could have brought them into the home.'

'Did Mr Swindlehurst have many visitors?'

'Not many. He had no family. But I can show you the visitors' book if you like.'

'Perhaps you could tell me a little more about him first? Was there any reason to suppose he might take his own life?'

'None, as far as any of us knew. Natalia knew him better than most.' Judith looked up at the young Polish woman encouragingly.

Natalia still seemed uneasy. She stood silently, her face giving nothing away.

'You cared for Mr Swindlehurst?' prompted Becca.

'Raymond, yes,' said Natalia. She clasped her hands together. 'Raymond was lovely man. Very kind. Always polite. Was true gentleman.'

'How was his state of health?'

'Good. I mean, for ninety-six years. Yes, he took tablets for blood pressure, for cholesterol... like many residents here. But he was fit and' – she tapped the side of her head – 'how do you say? He had his marbles.'

Becca smiled and nodded to show she understood. Her grandparents had lost more than one friend to dementia in recent years. It seemed to Becca like the worst way to go.

'We thought he would live to one hundred,' continued Natalia. 'I never expected this...' She trailed off and her voice caught.

Becca never went anywhere without a wad of clean tissues in her pocket. She fished them out and passed them to Natalia, who blew her nose on one. 'Thank you,' she said when she had recovered her poise.

'Don't worry,' said Becca. 'What can you tell me about Raymond's state of mind? Did he show signs of depression? Had you noticed any change in him recently? Had anything happened that might have upset him?'

Natalia hesitated before replying. She glanced over at Judith, who nodded encouragingly. Natalia looked at the floor as she spoke. 'He was happy man. And popular with other residents. But... he was strange in past few days. Bad weather on news all the time...'

'The flooding,' said Judith.

'It made him sad, I think,' concluded Natalia.

Becca doubted that a spell of heavy rainfall would make someone want to take their own life, but it seemed that Natalia had nothing more to say on the subject. 'Did Raymond have any particular friends at Larkmead? Someone he might have confided in?'

'Violet,' said Natalia immediately. 'He was very close to Violet. She will be very upset, poor lady.'

Natalia's lip was trembling again and Judith rose to her feet hurriedly. 'Thank you, Natalia. Unless the sergeant has any more questions for you...?'

'No, that's all for now,' said Becca, and watched as Natalia gratefully scurried away. 'She seemed very upset,' she said to Judith once they were alone.

'That's only natural. Natalia was Raymond's primary carer.'

'She also seemed nervous.'

Judith sighed. 'I think she blames herself. After all, she was responsible for administering Raymond's medication. But I've explained to her that this wasn't her fault. Raymond obviously went to some considerable trouble to hide what he was planning to do.'

'You think he planned it, then?'

'Buying the paracetamol and the brandy... it indicates some premeditation.'

'I suppose so.'

'You know, suicide among the elderly isn't so uncommon,' said Judith. 'It's rather a taboo subject but in fact suicide rates are particularly high among older males, especially men like Raymond who have no surviving family. They easily get depressed. With nothing to look forward to, what's the point in living?'

Becca made no reply. She thought of her own grandparents who always seemed so cheerful. The idea of an old man being so lonely that he would take his own life was difficult to face. Particularly one like Raymond, who Natalia had painted in such positive terms.

'Would you like to see the body?' asked Judith. 'He's still in his bed. We haven't moved anything.'

'That would be good, thanks.'

Becca followed Judith out of the office and along the corridor. Breakfast was now over in the dining room and the kitchen staff were busy clearing away. In a lounge someone had started playing the piano very loudly and a handful of warbling voices could be heard in a rendition of *The White Cliffs of Dover*.

'On Tuesdays and Thursdays we have music therapy,' explained Judith. 'A wonderful lady comes in to lead the residents in their favourite songs.'

Becca paused for a second to listen. At one level the feeble singing was comic, even tragic. And yet there was dignity there too. Here were men and women gathered together, nearing the end of their days, yet joined in common purpose. They had lived long and full lives and had experienced joys and hardships that Becca could only guess at. But they had been young once, like her. For a brief moment they were young again, reliving long-forgotten hopes and memories through music.

Judith was watching her. 'Even those with the most serious cognitive decline respond well to music. It has the power to reach that part of the brain lost to ordinary speech and memory.'

'It must be very rewarding working here.'

'We like to think we can make a difference.'

They stopped outside a closed door near the end of the corridor. Judith drew out a bunch of keys and unlocked it.

Becca went inside. The room was dim, the curtains drawn closed, and Judith turned on the lights.

Raymond lay in bed, his veined hands crossed over his chest, his eyes closed. His chalk white hair was brushed back from his face. A few sparse white whiskers protruded from his chin. His cheeks were sunken with age, but he had a fine, straight nose and a high forehead. Becca guessed that he would have been very good-looking in his younger days.

The cause of death appeared obvious. The locker drawer next to the bed was half open and inside were four empty blister packs of paracetamol. An empty bottle of brandy stood on top of the locker. But appearances could be deceptive.

Why would a man who was fit for his age, well looked after and with good friends decide to take his own life? It didn't make sense.

'It was Natalia who found him,' said Judith. 'She brought him his morning cup of tea and immediately saw that he was dead.'

Becca nodded, guessing that it was Natalia who had taken the trouble of positioning Raymond's body so that he resembled a king lying in state. It was obvious from what little she'd said that she had cared for him very much.

Becca quickly searched the room, including the writing desk placed before the window, but it appeared that Raymond had left no explanation for why he had taken an overdose.

'I already looked for a note,' said Judith. 'But there's nothing.'

The room offered a few clues to the sort of man Raymond had been. A bookcase well stocked with paperbacks – mostly thrillers and crime novels, a few political biographies. Copies of the *Times* newspaper turned to the crossword page. A small collection of classical CDs and a portable CD player. The only photographs were of a woman, presumably his late wife, and a black-and-white photo of a group of men standing by the seafront, Scarborough Castle just visible in the background.

Becca approached the bed again. Raymond lay beneath the bedclothes as if asleep. Apart from the pale waxy skin and unnatural stillness of the body, it would be easy to imagine that he might awaken at any moment and go downstairs to join the others in their singing.

Leaning in, Becca could clearly smell the alcohol. There were no visible marks on the body, nothing seemed out of place. Everything was exactly as Natalia and Judith had described, except...

Very gently, Becca lifted first one, then the other eyelid. What she saw confirmed her misgivings about the death.

If the post-mortem confirmed her suspicions, then Raymond Swindlehurst had not taken his own life. Instead, the suicide had been staged, and they were dealing with a case of murder.

CHAPTER 3

The doorbell rang promptly at nine o'clock in the morning. Raven had taken a few days off to get his life in "some semblance of order" as Superintendent Gillian Ellis had aptly phrased it. The move to Scarborough had been so sudden and so recent that he hadn't had time to sort out his domestic arrangements. He'd been living out of a suitcase, subsisting on a diet of fish and chips from a takeaway near the seafront, with barely enough clean shirts to see him through the week. All right – there was no point denying it – not enough clean shirts.

But now his temporary secondment with North Yorkshire CID had been made permanent, and he had travelled down to London the previous day to empty his apartment and bring all his gear up to Scarborough.

He had finished washing his breakfast dishes and was about to load his dirty laundry into the machine in the kitchen. Later, he planned to take his suit to the dry cleaners after the previous week's outing to Forge Valley Woods. The visit to the crime scene had left his shoes and trousers caked in mud, but it had been worth it to view the body *in situ* first-hand. It had also been good to make the acquaintance of Dr Chandice Jones. Raven hoped he would have cause to see the forensic anthropologist again during the investigation. He wondered if she might even make good on her promise to show him around the Rotunda Museum sometime.

The doorbell continued to ring and Raven went to answer it, leaving his laundry lying in a heap on the kitchen floor.

'Barry Hardcastle,' said the man standing on the doorstep, holding out a meaty hand. He was about forty, generously proportioned, and dressed in paint-spattered combats and a tight grey T-shirt. The van behind him, blocking the narrow road and pavement of Quay Street, was emblazoned with the slogan *Hardcastle Builders – for all your building and decorating needs*. Well, Raven certainly had plenty of those. The house he had inherited from his father was a wreck, and in urgent need of attention from a man of Barry's profession.

'There's a car park at the end of the road if you want to move your van out of the way,' said Raven.

'Nah,' said Barry. 'It'll be all right for a bit.'

Raven glanced up and down the road, but so far there was no one trying to get past. 'Well, you'd better come in then. Thanks for coming to see me at such short notice.'

'Yeah, no problem,' said Barry, wiping his boots on the mat in Raven's hallway. 'You want me to take these off?' He indicated his sturdy footwear.

Raven looked around at the threadbare carpet that scarcely covered the floorboards. 'No need. It hardly matters.' Raven led him into the living room.

Barry's mouth broadened into a grin as he took in the state of the carpet, furniture and outdated décor. 'All this lot going in the skip, then, is it? Best place, I reckon. You've got a bit of work ahead of you, by the look of it.'

Raven had been given Barry's details by his sergeant Becca Shawcross whose brother, Liam, was into doing up old properties and either selling them on for a profit or renting them out as holiday lets. 'I don't know what he's like,' Becca had warned Raven. 'But Liam uses him regularly, so he can't be too bad.'

Liam had previously recommended a guy to repair the bodywork of Raven's beloved BMW M6 after it had been scratched. The man had given the impression of being a cowboy but had done a good job in the end, so Raven was willing to give Barry a try. It wasn't as if he had any other local contacts. And at least Barry had turned up when he said he would, which was a good start.

'So, what needs doing, then?' Barry's hand now held a pencil and hovered expectantly over a clipboard.

Good question. The answer was *everything*. The house, located a few yards from the harbour in the heart of the old town, dated back to the eighteenth century, possibly earlier. It was a tall, narrow building arranged over three floors and hadn't been refurbished in decades. Raven had grown up here, but after leaving Scarborough at the age of sixteen he had never expected to find himself living here again. Certainly, when he'd returned to arrange his father's funeral, his only thought had been to put the house – the only thing of value that Alan Raven had left behind – on the market as soon as possible.

Yet the lure of his hometown had turned out to be too strong, so here he was.

His wife, Lisa, had been incredulous when he'd told her. 'You won't last long up in the north, Tom,' she'd told him dismissively. 'What are you going to do with yourself in a backwater like Scarborough? You'll be back in London before the year's out.' He had said nothing in reply, refraining from pointing out that she was the one who had walked out on him, leaving him with little reason to remain in the capital. Perhaps she was resentful that he was building a new life for himself without her.

He'd wondered if she would take the opportunity to broach the subject of a divorce, but the topic hadn't been mentioned. Was she still undecided? Having doubts about her accountant lover? Still hedging her bets? Neither of them really knew what the other was thinking. That was half the problem, really. They had forgotten how to talk to each other.

His daughter, Hannah, who was at university studying Law, had sounded much more enthusiastic when he broke the news to her by phone. 'That's cool, Dad. A fresh start. The move will be good for you.'

'Perhaps you could come and visit me sometime?' he'd suggested.

'Perhaps.'

It had been the most positive exchange that he and Hannah had enjoyed in years and had filled Raven with hope for a renewal of the father-daughter relationship. But if he was ever going to have visitors to the house, he would need to make it fit for twenty-first-century living.

'Shall we start in the kitchen?' he suggested to Barry.

'Lead the way, squire.'

On entering the tiny room, where nothing was fitted and everything was mismatched, Barry made no attempt to conceal his amusement. 'You don't see many of these around nowadays,' he said, tapping the top of the antiquated gas cooker with his pencil. 'You'll be chucking this out, I expect.'

'I was thinking of replacing it with an induction hob,' said Raven. Back in London before the split, Lisa had insisted on having all the most expensive appliances fitted in their designer kitchen. He hadn't agreed with all of her interior design choices, but the hob had been an excellent decision.

'Can't go wrong with one of those,' agreed Barry. 'And you'll need an extractor fan to go with it. Building regs have changed a bit since this thing was installed. In fact, whoever did this didn't follow any regulations at all, as far as I can tell.' He produced a tape measure from a back pocket and proceeded to jot down a series of numbers on his clipboard.

They worked their way through the kitchen, living room and downstairs bathroom, discussing what needed to be done. In every room, Barry managed to find jobs that Raven hadn't even considered. 'Damp,' he muttered, rapping the bathroom wall with his knuckles. 'We'll need to replaster this whole room, and repoint the brickwork on the outside.'

'Right,' said Raven.

Barry flicked the bathroom light switch on and off, listening to it crackle as a blue spark flickered behind the faceplate. 'This wiring's out of the ark. Best to get the whole lot replaced before it kills you.'

Raven couldn't disagree. 'Include it in the estimate.' His bank balance was going to fall off a cliff at this rate.

Having established that the house would need a whole army of subcontractors to make it safe and habitable – not just Barry's building and decorating skills, but also the services of a plumber, plasterer, electrician, gas engineer and damp specialist – Raven led the way up the steep staircase to the next floor. He had moved out of his childhood bedroom on the top floor and now slept in his parents' old room, having bought himself a decent bed to replace the one his father had slept in. He was considering turning the guest room on the middle floor into a bathroom, and knocking the downstairs bathroom through to make a bigger kitchen.

'Good thinking,' said Barry. 'I'll just need to take a look at the water tank. It'll be in the attic, I expect.'

Raven had never ventured up into the loft space at the top of the house and had no idea what it contained. It was reached by a trapdoor in the ceiling of the topmost landing, and on pulling it open he was surprised and pleased when a folding ladder lowered itself to the floor.

Barry tested it with a good shake, then proceeded to clamber up it with the ease of a man used to running up and down ladders all day.

Reluctantly, Raven followed him up, grimacing as the familiar twinge in his leg made itself known. Many years ago, he'd taken a bullet while serving as a soldier in Bosnia. The injury had cut short his army career, and had led to him joining the police. Most of the time the old wound was of little bother, but during any kind of physical exertion it came back to haunt him. Now as he lumbered up the creaking rungs of the ladder, he felt that old pain stabbing him in his right thigh.

Poking his head up through the trapdoor, he found Barry crouching amid piles of dusty boxes and old furniture, examining the water tank and its tangled array of connecting pipes and valves. The whole thing resembled a relic from the Titanic.

Barry turned to Raven with a look of dismay on his face. 'What a bloody mess. Know what I think?'

'It will all have to go?' guessed Raven.

Barry nodded gravely. 'You'd be better off with a modern tank. More efficient, better insulated. You'll be saving yourself a fortune in the long run.'

'Add it to the list,' said Raven, resigned by now to footing the bill for a mammoth restoration project on a par with refurbishing the Grand Hotel where his mother had worked.

Barry gestured at the mounds of junk that littered the floor of the attic. 'This lot will have to go before I can start work. Want me to clear it out for you?'

Raven surveyed the broken landscape of boxes, biscuit tins and picture frames with a sigh. Tempting though Barry's offer was, he knew that he couldn't just throw everything away without first seeing what was here. 'No, I'd better take a look at it myself before I get rid of it.'

'Suit yourself. As long as this place is empty before the plumber comes to replace the tank. I don't want him tripping over and putting his foot through the ceiling below.'

After saying goodbye to Barry, who drove off in his van promising to be back in touch "very soon mate, don't worry about that, I can see you're keen to get started", Raven made his laborious way back up to the top of the house and the dusty space of the attic. Having discovered the mess, he knew he wouldn't be able to put off clearing it.

Mess of any kind was anathema to Raven.

He suspected a psychiatrist would have a field day analysing why he was so obsessed with order and cleanliness. No doubt it had something to do with the habit his mother had ingrained in him from an early age of taking care over his clothing and appearance and always looking his best. But it was also deeply rooted in the guilt and self-loathing that he felt about her untimely death, not to mention the effect of growing up in a home with an alcoholic and violent father. Oh yes, Raven's past was fertile ground for a psychiatrist, who would no doubt trawl through his chaotic early years to explain why he had become a police detective and why he was so obsessed with solving his cases, even to the detriment of his home life and personal relationships.

Raven didn't need a therapist to tell him that. Nor did he need one to explain that this was why he had run from Scarborough and spent thirty years away. He certainly didn't need an expert to explain why he was once again clambering up the rickety old ladder to the dirty and cluttered space beneath the rafters.

With gritted teeth he ascended the steps until he was back amid the detritus of past lives. The house had originally belonged to his grandfather, Jack Raven, a fisherman who had drowned at sea. After Raven's grandmother died, the house passed to his father. And now it was his. For all he knew, this attic might contain family heirlooms of the Ravens all the way back to the beginning of the previous century. He'd better get cracking, otherwise he'd be here all day.

It got dark early at this time of year, and the light bleeding through a tiny skylight and coming from the forty-watt bulb hanging overhead was desultory at best. He lowered himself down among the boxes and lifted the flaps of the nearest one, swatting away the cloud of dust that rose up.

Under layers of old curtains and tablecloths, he found

a photo album with a white satin cover, yellowed with age, and embossed with the words *Our Wedding*. The spine creaked in protest as he eased open the album. On the first page, written in a sloping cursive script, were the names of the bride and groom: Muriel Kemp and Jack Raven – his paternal grandparents, neither of whom he had ever known. The album informed him that they were married on the sixteenth of June 1945 in Queen Street Methodist Church in Scarborough. The maid of honour was Jane Kemp, presumably a sister of the bride, and the best man was one Eric Roper. Raven turned a page and there was his grandfather, Jack Raven, in a double-breasted pin-striped suit and spit-polished shoes, grinning like the cat who'd got the cream, with his white-robed bride on his arm. Raven laid the album to one side, determining to take it downstairs and go through it at his leisure.

Most of the boxes appeared to contain nothing but junk – moth-eaten clothes, dried tins of paint and rusted tools. He had no idea how he was going to get all this stuff through the loft hatch and down the ladder. Perhaps he would leave it for Barry after all. In one corner he unearthed a wooden case with a curved top and the word *SINGER* engraved in gold lettering. His heart leapt at the sudden memory. He lifted the lid and there was his mum's old manual sewing machine, black and glossy and decorated with an ornate mother-of-pearl design. He had a vision of her then, sitting in their tiny living room, turning the handle of the machine as she sewed a pair of curtains. She'd made all the curtains in the house. Lightweight curtains for the summer months, thick velvet drapes for the long, dark winters. She'd saved the housekeeping money to buy material, or had accepted hand-me-downs from friendly neighbours. In London, Lisa had spent a fortune ordering made-to-measure curtains for every room, and still she hadn't been satisfied with the result.

It was cold in the unheated attic and Raven's thigh was starting to throb. Opening one more box that had been hidden behind the sewing machine he lifted out a flat cap and then a three-piece suit – trousers, waistcoat and jacket. This must have been his grandfather's demob suit, the one he got married in. There was something else at the bottom of the box, wrapped in an old tea towel.

Raven lifted it out and immediately perceived, from its weight and shape, the nature of the object he held in his hands. Carefully unwrapping the tea towel, he found himself staring at a gun.

A Walther P-38. An iconic weapon, instantly recognisable to an ex-soldier like Raven. A German pistol from World War Two. But still in pristine condition.

How on earth had his grandfather acquired an enemy weapon? And, more to the point, what was it doing in Raven's attic?

CHAPTER 4

'Yes, what is it?'

When Becca knocked on DI Derek Dinsdale's door and entered his office, she could have sworn that he was in the process of booking next year's summer holiday. Either that, or he was busy investigating a crime that had occurred at a resort somewhere on the Algarve or the Costa Brava. Whatever it was, he hastily closed down the website he'd been browsing and adopted an air of distracted helpfulness.

'Ah, DS... um...'

Had he really forgotten her name? Dinsdale ought to be in a care home himself, the way he was going. Becca wished that he'd just hurry up and retire. Retirement was obviously what he wanted. It was what all his colleagues wanted for him too. Perhaps a few more monthly payments into his police pension would see him good to go. It might even be worth having a whip-round in the office to see if they could get him across the line.

'...Shawcross,' he managed eventually. 'How can I help you?'

Becca would much rather have been working for DCI

Raven, despite Raven's infuriating tendency of keeping her in the dark about what he was thinking. At least Raven was dynamic and got things done, instead of hiding behind his desk hoping for an easy ride.

But Raven was busy investigating his mysterious skeleton, leaving Becca reporting to Dinsdale on the suspected murder at the care home. At least, Becca suspected it was murder. The tiny red dots – petechiae – that she had seen standing out like pinpricks in the whites of the dead man's eyes were caused by bleeding beneath the mucous membrane. A classic sign of death by suffocation.

Dinsdale remained convinced that it was suicide.

Suicide involved less paperwork.

'I was wondering if there was any news from the pathologist, sir?'

'The pathologist?'

'Raymond Swindlehurst's post-mortem?'

'Ah. Nothing yet.'

'But you did arrange for it to be done as soon as possible, sir?'

'Yes, of course. But you know what pathologists are like. It'll be done when it's done.'

Becca waited to see whether Dinsdale had any jobs to assign to her. Or any information to share. Or any enthusiasm for the investigation at all.

Nothing.

She squared her shoulders and prepared to rouse his interest in what she had to say. 'In that case I'd like to follow up a lead, sir. I took a copy of the visitors' log at the care home for the days leading up to Mr Swindlehurst's death. On the day he died, he had one visitor. A man called Craig Clarkson. I looked him up online and found that he writes books about local history. His area of interest is World War Two.'

Dinsdale was starting to look distinctly bored. 'Why is this relevant?'

'Well, sir, if Raymond really was murdered, then Craig

Clarkson was the last person to visit him. He may even have been the last person to see him alive.'

Dinsdale groaned. 'I don't know why you're convinced it's not a straightforward case of suicide.'

'Well, that would be because of the signs of asphyxiation, sir.'

'There could be a perfectly reasonable explanation for those. Maybe the result of some medication he was on.'

'It's possible,' said Becca. 'We'll have to wait for the post-mortem results to know for certain. In the meantime–'

'You want to go and speak to a historian.' Dinsdale's eyes were drifting back to his computer screen. Whatever he'd been browsing it was clearly far more interesting than investigating an unexplained death at a care home.

'If you have no objections, sir.'

'No, you go ahead,' said Dinsdale, clearly glad to be offered a quick way out of the conversation. 'Knock yourself out. Ask him all the questions you like.'

'I'll do that then, sir. I'll let you know what I find out.'

Even before she had pulled the door fully closed, Dinsdale's attention had switched back to his computer, and he was already clicking his mouse. She left him to the delights of sun and sand, pushing away the horrifying image that had suddenly entered her head of Dinsdale reclining in a deckchair, naked from the waist up, rubbing sun cream into the soft folds of his flesh.

*

The last time Raven had visited the city of York had been thirty-one years previously when, as a sixteen-year-old lad running away from his home town in search of freedom and adventure, he had got off the train and found himself in the army recruitment centre on Micklegate. There, across the table from a uniformed sergeant with a barrel chest and a voice that could wake the dead, he had signed up to join the Duke of Wellington's Regiment. After completing his training he had been deployed to Bosnia, only to be flown back two years later after a moment of madness – or heroism – left him with a bullet in his leg and the Conspicuous Gallantry Cross pinned to his chest.

Now here he was again, this time in the role of a senior police detective visiting the university to speak to a forensic anthropologist about an ongoing murder enquiry. As he left his car, rubbing his still-aching thigh, he wondered what the young Raven would have made of the way things had turned out. One thing he had learned over the years was that it was impossible to guess the twisty pathway that life had in store for you.

The university occupied a sprawling campus to the south of the city, some distance from the medieval Minster and tourist-filled streets. Set in landscaped grounds around a meandering artificial lake, buildings with radical modernist designs vied for attention with one another. Maybe it wouldn't have seemed so bleak on a bright summer's day, but in early November the grey buildings looked drab, and a gust of wind disturbing the surface of the water seemed to suggest the menacing presence of a junior Neptune about to rise from the shallows.

Dr Jones more than made up for the dreariness of the campus with the warmth of her greeting. 'Glad you could make it.' She clasped his hand and gave him a smile that lit up her face. Today she was dressed in a pair of tight black jeans and a crisp, fitted, white shirt, managing to look both professional and, Raven had to admit, ravishingly sexy at the same time. Nearly a week had passed since the discovery of the skeleton at Forge Valley Woods and she had invited him to go through her preliminary findings. Sealing the deal, she had also promised to brew him an espresso on her Gaggia Classic Pro.

'It's my pleasure,' he told her. 'I'll travel any distance for a good cup of coffee.'

She laughed, her voice tinkling like a bell. 'Come over to my office. I'll get the machine on straight away.'

Raven sensed that their initial misunderstanding was

firmly behind them and they would now get along just fine.

They walked around the edge of the lake, the water reminding Raven of the reason he had come here in the first place. The floodwaters that had ravaged the county had all receded now, but the human remains they had unearthed were somewhere on this campus. He felt a chill run down his spine. In a sense, the grave in which the victim had rested peacefully for so long had been desecrated, the human remains now reduced to evidence to be measured and studied. Every murder case was the same of course. The examination was a necessary part of the forensic process, a prerequisite for obtaining justice for the victim and their family. But still, the thought left him uneasy.

'Good journey?' enquired Dr Jones.

'Great, thanks.' When he'd lived in London, there had never been any opportunity to put the BMW through its paces. But since the move to Yorkshire, he'd taken the car onto the open road a few times and really opened up the throttle. The M6 was seventeen years old, but a real beauty, and still going strong. Its V10 engine was a beast when uncaged, and Raven had been able to put his foot to the floor on the journey here, enjoying the feel of raw power as he overtook slower vehicles on the A64.

Dr Jones's office was located within one of the more restrained edifices on the campus – recognisably building-shaped with reassuringly familiar elements like straight walls, square windows and a roof that wasn't trying to slope in every direction at once. 'Do you like modern architecture, DCI Raven?'

'Call me Raven, please.'

A smile curved her claret-coloured lips. 'You don't have a first name?'

'Everyone just calls me Raven.'

'Well, you can call me Chandice. And don't think you can dodge my question that easily.'

'Modern architecture?' Raven glanced around at the blocks, towers and domes of concrete that clustered around him. 'I think it can be very interesting.'

'You hate it!' She chuckled. 'Well, I love it.'

Raven followed her inside the building, dodging past a group of students emerging noisily from a seminar room. Dr Jones seemed to fit in well with the young crowd and Raven immediately felt his age. Suddenly his earlier joke about being a dinosaur no longer seemed funny.

Chandice seemed oblivious to his discomfort. 'My area of study is very much a cross-disciplinary field,' she explained enthusiastically. 'The department carries out work in bioarchaeology, human and primate anatomy, and we have links with the mass spectrometry centre and the departments of biology and chemistry.'

'Right,' said Raven, nodding sagely. 'Mass spectrometry.'

The smile lit up her face again. 'You have no idea what that means, do you?'

'Not a clue.'

'Well, let me show you something just as technologically advanced, but which you might be able to understand.' She led the way into her office and showed him a gleaming stainless steel machine that occupied pride of place on an area of worktop.

Raven grinned. 'It's the Gaggia. I used to own one just like it.'

'Used to?'

'My wife took it with her when she walked out on me.' He stopped, realising that he'd given away far too much information. It wasn't like him to volunteer anything about his private life. He appeared to have let his usual defences slip in Chandice's company.

She regarded him thoughtfully for a moment. 'Well, I think your wife made a huge mistake there,' she said at last. 'And I don't mean taking the espresso machine, I mean leaving you.'

Raven shrugged. 'Water under the bridge. So, let's see what this beauty can do.'

While she ground fresh coffee and fiddled with the

switches on the machine, Raven sat down on a small sofa and took in his surroundings. Reference books from the field of forensic anthropology filled a bookcase behind the desk. The desk itself was remarkably uncluttered – just a sleek laptop and a pile of papers weighed down with a fossil paperweight. An Egyptian print of the god Anubis hung on the wall, but there were no personal photographs on display. No clues as to Chandice's life outside of work. He realised he was searching for evidence that she might be in a relationship. Or not.

'Here you go.' She handed him a small glass of espresso, the aroma rich and aromatic.

He inhaled and took a sip. 'Delicious, thank you.' The smell and flavour transported him briefly to another age, to a time of his life when he'd thought he was happy. Settled in London, with a wife and daughter. The sensation left him feeling conflicted. He was still a married man. Lisa, for whatever reason, hadn't yet asked for a divorce, even though she had chosen another man instead of him. So what was he doing flirting with another woman? A woman much younger than him.

Because that's what he was doing. Flirting.

He had to admit, it felt like fun.

Chandice sat down at her desk, cradling her own shot in two hands. 'I first learned to love coffee when I was studying for my PhD in Milan.'

'You studied in Milan? Do you speak Italian?'

'Pretty well.'

Raven had encountered super-achieving women like Chandice before. Hell, he had even lived with them. His wife and daughter were good examples of the species. But that didn't mean he didn't find them intimidating. 'And have you worked in Egypt too?' He nodded towards the print.

'Only as an undergraduate. That was many years ago now.' She gave a laugh. 'And it was nothing glamorous like discovering the tomb of a pharaoh. I spent the whole summer cleaning blocks of stone while my supervisor claimed the credit for my finds. These days, much of my time is spent teaching undergraduates, and I supervise a couple of graduate students too. I work with the police sometimes, and I once spent a bit of time in Bosnia at the site of one of the mass graves near Srebrenica, helping to reassemble and identify human remains.'

Raven wondered if he should tell her that he'd been in Bosnia too, during the actual conflict. It wasn't something he ever spoke about. Most people couldn't begin to understand what it was like to be in a war zone so he'd given up trying to explain a long time ago. But perhaps Chandice would understand. She'd at least witnessed the aftermath of the atrocities. He opened his mouth to speak, but couldn't find the words.

'Anyway,' said Chandice, cutting off any possibility that he might broach the subject, 'I expect you're really keen to hear the results of my analysis.'

'Please.' He set the coffee aside and took out his notebook. He rarely needed to use it to take notes, but had learned over the years that its presence encouraged witnesses and experts alike to speak freely.

She took a file from her desk drawer and opened it. 'So the main findings are that Forge Valley Man was–'

'Sorry, who?'

She laughed again. 'I always give my skeletons a name. It helps to distinguish them. And also to remind me that they were once living and breathing people, just like you and me.'

Raven nodded appreciatively. So Chandice understood. These were not just bones in a laboratory. They were the mortal remains of a real person. They mattered.

'Our man was found in Forge Valley Woods, so I named him Forge Valley Man. Not very imaginative, I know, but I'm a scientist, not a novelist. Anyway, in the end an entire skeleton was recovered from the site. In some excavations, parts are missing. Animals sometimes remove pieces of the body, or perhaps part of the body is buried elsewhere. But in this case, the skeleton was complete.'

'That's something,' said Raven. 'At least there won't need to be any more searches.'

'Further examination of the bones has confirmed that the body was indeed male,' continued Chandice. 'He was tall too, a good six foot. Using the length of the femur and humerus I can estimate his height to within five centimetres. The skeletal anatomy indicates that he was what people used to call Caucasian. We no longer talk about race in modern anthropology, but in everyday language you could say that Forge Valley Man had primarily European ancestry. As for age, there are two questions we have to ask. The first is, how long have the bones been in the ground? The second question is, how old was he when he died?'

Now they were getting to the crux. 'Go on.'

'As for dating the find historically, the standard technique is carbon-14 dating. Unfortunately, the margin of error here is about fifty years, so all I can tell you is that the bones are not older than one hundred years.'

Raven had been hoping for a rather narrower timeframe. 'I think we already knew that. Because of the coin. Can't you pin it down any further?' He hoped his question didn't come across as too critical.

But Chandice was obviously used to fielding challenging questions. 'I'm afraid not. But when it comes to the actual age at the time of death, I can be a lot more precise.'

'Okay.'

'To determine the age of a person from their skeleton we need to consider growth and degeneration. In a child or young adult, there would be clear signs of immaturity in the skeletal structure. In a person past their prime, say over the age of forty, there would be obvious indicators of degeneration.'

Raven wondered what kind of indicators Chandice might find if she examined his own skeleton. At forty-seven he was well past his prime according to her scientific definition. Whereas she was still very much in peak condition, at least to his way of thinking. Soft skin, a mere trace of laughter lines around her eyes. Good posture, nice teeth. He tried to refocus his attention on Forge Valley Man.

'So,' she said, 'one of the key indicators that we use is the condition of the pubic symphysis. It's a joint that forms part of the hip bones. The symphyseal surface changes in a predictable way during adulthood, so it's a reliable way of determining age. There are other parts of the skeleton that we can examine too, such as the auricular surface of the ilium. I can tell you with some confidence that our man was aged between eighteen and twenty-five when he died. My guess would be around the middle of that range.'

Between eighteen and twenty-five years old. By Raven's reckoning, that made Forge Valley Man little more than a boy. His bones may have lain beneath cold earth for half a century or more, but when he died he'd been a young man full of vigour with his whole life ahead of him, scarcely older than those students who had jostled past Raven on the way in. Perhaps no older than his own daughter, Hannah.

'That's very helpful. And what about the cause of death? Any way of telling?'

Chandice beamed at him. 'Now there I think I can be almost a hundred percent certain.'

'Really?' In Raven's experience, pathologists were rarely certain of anything, even in the case of very recent deaths.

She opened a drawer and took out a clear plastic bag. Sliding it across the desk to Raven, she said, 'I found this inside the skull. I would say that it's pretty incontrovertible evidence.'

The bag contained a single bullet.

'The skull exhibits the trauma associated with a gunshot. The entry wound is located in the occipital bone at the rear of the skull.' She indicated the location with a slim finger pressed against her own head. 'Forge Valley

Man was shot in the back of the head, execution-style, at point blank range. I've seen this kind of thing before, in Bosnia.'

'I see.' Raven examined the bullet through the clear plastic of the bag. A 9mm round, by the look of it. Ballistics would hopefully be able to determine the nature of the weapon that had fired it.

While he pondered this latest piece of information, Chandice retrieved another bag from her drawer and placed it on the desk. 'This was also found with the body.'

The object in the bag was a large watch face, measuring at least five centimetres in diameter. The strap, which must have been leather, was missing, probably rotted away. Raven had never seen a watch quite like it. There were two sets of digits – an inner circle measuring the hour, and an outer circle measuring minutes. An alphanumeric code "FL 23883" was engraved on the back and left side of the case. On the back was a name, presumably that of the manufacturer – *A. Lange & Söhne*.

German. Or perhaps Swiss?

Chandice interrupted his thoughts. 'I know a good antiques dealer in York who should be able to tell us everything we need to know about this watch.'

'Sounds perfect,' said Raven.

'And if we're quick, maybe there'll be time for us to grab a bite of lunch afterwards?'

Raven wasn't going to argue with that.

CHAPTER 5

Craig Clarkson, the last person to have visited Raymond Swindlehurst in the care home before he died, didn't prove difficult for Becca to track down. Clarkson's books were available on Amazon and he even had a website with a contact page inviting readers to get in touch with him via email. Becca did just that and was pleased to receive a response before lunchtime.

She phoned the number Clarkson had provided and was duly invited to his flat. If only all witnesses could be so accommodating.

Climbing the stairs of the big Victorian terrace just off the Esplanade, she was reminded of the flat she'd almost moved into with her boyfriend, Sam. That had been almost a year ago. If all had gone according to plan, she'd be living there with Sam right now instead of stuck at home in her parents' Bed and Breakfast.

But then the accident had happened, and the bottom had fallen out of her world.

She was grateful for the support her family had given her. But although she loved her parents dearly, she knew she couldn't stay at home forever. Even if she couldn't be with Sam, she'd have to find a place of her own eventually.

The door to the top-floor flat stood ajar. Becca knocked and poked her head around.

'Come in,' said Clarkson, appearing in the hallway. 'I've just put the kettle on. Tea or coffee?' He was younger than Becca had expected – mid-thirties, with dark hair that curled over his collar. He wore an open-necked casual shirt, stylish jeans and a pair of moccasins. For some reason she had expected that a historian would be older, as if it were necessary for them to have first-hand knowledge of the period they wrote about. But that was obviously ridiculous.

'Tea, please,' she said. 'Milk, two sugars.'

'Coming right up.' He gestured towards the room at the front of the flat. 'Make yourself at home.'

Becca followed his directions into the living room, more than a little curious to see what a writer's abode looked like. Being in the attic, the flat was small with low, sloping ceilings. These rooms would once have been the servants' quarters in the days when the building was still a big house, before it was sub-divided into flats. Becca was reminded of her own top-floor room in the B&B. That too had a sea view, although in her case she enjoyed a wide panorama over the wilds of the North Bay, whereas Clarkson's flat offered a narrow glimpse of the more touristed South Bay. The sky was clear this morning after another night's heavy frost, and Becca could just make out a couple of dog walkers on the sands.

One wall of the room was completely covered in floor-to-ceiling bookcases. The shelves groaned under the weight of books arranged vertically and piled horizontally on top of each other in no order that Becca could discern. Clarkson appeared to be an avid and eclectic reader. *We Landed by Moonlight* stood next to *A Brief History of Time*. *Crime and Punishment* lay on top of the latest Dan Brown thriller. More books stood in heaps around the fireplace, or were scattered across the small sofa. A mess of papers covered in red ink were scattered across Clarkson's desk which stood before the window, enjoying the best of the light.

'Tea is served.' Clarkson bustled in with two mugs in his hands. He set one down on the desk, spilling a little over one of the papers. The mug was emblazoned with the words *Careful, or you'll end up in my novel!*

'Do you write novels as well as history books?' asked Becca, wondering if he penned thrillers or some such under a secret alias.

'God, no,' said Clarkson, grinning. 'It's hard enough writing books when all I have to do is get other people to tell me their personal stories. If I had to make it up as well, I'd never get past the first paragraph.' He took a comfy chair in the corner after dislodging a pile of newspapers onto the floor. 'So what can I do for you? You said it was a police matter. I can't resist a mystery.'

Becca took a seat by the desk and sipped the tea. It was nice and strong, just how she liked it. 'It's about Raymond Swindlehurst. He was a resident at the Larkmead Nursing Home. I don't know if you're aware of this, but he died sometime on Monday night or possibly Tuesday morning.'

Clarkson's smile faded. 'Ah yes, I was very sorry to hear about that. He was a fine old man. There aren't many like him left in the world.'

'How well did you know him?'

'I visited him a couple of times at the care home, and we met at a café on the seafront once. The Sun Court Café. Do you know it? It's part of the spa buildings. They put on outdoor concerts there during the summer months.'

'I know it,' said Becca.

'Raymond was fond of music. I think it reminded him of his heyday. He was a bit of a ladies' man, at least according to him. He was certainly a great spinner of yarns. A real character.'

'You visited him on the day he died,' said Becca, watching closely to gauge Clarkson's reaction.

The writer made no attempt to deny it. 'That's right.'

'I was hoping you could tell me why you went to see

him. What was your relationship to Mr Swindlehurst?'

Clarkson sat back, crossing one ankle over his knee, apparently at ease. 'I'm writing a book about local war veterans from World War Two. Ordinary men caught up in battle. I hope this doesn't sound tactless under the circumstances, but they're dying out quickly. Only a few are left, so I want to record their stories before it's too late. Raymond was a great guy. I'm truly sorry that he's gone.'

'How did you first meet him?'

'My grandfather introduced him to me. They were old pals from back in the day.'

'What did you talk about the last time you met him?'

'All sorts of things. Raymond was a fine raconteur. He served with the Royal Navy during wartime and he could tell you some hair-raising stories from the Battle of the Atlantic. You know, that man really did have nine lives. On his very first return voyage from America, his ship was torpedoed by a German U-boat. Raymond was convinced his time was up and he would go down with his ship. But he was rescued by another ship, a destroyer. Then that ship was also hit! What are the odds? Yet Raymond somehow managed to escape from that too. Afterwards, he said he asked God what he'd done to deserve being sunk twice on his first voyage. Do you know what he said to me? God told him he ought to be grateful he'd taken the trouble to rescue the poor sod twice!'

'And how was he the last time you saw him?'

'How was he?' A look of puzzlement crossed Clarkson's face. 'Actually, now you come to mention it, he wasn't quite his normal self.'

'In what way?'

'I don't know, he just seemed a little distracted, as if something was bothering him. He didn't have as much to say as he usually did.'

'Did he say what was on his mind?'

'No. And to be honest, I didn't think much of it. I just put it down to tiredness. He was an old man, after all.'

'And how was Mr Swindlehurst when you left him?'

'I'm not sure what you mean,' said Clarkson. 'But there's something going on here that I don't understand.'

'Oh?' said Becca. 'What's that?'

'Why is this a police matter?'

Becca phrased her reply carefully, using neutral police language. 'Because there are indications that Mr Swindlehurst may have taken his own life.'

Craig Clarkson's puzzlement deepened into a full-blown frown of disbelief. 'Suicide? Raymond would never do that.'

Becca decided to go for broke. 'Or that a third party may have been involved in his death,' she added, scanning Clarkson's face and body language.

'Murder? That's ridiculous! Who would want to kill a ninety-six-year-old man?'

'That's the question I'm asking myself, Mr Clarkson. So, let me ask you again. How was Mr Swindlehurst when you left him?'

Clarkson swirled his remaining tea angrily in his mug and swallowed it in one big gulp. 'If you're asking me whether he was still alive, then yes, very much so. And now I think it's time for you to leave. Like I told you before, I deal with facts, not fiction.'

CHAPTER 6

The antique shop looked like something out of a Dickens novel. The tall, thin house nestled among other similar buildings on Stonegate in the heart of York's historic centre, where gift shops and expensive chocolatiers jostled with pubs and tea rooms in the shadow of the Minster. The streets here were perhaps even narrower than Quay Street, scarcely wide enough for a horse and cart. Raven guessed that the Georgian façade of the shop probably concealed a much older medieval building beneath. A sign hanging on an elaborate wrought-iron bracket squeaked on its hinges in the breeze.

'After you.' Raven held the door open and Chandice walked into the shop with an amused smile on her face. Did she think him old-fashioned?

Inside, the walls were lined with glass cabinets, stuffed to overflowing with every conceivable type of jewellery, crystalware and silverware, so that the effect was rather like being inside Aladdin's cave. A tall, thin man who looked like he'd been fashioned in the same style as the house approached them.

'May I help you?' The shopkeeper's sharp eyes took in

Raven and Chandice at a glance, then alighted on a nearby cabinet glittering with diamond rings. 'Perhaps the lady and gentleman are looking to make a special purchase?'

Raven realised that the man had mistaken them for a couple in the market for an engagement ring. He soon put the matter straight, producing his warrant card. 'Actually, we were hoping to speak to someone who might be able to identify this.' He showed the man the watch, still in its plastic bag.

If the shopkeeper was disappointed not to be slipping diamond clusters onto the lady's finger, he was far too professional to let it show. 'My colleague upstairs would be the best person to advise you. Please, follow me.'

He led the way up the winding staircase to the second floor where he introduced them to his colleague, a Mr Watkins. The cabinets on this floor were filled with clocks and watches. A grandfather clock in a mahogany case slowly chimed the quarter hour.

Mr Watkins who, Raven observed with disappointment, wore an Apple Watch on his wrist rather than a pocket watch on a gold chain, was nevertheless very excited when Raven showed him the watch that had been found with Forge Valley Man.

'May I take it out of the bag?' he asked, pulling a pair of white cotton gloves from his trouser pocket.

Raven assented. If the man was wearing gloves, he could hardly do more damage than the watch had already suffered after years buried underground. In fact, the watch was in remarkably good condition given the time it had lain under the earth. That was German engineering for you.

Mr Watkins donned the gloves and slid the watch out of the bag, cradling it in the palm of his hand as if he were holding a rare species of butterfly. 'Remarkable. A genuine B-Uhr watch. It's a little grubby, and unfortunately the strap is missing, but apart from that it looks to be in good condition.'

'I'm sorry,' said Raven. 'What did you call it?'

'B-Uhr. It's short for *Beobachtungsuhr*, meaning

"observation watch". They were manufactured by a small number of German companies from the nineteen-thirties onwards and supplied to the *Luftwaffe*, the German air force, in World War Two. They were known for being, if you'll excuse the pun, deadly accurate – an essential requirement if you're in the business of bombing targets. The watch is instantly recognisable from its two dials.' He pointed with a gloved forefinger to the inner and outer circles of digits that Raven had already noted. 'It's very large – the diameter is 55mm – for legibility. And the crown is also large' – he pointed to the winder – 'so that it could be easily operated while wearing gloves. Where did you find it?'

Raven dodged the question and instead asked one of his own. 'What about the code on the side? Is that unique to this particular watch?'

'FL 23883,' read Watkins. 'Sadly no. "FL" refers to *Flieger*, the German word for "aviator". "23" was the code used for navigation, and if I'm not mistaken "883" refers to the German Aviation Research Institute. All of the B-Uhr watches had the same designation.'

'And you say they were issued to members of the *Luftwaffe* during World War Two?'

'That's right. They were navigators' watches.'

'So how might a watch like this turn up in Yorkshire?'

'I don't follow you,' said Watkins. 'Items like this are bought and sold by collectors all over the world. They're quite valuable in fact.'

'No,' said Raven. 'This one isn't from a collection.' It seemed impossible to avoid explaining the circumstances of the find. He lowered his voice, even though there was no one else around. 'It was discovered with human remains that we believe may date back to the post-war period.'

The man's interest quickened. 'Ah yes, I saw that story on the news a few days ago. The skeleton at Forge Valley Woods?'

'That's right.'

'Well, how intriguing,' said Watkins. 'But I believe that

can be easily explained. There were several prisoner of war camps in this part of the world, so it's quite possible that the watch may have belonged to a captured German flight navigator. There was a camp not far away, just outside Malton. Eden Camp. In fact, it's been turned into a museum. If you want to find out about prisoners of war in the local area, that would be a good place to start.'

Raven thanked Watkins for his assistance and headed back outside with Chandice. The cobbled street was thronged with tourists and early Christmas shoppers, but Raven hardly noticed. His mind was turning over what they'd learned in the shop.

Chandice was clearly thinking through the implications too. 'If Forge Valley Man was a German prisoner of war, that fits with the timeline based on the coin that was found.'

'It also fits that he was a young man, possibly in his early twenties.'

'Exactly. How exciting. So what's your next move?'

'My next move?' Raven pretended to think hard. 'I'm pretty sure that you promised to take me out for lunch.'

Chandice laughed. 'Take you out? I thought that gentlemen were supposed to take ladies out.'

'To foot the bill, you mean? After such a productive morning, I'm pretty sure I can stretch to that.'

It seemed that chivalry wasn't dead, after all.

*

Becca was considering calling it a day. The visit to Craig Clarkson hadn't exactly revealed a lot of information, other than confirming her impression that Raymond Swindlehurst wasn't the kind of person to have taken his own life. But Dinsdale was adamant that she was wasting her time pursuing that line of enquiry. 'If it looks like suicide, then nine times out of ten it is,' he'd declared before slipping away from the station at five on the dot.

Becca had been tempted to join him, but she was a

stickler for keeping on top of paperwork, and so she'd stayed behind to enter her notes from the Clarkson interview into the police database while they were still fresh in her mind.

Raven had been out of the office all day, trying to make progress on finding an ID for his skeleton. He'd mentioned something in passing about a visit to York. Becca wouldn't have minded going with him. She'd rather be working with Raven than with Dinsdale.

The phone in Dinsdale's empty office rang several times, and then was followed almost immediately by the phone on her own desk.

Becca picked up. 'DS Becca Shawcross.'

'Hi, Becca, Felicity here.'

Dr Felicity Wainwright was the senior pathologist at Scarborough Hospital. A prickly character who had taken an instant dislike to Raven, for some reason she had a soft spot for Becca.

'How can I help you, Felicity?'

'I was trying to get hold of DI Dinsdale, but he doesn't seem to be answering his phone.'

Becca had a strong inkling that Felicity knew exactly why Dinsdale's phone had gone unanswered. 'No, sorry. Dinsdale's already left the station.'

'No need for you to apologise on his behalf, Becca. I'm sure the inspector's had quite an exhausting day at work.'

Felicity's contempt for Dinsdale was legendary within the department. Come to think of it, the pathologist appeared to harbour a strong loathing for all men.

'Is it something I can help you with?' asked Becca.

'I just wanted to let you know that I've finished the post-mortem examination of Raymond Swindlehurst. I'll send you the full report by email, but I thought you might like to hear a quick summary of my findings over the phone.'

Becca reached for her notepad and pencil with her spare hand. 'Go ahead, please.'

'Well, I must say that whoever suggested to you that

this was suicide was very much mistaken. Toxicology shows no evidence of paracetamol in Mr Swindlehurst's system. Nor was there any alcohol in his blood. There were, however, signs that French brandy had been forced down his throat, quite possibly after his death. At least half of it had spilled over his clothing.'

Becca was quickly taking notes. 'So what was the cause of death?' she asked, already pretty sure what Felicity was going to say.

'I'm afraid that the answer to that question is unambiguous. There are various indicators that confirm my conclusion – bleeding in the eyes, high levels of carbon dioxide in the blood, cotton fibres recovered from the victim's nose and mouth. Mr Swindlehurst died from asphyxiation. He was suffocated.'

CHAPTER 7

When Becca opened her bedroom curtains the next morning, the view through her window was obscured by a thick mist. The grey of sea and sky merged into each other making it impossible to discern any horizon. It was a miserable start to the day.

She hadn't slept at all well, her night punctuated by disturbing nightmares. Once, she'd woken from a dream where she was on a ship in the middle of the Atlantic, tossed by storms and hunted by German U-boats. She'd felt cold water filling her lungs, dragging her down into the watery depths. Another time, she imagined a killer in her room, creeping up to smother her with a cushion. She'd woken gasping for breath, her face buried in her own pillow.

But as she went downstairs, the mouth-watering smell of frying bacon lifted her spirits.

She entered the large kitchen at the back of the house and found her mum busily cooking breakfast for the few guests currently occupying rooms. November was a quiet month, midway between the school half-term holidays at the end of October, and the run-up to Christmas, when a troupe of actors booked in for the duration of the annual pantomime would no doubt liven things up. But Sue Shawcross was always busy, whatever the season.

'Sleep well, love? You're looking a bit tired.'

'I'm all right, Mum.'

'Well, sit down and have a proper breakfast before you go to work,' said Sue, turning to the stove and her remedy for all of life's ills – comforting food. 'Scrambled eggs and bacon? And I've got some lovely fresh mushrooms to go with them.'

Becca had no willpower to resist. 'Yes, please.' The hot food would set her up for the day and if she had to go back to the care home, as looked extremely likely, then she wouldn't be craving bacon when she walked past the dining room.

The back door crashed open and Becca's brother, Liam, entered. 'That smells good, Mum. Got any spare?'

Sue smiled at him indulgently. 'There's always a cooked breakfast waiting for you here, Liam. You know that.'

'Of course he does,' said Becca, boiling the kettle for tea. 'That's why he never bothers making any for himself.' Despite having a place of his own, Liam always scrounged whatever he could from his parents, not only eating his mum's cooking, but also getting her to do his laundry. Becca sometimes wondered why he'd bothered to move out at all. Although really it didn't take a detective to work out the answer. To stay out late, never tidy up, and bring girls back to his flat without any questions asked.

Liam pulled a face at her. 'A mug of hot tea wouldn't go amiss either, sis.' He was incorrigible.

Becca poured boiling water into two mugs and carried them over to the table where Liam had already taken a seat.

'So are you working on this skeleton they found in Forge Valley Woods then, Becs?' he asked.

Before Becca had chance to reply, Sue bustled over with two plates piled high with food. 'Shocking, isn't it? We used to go walking through those woods when you two were little. You used to love playing hide and seek among the trees. Do you remember? And to think there was a dead body buried there the whole time. It might have been right beneath our feet.'

'I'm working on another case,' said Becca, slicing through a juicy mushroom that filled half her plate.

'With Raven?' asked Sue.

'Dinsdale.'

Liam grinned. 'Bad luck. So is Raven in charge of the Forge Valley case?'

Becca regarded him suspiciously. 'You seem very interested in this case.'

'Not really,' said Liam, cramming a fork load of bacon and egg into his mouth. 'More interested in Raven. Do you know how he got on with Barry?'

'Your builder? No idea. Raven never tells me anything.'

Liam seemed disappointed. 'Well, Barry's a good bloke. I'm sure he'll do an excellent job for your boss. Just as soon as he's finished the work he's doing for me.'

*

There was still no word from Barry, despite his promise to get back to Raven very soon with an estimate. Now that Raven had decided to make the old house his home, he was hoping the work could start without delay. It would be good to get it finished in time for Christmas. At present the house was barely habitable, and certainly not fit for guests. If he wanted to invite Hannah to come and stay with him he would need at the very least to get the guest room redecorated and the new bathroom installed.

And if he wanted to have other guests round... his mind drifted to Dr Chandice Jones, her dark eyes and smooth skin setting his imagination running wild.

He was aware that by taking her out to lunch the previous day he'd broken his cardinal rule of never mixing work with pleasure. Discreet questioning had established that she was single. And of course he had made her aware of his own rocky marital status. But he felt no guilt about spending time with the attractive forensic anthropologist. Chandice – Dr Jones – was highly intelligent with a great deal of relevant expertise, and they had devoted at least some of their time to discussing the case. She was very excited by the idea that Forge Valley Man might have been a captured German aviator.

'Do you think he could have escaped from the camp?' she'd asked, meaning Eden Camp, the old prisoner of war camp mentioned by the watch specialist, Mr Watkins.

It was certainly a possibility that Raven was willing to contemplate. But if so, who had shot him? Raven had never worked such an old case before, and doubted that it was solvable after so many years had passed, but he wanted to see if it was possible at least to identify his victim.

He and Chandice had parted with a promise that he would keep her up to date with progress on the investigation. There had also been a hope, on his part at least, that they might get together again soon. Maybe for dinner this time.

Arriving at the station the following morning, he called in to Detective Superintendent Gillian Ellis's office to give her an update on the case. Although his temporary secondment in Scarborough had now been made permanent, whenever he was in Gillian's presence he found it hard to push aside the feeling that he was still on probation, and he knew that she liked to keep a tight rein on her senior investigators.

He knocked at her door and entered.

'Ah, Tom. Sit down. Let's hear how your investigation's going.' Gillian was a woman who filled a room with her presence as much as with her physical self. She removed her reading glasses, laid aside the document she'd been working on and looked at Raven expectantly. She was clearly assuming that he had some progress to report.

Raven outlined his visit to the university, carefully omitting the fact that he'd taken Chandice out to lunch after speaking to the antiques dealer.

'Sounds like you had a productive time,' she said. 'Just as well, since you spent the whole day in York. So what's your next step?'

'I thought I'd pay a visit to the camp and see what records I can find.'

'Okay.'

'I was thinking I might take DS Shawcross with me.'

'I'm afraid she's working another case,' said Gillian. 'But I can spare you DC Tony Bairstow and DC Jess Barraclough.'

'All right.' Raven was disappointed to hear that Becca was unavailable, but he had worked with the two detective constables before and was glad to have them on his team.

'Just be aware that I can't give you unlimited resources, Tom. I know that this case has gathered some attention from the media, but a murder that took place such a long time ago is unlikely to lead to a prosecution.'

'I know that.'

Gillian was never one to mince her words or to hold back her opinion. 'I'll give you a few days to see how you get on. But if there's no progress...'

There was no need for her to complete her sentence. Raven knew that if he couldn't put a name to Forge Valley Man within the next few days, he would have to put the case aside. And that might mean no more visits to York.

CHAPTER 8

'Nice car, sir,' said DC Jess Barraclough, settling herself into the passenger seat of the BMW and stretching out her long legs in the roomy footwell.

Raven couldn't help a smile from spreading across his face at her evident approval. Lisa had never liked the M6, always complaining about its high running costs and its unsuitability as a family car, despite the fact that he had never stood in her way whenever she wanted to redecorate the house or upgrade the appliances in the kitchen. Needlessly, in his opinion.

Jess, by contrast, clearly appreciated its sleek lines and powerful engine. She obviously had good taste in cars. He put his foot down, enjoying the sensation as the car accelerated to overtake a lumbering tractor. 'What do you drive?' he enquired.

Jess laughed. 'My dad's old Land Rover. It still goes, that's the most I can say for it.'

They were heading west out of Scarborough, following the same road Raven had taken the previous day. This time, however, he would be turning off the A64 at Malton, roughly halfway to York. He had decided to take Jess with him to the camp, assigning DC Tony Bairstow the task of searching the archives for any records of missing prisoners of war.

'No problem, sir,' Tony had said. Most people would have been dismayed at the prospect of digging out files dating back to the 1940s, but Tony was the sort of detective who didn't mind that kind of nitty-gritty work. 'But the records from that time might be a bit patchy.'

'I know that, Tony. Just see what you can find.'

Meanwhile, Jess had been keen to get out of the station and go with Raven. 'I went to Eden Camp on a school trip, once, sir. Happy to go again.'

'So are you from Scarborough?' he asked her as they left the town behind. It was a forty-minute drive to Malton, and Raven thought he would spend the time getting to know the youngest member of his team a little better. When he'd been at the Met, he had invariably been told during appraisals that he needed to work harder at building rapport with his colleagues. Might as well start now.

'No,' said Jess. 'I'm from somewhere much smaller. Rosedale Abbey. Do you know it?'

'I've heard the name, but I've never been there.'

During the early years of his life in Scarborough, Raven had hardly ventured further afield than the nearby coastal town of Whitby, except for one memorable summer when he'd stayed with his maternal grandparents at a holiday park near Berwick-Upon-Tweed in Northumberland. But maybe it was time he got to know the area a bit better. 'Is it worth a visit?'

'It's fantastic,' enthused Jess. 'It's so beautiful, right in the heart of the North York Moors. They used to mine iron ore there, back in the nineteenth century. You can still follow the path of the old railway line on foot. My favourite route is up Ingleby Incline. The views from the top are amazing.'

'Is it a long walk?'

'About four hours each way.'

'Sounds like you're a keen hiker.'

Jess nodded enthusiastically. 'Walking, cycling, anything that gets me out and about.'

Raven, too, had been fit and active once, especially during his army days. Now his leg injury made long walks arduous, particularly anything involving rugged terrain or a steep hill. He didn't think he was cut out for a hike up Ingleby Incline, or for that matter anywhere else with the word "Incline" in its name.

There were no inclines around Malton as far as Raven could make out. Instead, the land thereabouts seemed relentlessly flat. As Raven turned off the main road and caught his first glimpse of Eden Camp across fallow fields of arable farmland and long, straight drainage ditches, he was struck by how bleak the camp looked in the implacable November weather. Apart from the single-storey huts that must once have housed prisoners, the only structures in evidence were a wooden watchtower and a line of electricity pylons that marched across the bare and frozen earth like sentinels. It was easy to understand why anyone would want to escape from this place.

'That school visit you went on,' he said to Jess, 'was it a punishment?'

Jess chuckled. 'It was a good day out, actually. Really interesting.'

Raven nodded gloomily. Jess's schooldays must have been a lot more fun than his own. No doubt she'd invested some of her boundless energy in her educational opportunities, instead of squandering them like he had. She'd probably chosen her friends more wisely too, instead of hanging out in beachfront amusement arcades with a bunch of ne'er do wells and juvenile delinquents.

Regrets. Raven had more than he cared to count, but this was no time to indulge in them.

The entrance to the camp was marked by an RAF Hurricane mounted on a plinth as if in flight. Beneath it, other military hardware was on display, including a field gun and other wartime vehicles. Raven felt his interest growing. He'd never been a big fan of museums, but as a veteran, the relics of warfare always held a certain fascination for him.

Raven pulled up at the ticket kiosk, produced his warrant card, and explained the reason for their visit to the woman on duty.

'Is there someone we can speak to about records of prisoners held at the camp?'

'The archivist knows most about the history of the camp,' said the woman. 'Let me see if he's available.' She dialled a number and explained the situation to the person at the other end. 'No problem,' she said, putting the phone down. 'He'll come and meet you in the car park.' She pointed the way to the parking.

The car park was empty today, except for a coach disgorging a party of schoolchildren defended against the elements in padded jackets and brightly coloured waterproofs. A couple of harried teachers were attempting to marshal them into some semblance of order.

Raven and Jess were saved from the rabble by the arrival of the archivist, a young man in his early thirties who introduced himself as Will and seemed very pleased to find that his expertise was in demand. 'Would you like me to show you around?' he offered. 'I can give you a guided tour if you like.'

'That won't be necessary,' said Raven. 'We just have some questions to ask.'

'Okay. You'd better come with me, then.'

They followed Will past rows of single-storey barracks, not dissimilar to those in concentration camps, which were lined up with regimental precision. On a drizzly, windswept November day it made a grim sight.

'You should come here in the summer,' said Will cheerfully as they crossed to the other side of the camp. 'We have lots of activities for families and young children. It makes a great day out.'

'I'm sure it does,' said Raven, throwing a sideways glance at Jess. She did her best to keep a straight face.

Will led them to one of the barracks, which was marked *Staff Only*. 'This is me. Come on in.'

Inside, the hut was surprisingly cosy and welcoming. Will's office was lined floor to ceiling with labelled boxed files. His desk was also piled high with papers and documents. On the back of the door was a poster of three determined housewives brandishing a curtain pole from which billowed a banner emblazoned with the slogan "UP HOUSEWIVES AND AT 'EM!" A determined little Scottie dog trotted alongside the women, a bone in its mouth, doing its bit for victory. The bottom of the poster exhorted women to put out their paper, metal and bones to be made into planes, guns, tanks, ships and ammunition. By bones, the poster presumably meant those left over from cuts of meat, but Raven couldn't help thinking of Forge Valley Man. Was this the place he had called home in the days before he met his untimely end?

Will offered to make them coffee in tin mugs. 'I've only got instant, I'm afraid, but at least it's not ersatz.'

Raven and Jess politely declined.

'So,' said Raven, taking a seat, 'we're hoping you can help us trace the identity of someone who was likely held prisoner here during the war.'

'Intriguing,' said Will. 'But unlikely.'

'Why is that?'

'Because there are scarcely any surviving documents listing the names of the prisoners. They were all lost or destroyed after the war. Sadly, in those days no one thought those records were worth preserving.'

The news came as a blow to Raven. If there were no lists of prisoners held at the camp, his chances of putting a name to Forge Valley Man were almost non-existent. 'What about the names of any who escaped? Surely there would be some record of those?'

Will chortled at his suggestion. 'No prisoners escaped.'

'None?' From what Raven had seen, there was no indication that the security measures at the camp had ever comprised much more than a wire fence around its perimeter. He found it hard to believe this would be enough to thwart a determined escape attempt.

'Perhaps a few kids on school trips have tried to get away over the years,' said Will with a grin, 'but no prisoners ever tried to escape, even though the security at the camp was very low-key.'

'Why not?'

'Because Eden Camp only housed low-risk prisoners. Captured German soldiers were divided into three categories. Firstly, there were hard-line Nazis, including senior officers and members of the SS. They were graded "black" and held in high-security camps like Island Farm in South Wales. Then there were so-called "grey" prisoners who had probably joined the Party because it was expedient to do so but weren't hard-line fanatics. But most of the prisoners wore a white patch. They were often just young conscripts who'd had no choice about joining the army. If they found themselves at Eden Camp, they could count their lucky stars. It wasn't the Ritz, for sure, but it was a lot better than being on a battlefield. They were safe here, and received the same food rations as British servicemen.'

It wasn't hard to get Will talking about his subject. He had his facts at his fingertips and imparted his knowledge with enthusiasm.

'What did they do all day?' asked Raven. 'Were they locked in the huts?'

'Not at all,' said Will. 'They may not have been given an easy life, but they were treated very fairly. There was a chapel and a literary club here, even lessons in mathematics. And a lot of the POWs did agricultural work on nearby farms.'

'They were allowed out?'

'Under supervision. And they were paid with tokens that could be spent in the camp.'

'Sounds like they had a fairly cushy time of it, all things considered. Were all the prisoners here German?'

'No,' said Will. 'When the War Office established the

camp in 1942, the first prisoners were Italians. At that time the camp was just tents surrounded by barbed wire. The huts were built later. In early 1944 the Italians were moved out and the camp was used to accommodate Polish forces before the invasion of Europe. The first German prisoners didn't arrive until the middle of 1944. And the last didn't leave until 1949.'

'Why so late?' History had never been Raven's strongest subject, but even he knew that the war in Europe had ended in May 1945 when Germany had surrendered unconditionally to the Allies.

'Repatriation was incredibly slow,' explained Will. 'After the war, Britain was on its knees. There was a shortage of labour because so many young men had been killed, so the German POWs were very useful. Besides, not all of them wanted to return home.'

'They didn't?'

'Not if their families had perished, or if they were from the eastern part of Germany, which was now under Soviet control. And of course a number of them found a girl and fell in love.' He glanced awkwardly in Jess's direction. 'They were young men. Who can blame them?'

Raven turned over the implications of what he had heard. He was glad to learn that Forge Valley Man probably wasn't a Nazi sympathiser. Instead it seemed that he had most likely stayed on voluntarily after the war. The silver sixpence dated 1945 certainly backed that theory up. Perhaps the young man had fallen in love with a Yorkshire lass.

'What did the locals make of POWs taking up with English girls?' Raven wondered if resentment among the local men had led to the young German's death. Yorkshire folk were often portrayed as being mean-spirited. According to one old joke, the typical Yorkshireman was like a Scotsman, but with all the generosity squeezed out of him. It was a stereotype that Raven's own father had done his best to live up to.

'Most people were welcoming,' said Will cautiously.

'But it's fair to say that not everyone warmed to what they still saw as the enemy.' He paused. 'Can I ask why you're so interested in what happened to the German prisoners after the war?'

Raven stood up. 'Let's just say that we have reason to believe that one in particular may not have found Yorkshire hospitality quite to his liking.'

CHAPTER 9

Even DI Dinsdale couldn't ignore the results of the post-mortem on Raymond Swindlehurst when Becca confronted him about them over his morning coffee and biscuit. He had no choice but to grudgingly agree that this was now a murder enquiry and that they should begin their investigation at the care home.

Becca drove them there. Unlike Raven, who liked to be behind the wheel of his monstrously large, fuel-guzzling car, Dinsdale was happy to be chauffeured around. He seemed to regard it as a perk of the job. Becca didn't mind. She felt more in control when she was driving her Honda Jazz, as if she was the one taking the lead on the case. In many ways, she was.

'You talked to that writer chap yesterday,' said Dinsdale as she drove. 'What did he have to say for himself?'

'Not a great deal, sir. He confirmed that he visited Mr Swindlehurst on the afternoon of his death. He noticed that the old man was a bit out of sorts, and also expressed the view that he wasn't the type to take his own life.'

'Yes, well we know that *now*, don't we?' snapped

Dinsdale. They drove the rest of the way in silence.

Becca parked under the yew tree and waited for Dinsdale to clamber out of the small car. The last of the autumn leaves had dropped now and lay strewn over the lawn in a carpet of yellow and brown beneath a large oak. As they walked to the entrance of the home, Becca heard voices coming from the other side of the tree.

Pausing a moment, she saw the nurse, Natalia Kamińska, standing behind the trunk. She was shivering in her short-sleeved uniform, her thin, pale arms wrapped around her. She was with the gardener Becca had noticed on her first visit to the care home. He held a rake in his hand.

The pair appeared to be having a heated discussion, facing one another with furious expressions. 'Why not?' hissed Natalia, and the gardener replied, 'I've told you why!' He shook the rake at her.

They must have heard Dinsdale's feet crunching along the gravel path, because they stopped their argument and fell into a stony silence as he walked past. Becca attempted a casual, friendly wave, but Natalia didn't respond and the gardener just scowled, turning away and striding off across the lawn with his rake.

A lover's tiff? Or something more serious? Becca was attuned to signs of domestic violence, and didn't like the way the gardener had raised his voice, nor the way he had brandished his rake like a weapon.

But there was nothing she could do about it now. Natalia was walking away around the side of the building and Dinsdale was already at the entrance. He turned back to see what had happened to her. Becca caught up with him and went inside.

Almost immediately she was stripping off her outer layers in the entrance hall of the overheated building, before signing in as before. Five minutes later she was back in Judith Holden's office, seated once again on the L-shaped sofa facing the care home manager across the coffee table.

'How dreadful,' said Judith after Dinsdale had outlined the reason for their visit. 'And you're sure there's no mistake, with the post-mortem, I mean?'

'No,' said Dinsdale. 'Unfortunately, it would appear that Mr, uh...'

'Swindlehurst,' prompted Becca.

'... was murdered.'

Judith looked shaken and confused in equal measure. 'But who would want to murder Raymond? He was very popular. There was no history of any quarrel with another resident. In any case, it seems inexplicable. This is a care home. And Raymond was ninety-six.'

'I'm afraid there's no doubt,' said Becca. 'Dr Felicity Wainwright is a very experienced pathologist.'

Dinsdale took out his notes and a pencil. 'So now we'll need to speak to everyone who knew Mr Swindlehurst or had access to his room.'

'I suppose so,' said Judith. 'But really that's everyone. All our residents and staff, I mean. Plus visitors too.'

'Perhaps we can narrow it down a little?' suggested Dinsdale.

'Yes, yes, of course.'

Judith pulled a pad of paper towards her and unscrewed the lid of her fountain pen. She was obviously trying to deal with the situation by reverting to type – taking charge and making plans. 'You'll want to know who was here at the time of his death. Have you established when that was, exactly?'

'It was sometime on Monday evening,' said Becca, who had memorised the details from the post-mortem report and wasn't going to wait while Dinsdale searched through his notes. 'Between the hours of 6pm and 11pm.'

'Right,' said Judith. She noted down the times, and below them wrote three words – *Residents*, *Staff* and *Visitors*. 'I believe that all our residents were here on Monday evening. That's forty-eight people in total. Or forty-seven, not including Raymond. I'll print a list of names for you. As for staff, I'll need to check the rota.

Again, I can supply a list. And in the case of outsiders, I believe you already have a copy of the visitors' log.'

'That's right,' confirmed Becca. 'But would everyone in the building have access to Raymond's room? When you showed me his body, the door to his room was locked, so surely only those with a key would have been able to gain entry?'

'No, I'm afraid that's not the case,' said Judith. 'Normally residents' rooms are kept unlocked at all times for ease of access. We only lock them when a resident is off-site for some reason, such as a hospital visit. Or, as in Raymond's case, if they've passed away.'

'So who discovered the body?' asked Dinsdale.

'Natalia Kamińska, one of our nurses.'

Dinsdale frowned, and Becca spelled the name out for him. 'I've already talked to Natalia,' she said, 'but in light of this new information, we'll need to speak to her again. Alone, this time.'

If Judith took any offence at Becca's comment, she showed none. 'Of course. I'll send for Natalia right away. There's a meeting room next door that you can use to carry out your interviews. Do you need anything else?'

Becca looked to Dinsdale. 'Well,' he said, 'since you're offering, a coffee would be lovely. Milk with two sugars. And do you have any biscuits? Chocolate digestives always go down a treat, I find.'

*

The meeting room was a dark wood-panelled affair, hung with the head of a stag. Becca seated herself opposite the dead animal, whose glassy eyes seemed to regard her with an accusing air of despondency. Dinsdale sat at right angles to her, his weight sinking into a huge leather armchair, a plate of biscuits on the desk before him. He pushed the plate in Becca's direction, but she politely declined. Dinsdale shrugged and helped himself to a second digestive.

The first person to be interviewed was Natalia. When she entered the meeting room, the nurse's eyes and nose were red, whether from crying or just being outside in the cold, Becca couldn't tell.

Either way, Dinsdale didn't seem to care. He brushed biscuit crumbs off his brown tie and launched straight into his questioning. 'So. You worked the night shift on Monday evening, the time the victim was killed. Correct?'

Natalia hugged herself with her thin arms. She nodded, looking uncertainly from Dinsdale to Becca. Becca knew she must be wondering what this was all about. Dinsdale hadn't bothered to explain to her that Raymond's death was now being treated as murder. And he hadn't exactly adopted a gentle approach to questioning.

'And were you the one who discovered the body?'

'Yes.'

'What time was that?'

'It was seven o'clock Tuesday morning.'

Dinsdale consulted his notes. 'By which time the victim had already been dead some – what? – nine hours or so?'

Natalia shrugged. 'I found him lying in bed, with strong smell of brandy. I knew it was not right. His body was already cold. I straightened bedclothes, put empty bottle back on top of locker–'

'Wait,' said Dinsdale. 'You moved the body? You tampered with evidence?'

A look of fright passed across Natalia's face. 'Tamper? With evidence? No.'

'You understand that this is now a murder enquiry?'

Natalia's hand flew to her mouth. 'Murder?' Her eyes began to fill with tears.

Becca passed her a tissue and she dabbed at her eyes and blew her nose. Dinsdale folded his arms across his chest, either embarrassed or annoyed by the nurse's reaction. Becca knew exactly what he was thinking. *A stupid woman.* But there was only one stupid person in this room.

'Raymond didn't drink the brandy,' she explained to

Natalia before Dinsdale could ask any more questions. 'And he didn't take an overdose. Somebody killed him and made it look like suicide.'

Natalia shook her head. 'No, that's not possible. Not here. This is good home. He was safe here.' Her eyes shifted to left and right as if she was afraid somebody might be listening.

'Is there something you want to tell us, Natalia?' Becca asked. 'You don't need to be afraid.'

But Natalia shook her head again.

Dinsdale sighed loudly. 'Let's try again, shall we? When was the last time you saw Mr Swindlehurst alive?'

Natalia flinched at the question. 'Alive? I saw him Monday evening.'

'At what time?'

She shrugged. 'I... can't remember.'

'You can't remember,' repeated Dinsdale sceptically, scribbling a note for himself. 'Well, where did you see him?'

'In his room. He was with...' She trailed off.

Dinsdale's brows knitted together in a frown. 'Who? Who was he with?'

Natalia shook her head again. 'A man. A visitor.'

Dinsdale consulted his notes. 'That would be this writer you mentioned, DS Shawcross.'

Becca ignored him. 'Natalia, had you ever seen this visitor before?'

Natalia thought for a moment, then nodded. 'I think so. Yes.'

'Can you describe him?'

'He was aged... about thirty, maybe thirty-five. Dark brown hair, quite long.' She indicated shoulder length hair with her hands. The description matched that of Craig Clarkson, the historian.

'And did you see this man leave the home?' asked Becca.

'No.'

'So you didn't see Raymond alive after the visitor had

gone?'

'I...' Natalia seemed on the brink of saying something, but then thought better of it. 'No.'

Becca sighed. Natalia knew something, she was certain of it. But she was too afraid to speak freely. If Dinsdale hadn't jumped in, interrogating the young nurse as if she were the prime suspect, perhaps she would have opened up. Becca would just have to try again later, when she was alone.

'Can anyone vouch for your whereabouts on the evening of the murder?' asked Dinsdale.

Natalia looked confused. 'I was here. Working.'

'Yes, but were you with someone the whole time?'

'No. We work alone. Is no need to be with someone else.'

'So you have no alibi. You had easy access to the victim's room. And it would have been a simple matter for you to slip inside, smother him with a pillow and then leave.'

Presumably Dinsdale's tactic was to frighten Natalia into revealing some fresh piece of information, maybe even trigger a full-blown confession. But Natalia was already terrified. 'But I... no! I did not kill him! Why would I do that?'

'Just the question I was about to ask,' said Dinsdale, as if his case was proven. 'Why would you? What reason did you have for wanting him dead?'

But it was no good. Natalia dissolved into tears and just shook her head when Dinsdale repeated his question. She got up and fled from the room, letting the door slam shut behind her.

Dinsdale folded his arms across his belly with a satisfied look. 'Well, I think we might have just found our murderer, don't you, DS Shawcross?'

'Do you really think so, sir?'

'Means, opportunity... all we have to do now is work out her motive. Perhaps this Raymond Swindlehurst left everything to her in his will. After all, he had no family to leave his money to, did he? I suggest we try to find out the contents of his will as a matter of urgency.'

Becca said nothing.

'So, who's next?' asked Dinsdale, examining the list of names Judith had printed for them.

'I'd quite like to speak to a woman called Violet,' said Becca. 'She's one of the residents.'

'Whatever for? You don't think some old woman suffocated him, do you?'

'When I first spoke to Natalia, she told me that Violet and Raymond were very close. She might know something that will help us.'

Dinsdale snorted. 'I don't want to waste time talking to the residents. Most of them probably can't even remember what happened as long ago as Monday. Why don't you talk to this...'

'Violet.'

'... and let me interview the rest of the staff myself.'

'Good idea, sir,' said Becca, getting up. 'I'll go and see if I can find her.'

★

The trip to Eden Camp had quashed Raven's theory that Forge Valley Man might be an escaped prisoner of war, but had opened up a new line of inquiry. One that was less likely to yield a positive ID, but that he nevertheless was determined to get to grips with. As soon as he and Jess returned to Scarborough, he went to look for DC Tony Bairstow.

He found Tony at his desk, exactly where he'd been that morning, and Raven wondered if he had ever left it. A foil-wrapped stack of homemade sandwiches stood beside his computer screen, indicating that he hadn't even stopped for a lunch break. He looked up as Raven entered. 'I chased up those records of escaped POWs in North Yorkshire, sir, just as you requested. Unfortunately I drew a blank.'

'Never mind that, Tony,' said Raven, aware that he had sent the detective constable on something of a wild goose chase. 'We're now looking for a German ex-POW who stayed on after the war.'

To his credit, Tony didn't bat an eyelid at the news that he had wasted his morning. Police work was like that sometimes. You had to follow up every lead, even though most of them led nowhere. 'Do we have anything more to go on, sir?' he asked, a pencil in his hand, ready to jot down details.

'We're looking for a young man, aged between eighteen and twenty-five, most probably with a German-sounding name. He would have been an airman – a navigator with the *Luftwaffe* – captured sometime during 1944 or 1945, and was most probably working on a nearby farm as an agricultural worker, or possibly a labourer.'

Now that Raven put together all the known facts, a fairly clear picture of the murder victim was beginning to emerge. They had almost everything they needed, except – tantalisingly – a name.

'I suggest you start with missing persons reports dated 1945, and work forwards. We can't rule out the possibility that he was killed as late as the fifties or even the sixties.'

Tony was busy writing it all down. 'I'll get straight onto it. I might need to speak to the archive offices at York and Northallerton.'

'Whatever you need, Tony.'

Raven was mindful of what Gillian had told him – that there was a limit to the resources she was willing to commit to the investigation. But that was a good reason to pull out all the stops before she decided that enough was enough.

'What do you want me to do, sir?' asked Jess. 'Do you think it's worth asking around the farms and villages close to Malton? See if anyone remembers?'

'Someone who was alive at the time, you mean?' Raven considered the proposal. He wished he had some more reliable way of identifying his victim, but with such an old case it was hard to know which way to turn. Jess's suggestion was a long shot, but he could see that she was keen to get back out into the countryside in her old Land Rover, and it wasn't like he had any better ideas. 'Go on then, Jess. It's worth a try.'

She shrugged her jacket back on, and headed out.

Raven was pleased to see that he could rely on the continued enthusiasm of his small team. Tony and Jess weren't giving up, and neither was he. Forge Valley Man might be nothing more than a pile of old bones, but to Raven he seemed very real indeed. He realised that as an ex-soldier himself, he had formed a strong affinity with the young German, who had died a long way from the land of his birth at a time when he ought to have felt safe after the war had ended.

Gillian might talk about resources, but for Raven a principle was at stake.

Justice still mattered, even if a man had been dead seventy years.

His phone rang in his jacket pocket and he pulled it out. It was Chandice. With a smile, he answered it.

CHAPTER 10

The enormous wood-panelled lounge at Larkmead might have lacked the privacy of the small meeting room, but without the head of a stag it was a much less oppressive place to conduct a police interview. Becca made herself comfortable in a wing-backed chair in front of a grand stone fireplace – mercifully without a fire – and gladly accepted a cup of tea and a biscuit when they were offered to her by one of the care home's catering staff.

Waistline be damned! She deserved a custard cream after having to put up with Dinsdale's nonsense.

She was glad to be on her own again and away from her boss. The man made her furious, the way he always jumped to conclusions and seized on the most obvious answer to any question. He did more harm than good and had completely ruined any chance of getting Natalia Kamińska to reveal what was bothering her. Becca would just have to track the nurse down later on her own.

For now, she had managed to locate Violet Armitage, the resident Natalia had described as Raymond's best friend in the nursing home.

The old lady was a petite figure in a cream satin blouse,

pleated skirt and smart court shoes. Snowy white hair as delicate as dandelion seed framed features dusted in a layer of face powder. Her lipstick was fuchsia pink and her nails were painted to match. Her perfume was lily of the valley. Becca felt positively underdressed in her black work trousers, plain shirt and lace-ups with no make-up.

But there was nothing snooty or superior about Violet. She seemed delighted to talk to Becca, despite the sad circumstances of her visit, and Becca sensed that she and the old lady were going to get along like the proverbial house on fire.

The handful of other residents dotted around the lounge were sitting quietly, reading. One old chap a couple of seats away appeared to have nodded off, but despite her obvious age Violet was alert and keen to chat.

'Raymond was a lovely man,' she said. 'Such a gentleman, and very good company. I was so sorry to hear of his passing. I will miss him more than I can say.'

'I'm sure you will, Mrs Armitage.'

'Oh, Violet, please. Calling me Mrs Armitage makes me feel even more ancient than I am.'

Becca smiled. 'Violet, then.'

'Was it his heart that gave out in the end?' she asked. 'I did question Judith, but she wouldn't give me a straight answer. She said it was up to the coroner to make a formal announcement after the inquest.'

Judith's efforts to keep the circumstances of Raymond's death under wraps were obviously paying off, and Becca didn't feel that it was her place to reveal any information. 'That's the procedure, yes.'

Violet studied her carefully. 'But if it was his heart, the police wouldn't be here asking questions, would they?'

There was clearly no chance of fooling the old lady. 'There are certain circumstances that indicate the death may have been unnatural,' said Becca.

Violet shook her head sadly. 'I can't understand why anyone would want to harm Raymond, but if that's what happened, then I want to do all I can to help.'

'Thank you very much,' said Becca. 'Can you tell me how long you'd known him?'

Violet chuckled. 'Why, Raymond and I went all the way back. We grew up together in Malton. The town isn't large and it was even smaller back then. This was in the nineteen-thirties, you understand. I knew practically everyone in the area because my father was the vicar of St Michael's on the market square. Raymond's parents ran a grocery shop. Swindlehurst's, it was called. You could buy everything there once upon a time. That was before they built the supermarket of course.'

She dipped a ginger snap into her tea and took a delicate bite.

'So, were you at school with Raymond?' prompted Becca.

'We went to the same school but Raymond was two years older than me. All the lasses were sweet on him because he was such a handsome lad.' Violet giggled, revealing a glimpse of the vivacious young girl she must once have been. 'I was too,' she admitted.

'So were you and Raymond ever...'

'Oh, no. It wasn't to be. The war saw to that.' Violet sighed and looked wistful. Becca waited patiently for her to continue, which she did without prompting. From the faraway look in her eyes, Becca could see the old lady was reliving her youth.

'We had a happy childhood, growing up in Malton. No one there was very rich, but we all had what we needed. There was nothing to complain about. But then the war came and changed everything. I can still remember that Sunday as if it were yesterday. Church finished early that day so that everyone could go home and listen to the radio. When Neville Chamberlain said, "this country is at war with Germany" we all expected bombs to start falling immediately. I was eleven when war broke out and seventeen when it ended. Can you imagine that?'

'No,' said Becca. 'It must have been a very difficult time for everyone.'

'It was. There was food rationing and you couldn't get nice clothes' – Becca wondered if that was why Violet took such good care of her appearance now – 'and the death toll was horrendous. But I was young, and life's always better when you're young. You're probably not old enough to understand that.' She smiled gently. 'There were also good opportunities for women. Do you know, in 1944 I joined the Auxiliary Territorial Service, the women's branch of the British Army.' Violet dropped her voice to a conspiratorial whisper. 'I pretended I was a year older than I really was!'

Becca laughed. 'Good for you.'

'The late queen was in the ATS, you know, when she was just Princess Elizabeth, and so too was Churchill's daughter, Mary.'

'Quite an elite club,' said Becca.

'It didn't matter if you were posh or poor, everyone had to muck in. Women weren't allowed to take part in combat, but I drove trucks and worked at the radar station in Ravenscar. It was bleak there, I can tell you. We lived in a barracks in a farmer's field next to the radar station. The field turned to mud whenever it rained, and in winter we had to de-ice the radar aerials. But there was a camaraderie between us girls. We knew that we were making a real difference to the war effort. Meanwhile, Raymond joined the Royal Navy and went off to sea. He did look smart in his uniform. I remember that day very well.' She paused. 'But by the time he returned, everything was different. The war had changed us. Some never came back at all. I met a young lad from Ravenscar, Billy. He wasn't quite as good-looking or charming as Raymond, but, well, there was no point waiting in the vague hope that Raymond might come back from the sea and ask me to marry him. You have to hold on to what you've got, don't you?'

Becca nodded.

'A friend of mine, Eileen, got engaged to a German lad. He was from the nearby prisoner of war camp – one of those who stayed on after the war ended. Imagine that!

German POWs living right under our noses! Some of the townspeople weren't too happy about it, but most folk realised they were just young lads who hadn't chosen to fight. But in Eileen's case it didn't work out. He abandoned her and went back to Germany. It broke her heart, it did. She was in the family way, and back then having a child outside of wedlock was scandalous, even though it went on more than people liked to admit. At least we're more relaxed about that sort of thing nowadays.' She leaned over and tapped Becca's hand. 'What about you, dear, do you have a young man?'

Becca was saved from having to answer by the old chap sitting close to Violet suddenly rousing himself from his slumber. He sprang to life, veined hands flying into the air. His eyes opened wide, fixing Becca with his gaze. 'Who are you? What are you doing here?'

'Now, now, Eric,' said Violet, speaking slowly and clearly in a loud voice. 'There's nothing to worry about. This young lady is from the police. She's here to ask about Raymond.'

'Raymond?' Eric scratched his head.

Violet leaned towards Becca and lowered her voice. 'Eric's from Malton too. He used to know Raymond well, but he hardly knows anyone anymore. He suffers from dementia. He has occasional good days, but most of the time he doesn't know which way is up.'

The old man narrowed his eyes and levelled a bony finger at Becca. 'Never mind Raymond. What are you going to do about catching the person who nicked my money?'

Becca was so startled, she didn't know what to say.

'Shush, Eric,' said Violet. 'Not now.'

Eric gave her a mournful look, then closed his eyes once more.

'Has someone really stolen his money?' asked Becca.

'Of course not,' said Violet. 'He always says that.'

Eric's head once again lolled onto his chest and a snore emanated from his open mouth.

At least the interruption had given Becca an opportunity to guide Violet away from wartime reminiscences and onto more recent events at the care home. 'Raymond had no family, is that right?'

'No, his wife died some years ago, and they had no children.'

'So there were no relatives he could leave his money to?'

Violet gave a half-smile. 'I don't think he really had any money, apart from some small savings squirrelled away for a rainy day. Raymond used to say, "What do I need money for? There's no time to spend it. I'll be dead any day now."' Violet lapsed into silence, Raymond's words clearly taking on a new and prophetic ring given what had happened.

'Do you think he expected to die?' asked Becca.

'No. He'd been saying that for the past ten years.'

'You hadn't noticed any change in him recently?'

Violet thought for a moment. 'He didn't say there was anything wrong, but just these last few days he did seem a little preoccupied. Not quite his normal cheery self.'

'Do you know what might have upset him?'

'I'm sorry, I really have no idea. Raymond didn't normally keep secrets. But now I wish I'd asked.' Violet looked quite crestfallen and Becca squeezed her hand. The old lady squeezed hers back with surprising vigour. 'You know, dear, when you get to my age you realise that all we have in the end are joys and regrets. I've done my best to hold on to the joy and not to carry my regrets with me. Try to make sure that you do the same.'

CHAPTER 11

'So who exactly is Chandice Jones?' asked Raven.

He and Chandice were seated in a French restaurant named *Peut-Être*, tucked away amid the old streets of York behind the Minster. The place had been Chandice's choice. To Raven's way of thinking, its name suggested all manner of possibilities, a fact that both excited him and made him feel rather uncomfortable. After all, he was SIO leading a murder investigation, and she was a forensic expert, certain to be called as a key witness should the case ever come – by some small miracle – to trial. Yet he had followed his heart over his head many times before, and this would surely not be the last occasion.

When she had phoned to invite him out for dinner, he'd briefly considered declining. But then a vision of her long dark hair and shapely curves had formed in his mind and his resistance had crumbled in an instant.

At least he hadn't picked her up from her home. There was still some vague chance of pretence that this was something other than what it appeared to be – a dinner date. He had arrived, as was his habit, unfashionably early, and had been shown by the waiter to a corner table. 'Would *Monsieur* like to see the wine menu while he waits for *Mademoiselle*?'

'I'll just wait, thank you,' Raven had told him, resisting the temptation to tell the smug git that he was waiting for *Docteur*, not *Mademoiselle*, and already certain that this place would never make his list of favourite restaurants. Not that he had a list of favourites. Only least favourites.

Chandice had arrived some twenty minutes later, wearing a dress that made Raven gasp. He'd risen to his feet to greet her with the words, 'You look stunning,' and had been rewarded with a smile that could melt ice-cream.

And so here they were. And as they gazed into each other's eyes over twinkling candlelight, there really was no hope at all of hiding the fact that he was having a romantic *liaison* with a woman he should never have agreed to meet outside working hours. It was, he admitted to himself, a *liaison dangereuse*.

They had started the evening safely enough, with Raven telling her about his visit to Eden Camp and the likelihood of finally putting a name to the skeleton. But now, almost imperceptibly, they had moved into deeper and more dangerous waters.

She regarded him playfully, the candlelight making her eyes glint a warm caramel. 'You want me to tell you all about myself? Where should I start?'

'At the beginning?' he suggested.

'That might take a while.'

'I'm in no hurry.'

'Let's start with my grandmother, then. Her name was Glory. She was one of the Windrush generation. She came to Britain in the early fifties from Jamaica. My middle name is Glory, after her.'

'It's lovely.'

'Thank you.'

'And the name Chandice?'

'It's a traditional Jamaican name. It means "one who is extremely smart and talented."'

'Well, that figures.'

He took a sip of mineral water, and she raised a glass of Beaujolais to her lips. When ordering drinks, he had made his usual excuse about not drinking when driving. It always seemed easier than explaining the true reason.

'Anyway, now I want to hear all about DCI Raven. Who is he when he's not trying to identify skeletons?'

Raven shrugged. 'There's not a lot to tell.'

His usual opening gambit when asked about himself.

'I don't believe that for a moment.'

Raven knew that he was beaten. He wasn't getting out of here without revealing some morsel about his life.

'I grew up in Scarborough. My dad was a fisherman and my mum worked as a chambermaid at the Grand Hotel.'

Shorthand for a life of poverty.

Chandice nodded encouragement for him to keep going.

'My mum died when I was sixteen.'

Best to get that out of the way.

'I'm sorry to hear that.'

Chandice didn't ask how she'd died, and Raven wasn't going to volunteer the information that she'd been killed by a drunk driver when out at night looking for him when he should have been home revising for his exams. Nor was he about to admit to the thirty years of guilt and self-loathing that had followed.

'After that, things weren't too good between me and my dad.'

Understatement of the year. But there was really nothing to be gained from explaining that the reason he shunned alcohol was because of his father's heavy drinking and violent outbursts.

'I left home at sixteen and joined the army.'

'That must have been tough at such a young age.'

'The army taught me a lot. The value of discipline and structure. Self-respect and self-reliance.'

'Did you see active service?'

'Some.' He considered again telling her about Bosnia. But the prospect of engaging in a discussion of war crimes, genocide and mass graves held little appeal right now. 'After serving for a few years, I moved back to London and joined the police.'

Again, there was no need to mention the leg injury, the medal for bravery, the long and agonising path from military hospital back to a semblance of fitness, health and normal life. None of these were congenial topics for a romantic dinner, so he left them under the table.

'So where do you come from originally?' he asked, keen to deflect attention away from himself. 'I detect a southern accent.'

'Spot on,' she said. 'Brighton.'

'You still have family there?'

She nodded. 'I visit my parents whenever I can. In practice that means fitting in around the academic year. Christmas, Easter, Summer. What about you? Did you ever patch things up with your father?'

Once again she had struck a soft spot in Raven's armour. His father was one of his least favourite topics of discussion, second only to himself. But he had a quick way of shutting down questions. 'He's dead too.'

'Sorry,' said Chandice. 'But you do have a wife?'

'And a daughter. But I don't see either of them.'

He could see her trying to figure out how best to get past his defences. 'You said your wife left you...'

'...for an accountant called Graham.'

That produced a wry grin. 'Would you be happier if she'd left you for a stunt man called Clint?'

'I'd be happier if she hadn't left me at all.'

Silence.

Raven really sucked at this. He was so out of practice. Was he really going to sabotage Chandice's every attempt at conversation?

He was saved from his embarrassment by the arrival of the main course – an elaborate-looking *bouillabaisse* for Chandice, and an unimaginative *steak frites* for Raven.

Steak and chips. The go-to choice for all males when faced with a complicated restaurant menu. Lisa had always complained about his boring predictability. But to Raven's mind, predictability was a virtue. It was people who went off the rails without warning that you had to watch out for. People like Lisa herself whose act of rebellion had been to leave him for a professional bore. Ironic or what?

Chandice took a mouthful of fish stew and then set her spoon aside. 'At least your wife stayed around long enough for you to get married and have a daughter. I've never even come close. Academics aren't great at relationships. We move around too much, always looking for the next post, not even knowing if it'll be in the same department or in another country.'

'Like Milan?'

'Like Milan.'

Her words had poured out nervously, and she followed them with a large gulp of wine. Raven knew that she was doing her best to make up for his lack of tact and general reluctance to open up about himself. She was offering him an insight into her private life. Making herself vulnerable.

He wasn't good with vulnerability.

'If you think academics aren't good at relationships,' he quipped, 'then you've obviously never dated a police officer.'

He was hoping she would laugh at that, but instead she said, 'You mean until now.'

Silence again.

But this time it was his turn to break it.

'Is that what this is?' he asked. 'A date?'

'It can be whatever you want, Mysterious Man Called Raven.'

It was impossible for him not to smile at that. 'If you feel more comfortable, you can call me Tom.'

'Tom.' She tested the word, seeming to like it. 'Well, Tom, what do you say? Is this a date?'

★

'I met a lovely old lady today,' said Becca. 'Her name is Violet.'

She was sitting at Sam's hospital bedside, holding his hand in hers as she always did when she came to see him.

'She had a lot to tell me, all about life during wartime. She would have gone on a lot longer if I'd let her.'

Becca stroked Sam's palm, trying to ignore the various tubes, machines and monitors that were keeping him alive and confirming the fact that he was breathing, that his heart was still beating, and that his brain was functioning. That Sam was still in there, somewhere.

He had been in a coma for nearly a year now, ever since the hit and run accident that had left him with a traumatic head injury. His eyes remained closed, his fingers indifferent to Becca's touch.

The same, every day.

Yet still Becca came to see him. The doctors had told her not to give up hope, that talking to Sam might help to rouse him from unconsciousness, that he might be able to hear her words even though he gave no outward sign of awareness.

At least that's what they had told her at the beginning. Now, when she saw them, they said little, just regarded her with sad looks.

But Becca wasn't giving up that easily. What had Violet said to her just that very day?

You have to hold on to what you've got.

Becca gripped Sam's hand harder. 'She's a very wise old lady. And even though she's in her nineties, she's still trying to live the best life she can, every single day. That's how I want us to be, when we're in our nineties. What do you say, Sam?'

Sam said nothing, of course. But that no longer seemed to matter.

She could talk freely to him, relating the mundane events of her day, telling him of her hopes and her achievements, unburdening herself of her worries when life was getting her down. She always felt calmer after she'd talked to Sam.

She wasn't able to visit him every day, but she came as many evenings as she could. It wasn't just a sense of duty that brought her here. It was a longing to be with her best friend. Because that's what Sam was.

She'd long since lost touch with most of her school friends. They were either settled down with their own partners – some even had children – or were still living the free-and-single life, partying and clubbing every weekend. Becca and Sam would have been living together by now – might even have become engaged – were it not for the accident.

One instant of bad luck that had turned everything upside down.

She felt a hand on her shoulder and looked round to see Greg and Denise, Sam's parents standing behind her.

'We thought we might find you here,' said Denise. 'You're so good at coming to visit Sam.'

'I like talking to him,' said Becca. 'I was having a good old natter.'

Denise gave her a wan smile. She'd been a good-looking woman once, but the last year had taken its toll on her. The lines on her forehead had deepened. Her hair, once carefully coiffured and maintained a rich auburn colour, was now neglected and had been left to return to its natural grey, making her appear older than her years. Greg was a man of few words. He looked on, tight-lipped, unable to meet Becca's eye.

'We were hoping to have a word with you,' said Denise.

'Of course,' said Becca. 'I'll fetch a couple of chairs for you.'

'Not here,' said Denise, glancing awkwardly at her son. 'Come to the visitors' room.'

'Okay.' Becca leaned over Sam and whispered in his ear. 'Don't go anywhere'. They were the words she always said to him when she left his side. A private joke between them.

She followed Sam's parents to the room down the corridor set aside for visitors. Mismatched chairs were arranged around a low coffee table on which a pot of winter pansies in need of water were starting to shrivel. Becca sat across the table from them, a sense of dread growing in the pit of her stomach.

Denise fussed with her handbag. Greg leaned forwards, his elbows resting on his knees, staring at the floor. Becca waited for one of them to speak.

It was Denise who broke the silence. 'The thing is, Becca, we've been talking to the consultant and...' Her voice cracked and a tear appeared in one eye.

Greg cleared his throat. 'The doctors say there's no hope for Sam.'

'No!' said Becca. 'That's not true. They said there's always hope, that we should keep talking to him, that familiar voices can be crucial to his recovery.'

'That's what they said at the beginning. They also said that the longer Sam remains in a coma, the less likely he is to recover.'

'Yes, but–'

'It's gone on long enough,' said Denise, tears rolling down both cheeks now. 'I – we – can't stand it anymore. It's time to bring this to an end, Becca.'

Becca felt like she'd been slapped. She stared at Greg and Denise, wordless with shock.

Greg spoke again. 'The consultant has told us that if family and doctors are in agreement, then treatment can be withdrawn. Sam's breathing and feeding tubes will be removed. Without them... Sam won't suffer, Becca. He can no longer feel anything. He hasn't been able to feel anything for a very long time.'

Becca shook her head, unwilling to accept what she was hearing.

'Do you understand what we're saying?' asked Greg.

But all Becca understood was that Sam was still alive and that she wasn't giving up on him. There was still a chance, however slim...

'It's a joint decision between the family and the doctors,' said Denise.

'Family?'

'Parents,' said Greg.

What about me? Becca wanted to scream. *Don't I get a say in any of this? And what about Sam? Who is speaking up for him?*

'Is this really what you want?' she croaked, close to tears herself now.

'It's not about what we want,' said Denise. 'It's about what's best for Sam.'

For a minute, no one spoke. Becca felt as if she had entered a weird, parallel universe that she didn't know how to navigate. She was completely at sea, without a rudder or a compass to guide her. In the end, she managed one simple question. 'When?'

'There are still some formalities to complete,' said Greg. 'But it's one week until the anniversary of Sam's accident. We don't want to prolong this agony any longer than that.'

'One week?' said Becca.

'You're still young,' said Denise, leaning forward and giving Becca's hand a squeeze. 'It's time you got your life back. You need to move on, and put all this behind you.'

Becca said nothing. This *was* her life. What if she wasn't ready to move on?

CHAPTER 12

Jess padded briskly along the hard, wet sand of the North Bay, the salty air that blew in from the sea gently stinging her face. Scott kept pace at her side. The tide was on its way out, drawing back to reveal a mile and a half of clean, virgin sand just waiting for them to leave a trail of footprints. She turned back to see how far they'd come, the wind catching stray strands of her blonde hair and whipping them across her face.

They had started near the castle gatehouse, following the twisting path that led down the steep side of Castle Hill, and were headed towards the Old Scalby Mills pub. The plan was to stop there for lunch before continuing on up the coast. Jess was keen to see how far they could walk before having to turn back.

She had first met Scott, the youngest member of Holly Chang's CSI team, on a previous murder enquiry. He had caught her eye immediately, and she could tell that the attraction was mutual. But Scott was very shy and if things had been left to him they might still not have exchanged a single word.

Jess wasn't prepared to leave life to chance, however. If

you wanted something you had to make it happen.

So here they were, enjoying a shared interest. Walking. Jess hoped that in time they would discover other things that they had in common.

As first dates went, she had no doubt that this was unconventional. Her friends always did the predictable thing, hooking up with lads in bars. Cocktails, shots, loud music. Yet Jess had never been the same as most girls her age, and she suspected that Scott was different to other guys too. So if they wanted to walk along a windswept beach in November, why not?

There was an icy chill in the air this morning but Jess was an outdoors person and had come prepared for the weather with a hat and gloves. Scott, too, was dressed in a warm fleece, but was wearing shorts, revealing tanned, muscular legs. 'I don't really feel the cold,' he told her. 'Not unless there's snow on the ground.'

Scarborough was no stranger to snow, sometimes even on the beach itself in the depths of winter, when arctic winds could bring the temperature down to ten below freezing. If that happened, perhaps even Scott would be forced to wear long trousers.

'Have you always lived in Scarborough?' she asked. It seemed like a good place to start, since she knew next to nothing about him. And it was clear that if she wanted the conversation to move beyond a discussion of the weather she was going to have to do the heavy lifting.

'Yeah. Born and bred. You?'

'I'm from the North York Moors originally. Rosedale Abbey.'

Scott gave her a dreamy smile. 'Ingleby Incline.'

'You've walked it?'

He nodded.

'Awesome.' She waited to see if he would volunteer any more information, but it seemed like that was it for now. 'So,' she said, 'I moved to Scarborough to join the police. But after a year I realised I didn't want to be just a bobby on the beat. I fancied becoming a detective and solving real crimes. It does mean that I have to spend more time in the station, but I still manage to get out and about quite a bit.'

Scott nodded, seeming content to listen to her talk.

'I've grown to like it here, especially out of season.'

In truth, Jess had found the move to Scarborough tough at first. After the peace of Rosedale, the seaside resort had felt brash and noisy. She had almost packed her bags and returned home on more than one occasion. But Jess wasn't a quitter. Instead, she had made an effort to explore the town and its surroundings on foot, and had begun to appreciate its charms. The sands were a good place to walk, almost as open as the moors. And she'd developed a liking for the flat expanse of the sea. Sometimes blue and sparkling beneath the sun, at other times grey and dull, it was as changeable as the moorland. Today the wind was stiff, and grey clouds scudded overhead. Gulls soared and dived on the gusts, filling the sky with a cacophony of cries, and white horses galloped towards the shoreline, dissolving into foam and froth as they broke. It was an invigorating sight.

She wanted to put what she felt into words, but sometimes it was easier just to look. 'It's beautiful, isn't it?' she said to Scott.

'Yeah, it is.'

She could tell from the way his eyes lingered on the faraway horizon that he understood.

'So what made you want to become a crime scene investigator?' she asked. 'Did you watch one of those TV shows and get sucked in by the glamour?'

'No. It was because of my mum.'

'Your mum? Did she encourage you?'

'No, she was murdered.'

This was the last thing she'd expected him to say. 'Oh, Scott, I'm really sorry. I had no idea.'

'No worries. There's no reason for you to know.'

This definitely wasn't first-date material by any conventional measure. If Jess's friends were any guide, she and Scott ought now to be discussing their favourite songs and where they'd been on holiday that summer. Perhaps they would move on to chatting about popular TV shows.

'The CSI team messed up the investigation,' Scott continued. 'Key evidence was lost or contaminated. So her killer was never caught.'

'I'm so sorry,' said Jess. 'But did this happen in Scarborough? Holly Chang has a reputation for being really thorough.'

'Holly's great,' said Scott. 'But this was seven years ago, before Holly took over. It's why I decided to train as a crime scene investigator myself. I didn't want the same thing to happen to anyone else.'

Jess nodded. Suddenly her own reason for joining the police – to get out and about instead of being stuck in a boring desk job – seemed completely trivial.

She took his hand in hers, and they continued to walk across the sand in silence.

*

The old man dragged his rake across the lawn, clearing away the last of the leaves. At this time of year they were falling thick and fast, all brown and golden, not just from his own well-tended trees but across the fence from the overgrown jungle in his neighbour's garden too. The thought of that made his blood boil, and he tugged harder at the rake, making sure to gather every last leaf. Even the ones that had fallen onto his lawn from next door.

Especially those.

There would be more to clear the following day, but that was how life was. Always more jobs to do. If they didn't get done, they simply mounted up. Leaving jobs was the fool's way out. If a task needed doing, it was best done straight away. It was how he had lived his life, and he wasn't a young man, so he must have done something right.

He swept the leaves into a neat pile, then scooped them into the wheelbarrow. The bonfire was still smouldering at the back of the house, and he tipped the latest load on top and stood back to watch.

Soon the tips of the leaves began to blister and grey smoke emerged, curling into wisps in the cold air. He coughed once as it caught in his throat. An acrid smell that reminded him of long ago.

Smoke coming from the direction of the cockpit. The crackle of flames as they took hold. One engine down, and the judder and roar of the remaining three as they struggled to keep the plane aloft. Men's screams.

He scowled at the memory, pushing it back to where it had come from. To where it belonged. At the back of his mind.

Let those kinds of memories out and they would take over. He had seen it happen to weaker men. But he wasn't weak. Not like them.

The leaves were catching now, crisping and bursting into flames as the fire took hold. Soon they would all be gone.

He reached into his coat pocket and pulled out the letter. He'd known what it contained as soon as he'd seen it arrive through his letter box. The Scarborough postmark. The familiar handwriting.

Foolish nonsense. Reading it had made him furious, and the thought made his anger boil once again.

But that threat had passed. The fool who'd written it was no more, just like the leaves, crisping into oblivion.

He crushed the letter in his fist and tossed it into the flames. The fire was burning nicely now and the paper caught in seconds. He watched with satisfaction as it twisted and writhed, the flames devouring it.

Soon the letter was gone, and so was the threat it contained.

He felt a spot of rain and turned his face to the sky. Grey clouds rolling in. It would rain soon, just as he'd expected. It was a good job he'd burned the leaves before it started.

CHAPTER 13

Remembrance Sunday fell on the thirteenth of November this year and Becca had promised to take her grandparents up to the top of Oliver's Mount where the Act of Remembrance would take place around the war memorial.

'It's good of you to bring us,' said her grandmother as she got out of the car, the wind almost snatching her hat away.

'It's no trouble,' said Becca, going round to the other side of the car to help her grandfather.

He ducked low as he struggled to clamber out. At times like this, Becca wished she had a slightly larger car, though definitely not one like Raven's sports coupé. His BMW was almost impossible to squeeze around the tight corners of the old town and was a nightmare to park. Unlike the Jazz, which could slot into the tiniest of spaces.

As she held the passenger door of the Honda open for her grandfather she noticed a minibus from Larkmead parked nearby. Some carers were helping a few of the residents out of the bus. Violet was among them, and her friend Eric too, but they were too busy to notice Becca.

She helped her grandfather to his feet and handed him his walking stick.

'Thank you, Becca, love.'

The annual event was something of a family ritual. Becca's parents weren't easily able to get away from the guest house, and Liam never bothered to attend such things, but Becca always brought her grandparents to the service if she wasn't working. Afterwards they would go back to the B&B for a traditional Sunday roast.

This year the day seemed especially poignant. It was partly because of the death of Raymond Swindlehurst and the long conversation she'd had about the war with Violet. But it was mostly because of the news about Sam. She'd spent all Saturday by his bedside, talking to him and willing him to wake up before it was too late. But he'd lain there oblivious, the same as he always did.

Her grandparents linked arms and set off towards the cenotaph. Becca followed just behind. Her grandfather was a tall, dignified man who'd developed a stoop in recent years. His wife was rounder and softer and barely came up to his shoulder. They'd been married sixty-seven years and were utterly devoted to one another. It was the sort of long-lasting relationship that Becca could only dream of.

The thought of Sam's life-support machines being turned off filled her once again with terror.

The top of the Mount was packed with Scarborians muffled up against the wind that gusted off the North Sea. Veterans in wheelchairs proudly displayed their war medals on their chests. Becca and her grandparents found a space at the edge of the crowd with a view across the South Bay to the ruined castle on the headland. It was the most spectacular sight in Scarborough, but today even that dramatic vista failed to lift her spirits. She clutched the service sheet as it flapped in the wind and tried to stop herself from breaking down completely.

A hush fell on the crowd as representatives of the armed forces and the Royal British Legion carried their respective flags up the steps and took their places at the base of the memorial. Then the brass band of the Salvation Army led everyone in the hymn beloved by all seafarers, *Eternal Father, strong to save*. Becca's grandfather, who still possessed a rich baritone voice at the age of eighty-seven, led the singing in their little corner of the crowd, encouraging others to join in.

> *O hear us when we cry to Thee,*
> *For those in peril on the sea.*

The mayor led the laying of the poppy wreaths, and the preacher read the words of *The Ode of Remembrance*.

> *They shall grow not old, as we that are left grow old:*
> *Age shall not weary them, nor the years condemn.*
> *At the going down of the sun and in the morning*
> *We will remember them.*

When a lone bugle player embarked on the *Last Post*, the sound was so haunting and full of sorrow that Becca found herself overcome with emotion. She let her tears fall freely, no longer trying to hold them back. Her grandfather put his arm around her shoulders and held her tightly.

Afterwards her grandmother said, 'Let's go home and put the kettle on. Then you can tell us all about it, love.'

Back in the comfort of her grandparents' house on Scalby Mills Road, Becca sat on the sofa in front of the gas fire in the lounge and, between mouthfuls of strong Yorkshire tea, told them about her visit to Sam on Friday evening and the conversation with Sam's parents.

'What a terrible shock for you,' said her grandmother.

Becca nodded. 'I had no idea they were thinking of this. I can't believe they're giving up on Sam.'

'How long has it been since the accident?' asked her grandfather.

'Almost a year,' said Becca. Not a day had passed during that time when she hadn't thought about Sam, when she hadn't longed for his recovery.

'We've worried about you all this time,' said her grandmother. 'We didn't know how you'd cope, visiting him in hospital the way he is. We thought it would all be too much for you, but you've done so well. You've never given up hope. You're very brave.'

'Do you think I've been a fool?'

'Good gracious, no!' exclaimed her grandmother. 'Whatever makes you say that?'

'Maybe there really is no hope for him.'

Since speaking to Sam's parents, Becca had begun to doubt the wisdom of what she was doing. Was she clinging to a lost cause? Would it be kinder to Sam to let him die? Her thoughts turned to the old man, Eric, at the nursing home. He was alive but seemed to have lost his wits, believing that people were stealing his money.

They shall grow not old, as we that are left grow old.

Was a life like Eric's still worth living? Was such a life worth less than a young, healthy life? Would Eric – and Sam too – be better off dead? She felt so confused.

'There is *always* hope,' said her grandmother decisively.

'You need to tell Sam's parents how you're feeling,' said her grandfather. 'And they need to listen to you.'

'Thank you,' said Becca. It was a relief to know that her grandparents believed in her and supported her.

Her phone buzzed to indicate an incoming text message, and she glanced at the screen. It was from an unknown number.

We need to talk. Not by phone. Can we meet? Natalia

So Natalia did have something to tell her. Becca quickly texted back.

Can meet you tomorrow. I'll text in the morning.

She put the phone away in her bag. Now wasn't the time to think about work. Becca wanted to spend the rest of Sunday with her family, and to visit Sam again later that evening. But the confirmation that her hunch about Natalia was correct gave her a much-needed confidence boost. She dabbed her tears away with a tissue and stood up. 'Now, shall we all go round to Mum and Dad's? I don't know about you, but I could really tuck into roast beef with all the trimmings.'

CHAPTER 14

Monday morning. The start of another week. Raven woke to the screeching of gulls outside his bedroom window and arrived at the office early after a quick shower in his dysfunctional bathroom and a breakfast cooked on the ancient gas stove. He could hardly wait for the old kitchen and bathroom to be ripped out and replaced.

It had been an eventful weekend. The investigation into the murder of Forge Valley Man may have been moving at a glacial pace, but his relationship with Dr Jones – Chandice – had become sizzlingly hot.

What have I done?

He should never have agreed to go out with her on Friday evening. When she'd asked him whether or not the evening was a date, he should not have answered in the affirmative. And he should never, absolutely not, no way, have ended up in bed with her that night.

He had driven her back to her flat in York, agreed that a coffee would be the perfect way to round off the evening – turned out, she owned a second Gaggia machine at home – and then...

Well, suffice to say that it had all been an inexcusable lapse of professional judgement on his part.

And an absolutely unforgettable night that he couldn't regret.

It was the first time he'd spent a night with a woman since Lisa had left him. And apart from Lisa herself, Chandice was the only woman he'd slept with in almost twenty-five years.

He wasn't going to forget that in a hurry.

They'd woken up in bed together, made love again, then put the coffee machine on. *Expresso love*, he'd called it, but that had only shown his age. Chandice hadn't understood the reference. She was only thirty-five, for God's sake. She hadn't even been born when Dire Straits recorded their hit song. When he'd asked her what kind of music she liked, none of the names she reeled off had meant a thing to him. But she'd played him some tracks and he quite liked what he heard. He was willing to make an effort.

They'd spent the rest of Saturday together, going out again that evening and returning to her flat for another round between the sheets.

An inexcusable lapse of professional judgement.

Sod that. It had given him a buzz better than a whole week's worth of espresso packed into one morning.

He just hoped that what he had found with Chandice would last longer than a single weekend.

On returning to his home in Scarborough, he'd been struck by the contrast between the run-down old cottage and Chandice's trendy modern apartment. He desperately needed to get the place fixed up. Fortunately, Barry had dropped a quote for the work through his front door while he'd been gone.

After sitting down and checking the total amount for a second time, Raven decided to bite the bullet. The figure was eye-popping, even worse than he'd feared, but if he ever hoped to invite Chandice round to his place, he couldn't put it off. He called the builder and agreed the work.

'How soon can you start?' he asked.

'ASAP,' promised Barry. 'I'll call round later and pick up a key if that's okay. That way I can pop in and get cracking while you're at work.'

'Excellent,' said Raven. He was keen to get the work underway as soon as possible.

After speaking to Barry, he'd sent an email to his daughter, Hannah, telling her about the building work and suggesting that she might like to visit him once it was done. He began to tell her about Chandice too.

I've met someone. I'll think you'll like her. I like her very much.

But the more he stared at the words, the less sure he became. Would Hannah appreciate the fact that there was someone new in his life? A woman who wasn't her mother? Would she understand how lonely it could be when your wife had left you? And would she and Chandice really hit it off as smoothly as he imagined, or would there be complex undercurrents that would be tricky to navigate? Perhaps it was premature to broach the subject just yet. He deleted the words he'd written, confining his message to house-related matters.

In the morning when he checked his emails, there was no reply from Hannah. But Chandice had sent him a message on his phone.

Enjoyed our time together very much. Hope to see you again soon.

He tapped out a quick reply.

Definitely.

The door to his office opened and Becca came in. 'You're looking very pleased with yourself this morning.'

He tucked his phone away out of sight in his jacket pocket. 'Am I?' Raven was aware that a huge grin had spread across his face as he recalled the events of the weekend.

'Have you made a breakthrough with your skeleton?'

'Oh, that,' said Raven. 'Not really.'

'Jess told me that she'd driven out to Eden Camp with you.'

'Yes, we had an idea that our man was an escaped POW.'

'And was he?'

'No. But he may well have been a captured airman who stayed on after the war.'

'A German?'

'That's right.'

She gave him a half-smile.

'What is it?' Raven asked.

Her smile broadened. 'Go and speak to a woman called Violet Armitage. She's a resident at Larkmead Nursing Home. I have a hunch she might be able to give you an ID for your skeleton.'

'Who do you–' Raven began, but his words came to a halt as the door burst open.

DI Dinsdale rushed in, red-faced and out of breath, his hair a mess and his tie askew. Raven didn't think he'd ever seen him move so fast.

Dinsdale scanned the room and his eyes alighted on Becca. 'There you are! Come on, get your coat on, we're going out!'

'Where to, sir?'

Dinsdale was already turning to leave. 'There's been another murder.'

'What? Who?'

Dinsdale gestured impatiently for her to get a move on. 'That Polish woman who worked at the care home. Natalia…'

'Kamińska?' said Becca. 'There must be some mistake. I was just about to call her.'

'Well, it's too late for that,' snapped Dinsdale. 'Now are you coming or not?'

*

The lane was already cordoned off by the time Becca and Dinsdale arrived. It was a back alley behind a row of four-storey Victorian terraces that had been converted into flats.

Seen from this side, the houses were an ugly mishmash of bolted-on extensions, metal fire escapes and untidy backyards cluttered with wheelie bins. The alley itself was a scruffy affair, not even tarmacked, and full of potholes and litter. Police cars with flashing lights were parked at both ends, cutting off access.

The crime scene was halfway down the alleyway, protected from prying eyes by a white tent. An abandoned bicycle lay on its side a short distance away, flagged by a yellow evidence marker. Members of Holly's team were already there, scouring the area for evidence – perhaps a dropped cigarette butt or a tissue that could be tested for DNA, a used bus ticket, maybe even the murder weapon itself, although only a prize idiot would leave it lying around at the scene for the police to find. Becca and Dinsdale donned protective clothing and approached the tent.

Becca's mind was in turmoil. She'd driven to work that morning feeling calmer and stronger after spending Sunday with her grandparents. She'd resolved to speak to Sam's parents, to better understand their point of view but also to put across her own argument. They had to give Sam until the end of the year at least. They had to give him a fighting chance.

But now a young woman had lost her life and all thoughts of Sam needed to be put aside for the time being.

How could Natalia be dead? Her text message the previous day had indicated that she'd been afraid of something, or perhaps someone.

We need to talk. Not by phone. Can we meet?

Becca ought to have picked up on Natalia's concern and arranged to meet sooner. But she'd been so preoccupied with her own problems that she'd delayed meeting Natalia and now it was too late.

A uniformed PC standing guard at the scene filled them in on the details. 'IC1 female in her twenties. Found this morning at seven o'clock by a neighbour on his way to work. He ID'd her as Natalia Kamińska, a Polish worker at a nearby care home. She lived in that flat over there with her boyfriend.' He pointed to one of the nearby ground floor flats.

Dinsdale's nostrils flared at the mention of a boyfriend. 'Where is this boyfriend now?'

'In the flat, sir. And there's a copper making sure he stays there.'

'You think he did it, this boyfriend?'

'He says not, but he looks capable.'

'Right,' said Dinsdale gruffly. 'Let's take a look at the body.' He gestured for Becca to go first.

She lifted the flap of the tent and stepped inside. Holly Chang was supervising a photographer taking pictures of the body. Until that moment, Becca had been hoping against hope that it wasn't Natalia lying there. But one look at the victim told her the terrible truth. She took a breath to steady herself.

Dinsdale pushed forwards and stood over the body. It didn't take him long to come to a conclusion. 'Blunt force trauma to the back of the head with a heavy object.' He crouched down and tilted Natalia's head to one side with his gloved hand, revealing a nasty head wound. Natalia's hair was a sticky mess of dried blood mixed with grit from the lane. A circle of deep crimson had spread out beneath her head.

'She must have bled out quickly,' said Holly.

'Was anything taken?' asked Dinsdale. 'Was this a robbery?'

Holly showed the evidence that had been recovered from the body. 'Her phone and wallet were still on her, and the wallet contains a bank card and some cash. She was also wearing a lanyard around her neck that confirms her ID.'

Natalia's coat was unzipped at the neck and Becca saw that the dead woman was still wearing her blue nurse's uniform underneath. 'Looks like she was just going off to work, or just returning.'

'Any luck locating the murder weapon?' asked

Dinsdale.

'Not so far.'

'Any indications of a sexual assault?' asked Becca.

'Not that I can see,' said Holly. 'She's still fully clothed. We'll check her fingernails for fibres, but it looks as if she was attacked from behind and wouldn't have had a chance to defend herself. She might not even have seen her attacker coming.'

Dinsdale stood up. 'All right, I think we've seen enough here.' He stepped out of the tent and took in a gulp of the cold morning air.

Becca followed him. 'What now, sir?'

Dinsdale gave her a nasty smile. 'The boyfriend, of course. I don't think we'll need to look much further to find out who did this.'

CHAPTER 15

Natalia's boyfriend sat slumped on an old sofa in front of a TV, his feet propped up on a stool. Becca immediately recognised him as the gardener from the care home. He was wearing a pair of grey jogging pants and a stained grey T-shirt. He had no socks on his feet, and looked as if he'd just crawled out of bed.

A single overhead lightbulb struggled to illuminate the dingy surroundings. The remains of a takeaway curry littered the floor, along with some empty beer bottles. A Formica-topped table was pushed against one wall with a couple of chairs. On the way in, Becca had spied a kitchen just big enough to rustle up a modest meal, a bedroom with an unmade double bed, and a tiny bathroom.

This was not a luxury apartment by any stretch of the imagination.

Dinsdale pulled up one of the chairs and sat down in the middle of the living room. The chair creaked under his weight as he leaned towards the young man on the sofa. 'What's your name, son?'

'Troy.' He glowered at Dinsdale, clearly resenting the

patronising tone that the detective had adopted.

'Troy what?'

'Woods.'

'And you were the boyfriend of Natalia Kam...'

'Kamińska,' said Becca.

'Yeah.' Troy sniffed loudly and folded his arms over his chest. His eyes were puffy and a little bloodshot, either from grief, a heavy night, or both. He wasn't giving much away, but she sensed that beneath the defensive attitude he was upset.

Which didn't mean that he wasn't guilty, of course.

'Did she live here too?' asked Dinsdale, glancing around the small apartment, 'or is this your place?'

'We shared the flat.'

'Rented?'

'What do you think?' Troy didn't try to hide his contempt. 'Do we look like we earn enough to buy a place of our own?'

'Do I look like the kind of person who enjoys speaking to rude bastards like you?' countered Dinsdale. 'Show some manners, son, or I'll make your life even harder than it already is.'

Becca tried to defuse the tension. 'I've seen you working at the care home,' she said in a conversational tone. 'You're the gardener, aren't you?'

Troy glanced up at her. 'Yeah, I do the garden, and odd jobs around the house.'

'Do you work full-time there?'

'Full-time at Larkmead. There's plenty to keep me busy.'

'Do you enjoy your job?'

'It's all right.'

'So,' said Dinsdale, bringing Becca's attempt to get Troy talking freely to an abrupt halt. 'Tell me when you last saw Natalia.'

Troy shrugged. 'Yesterday.'

'What time?'

'I wasn't looking at my watch.'

'Morning, afternoon, evening?'

''Bout five o'clock, I guess.'

'And where did you see her?'

'At work.'

Becca could see the young lad withdrawing into himself, putting up barriers. He didn't like Dinsdale's aggressive style of questioning any more than Natalia had.

'Was that the time you finished work, Troy?' asked Becca.

Troy looked up again. 'I was finishing, but Natalia had just started her shift. She wasn't supposed to be working nights this week, but one of the girls was off sick and they couldn't get agency staff in. She should have refused, but she was too kind like that. She loved them old people, loved chatting to them. Loved hearing their stories.'

'What did you do after leaving work?' asked Dinsdale.

Troy redirected his gaze back to the detective as if it pained him to do so.

'Came back here.'

'And then?'

'There's no point cooking for one, so I picked up a takeaway.'

Dinsdale's gaze briefly roamed the carpet. 'And some beers by the look of it.'

'Ain't no law against that.'

'So what time did you go to bed?'

'Dunno. Midnight?'

Dinsdale nodded as if he were closing in on his quarry. 'Tell me about this morning. What time did you wake up? What did you do?'

Troy shifted uneasily on the sofa. 'I got woken up when your lot banged on my door about half past seven.'

'And was there any indication that Natalia had returned to the flat overnight?'

'No.'

'So you claim you didn't see her since yesterday at five, and the first you knew of her death was when the police came to your door this morning?'

'I don't claim it,' said Troy angrily. 'It's what bloody well happened.'

'I'm warning you. Don't you get all shirty with me, son.' Dinsdale pushed his face closer to Troy's. 'Or you'll regret it.'

Troy seemed suddenly to become aware that although Dinsdale was thirty years older than him, he was also well over thirty pounds heavier. 'Is that a threat?' he said nervously. ''Cos if it is, I'll be telling a lawyer everything that happens to me.'

Dinsdale chuckled unpleasantly. 'Don't be such a big girl's blouse. You're not going to accidentally fall down the stairs or something. That kind of thing doesn't happen anymore, more's the pity.' The smile left his face and he grabbed a fistful of Troy's T-shirt with his thick, stubby fingers. 'But if you raise your voice at me again, I'll have you banged up in the cells faster than you can say "police brutality".'

Wow, thought Becca. Casual sexism and sinister menace all in one package. Dinsdale could do bad cop without breaking a sweat. She really ought to shut him down, but she was so mesmerised by his performance that she was unable to say a word.

Besides, it seemed to be having an effect on Troy. The lad had lost all his bravura and an edge of desperation had entered his eyes. When Dinsdale let go of him, she took her cue. 'How long were you and Natalia together?'

In the wake of Dinsdale's hostile interrogation, Troy needed no further encouragement to talk to her. 'It's 'bout two years now.'

'How did you meet?'

'At the care home. I was already working there when she started as a nurse.'

'When we visited the care home on Friday,' said Becca, 'I saw you and Natalia outside. You were standing under an oak tree. Do you remember?'

Troy started to look uneasy again. 'Yeah.'

'You looked like you were having an argument.'

'Oh, that? It was nothing.'

'It didn't look like nothing.' She raised her eyebrows, inviting him to continue.

Troy was beginning to visibly perspire. 'She was just cross because the flat is always such a mess, that's all.'

Becca glanced at the empty curry cartons and beer cans on the floor. 'Did you ever hit her?'

Troy looked indignant at the suggestion. 'Of course not.'

'Then how did you get that scratch on your face?' One of Troy's cheeks was marked with a red line, about an inch long. Could Natalia have done that to him? Perhaps with a fingernail?

Troy put his fingers to his cheek. 'Scratched myself cutting back some brambles.'

'That was careless,' said Dinsdale. It was obvious from his tone that he had already decided he didn't believe a word Troy said.

'It's true,' protested Troy.

There was a tap at the door and Holly stuck her head around. 'Sir, we found something in one of the wheelie bins a couple of doors down.' She held up an evidence bag. Inside was a hammer, stained with what looked like blood.

At the sight of the hammer, Troy visibly paled. Then, without warning, he leapt to his feet, pushed past Becca, and ran out of the room, almost sending the diminutive Holly flying.

'Get that bastard!' roared Dinsdale.

Becca gave chase.

Despite having no shoes on, Troy was already out of the flat. Becca dashed through the small hallway and emerged outside. Troy was running across the backyard heading for the gate that led into the alleyway.

She didn't know what he hoped to achieve with this stunt, but it was obvious that he had recognised the hammer, and its discovery as the likely murder weapon must have freaked him out.

'Stop!' she shouted.

He must have known that his chance of escape was zero. Or was it?

Where were the uniformed guys when you needed them? Becca could see the blue flashing lights at the end of the lane, but the attention of the police officers was on keeping passers-by away from the crime scene rather than preventing anyone from escaping. Still, they could hardly fail to notice a barefooted man sprinting past.

Troy was almost at the end of the lane when he realised his mistake. He spun around, looking for another route and spotted a rickety-looking fire escape that led up the side of a nearby building. By the time the uniformed officers had woken up to what was happening, he had already started to climb.

Damn it. Troy was fitter than Becca, and was scaling the ladder at a pace. The fire escape led all the way up to the rooftop, and from there he might go anywhere. Across the roof, down the other side, along the row of terraces. Or just as likely, plunge to his death. Becca wasn't about to follow him up and engage in a rooftop chase.

'Let me!'

A figure flashed past her and began to climb the ladder. It was Scott from Holly's team. Becca watched in astonishment as the young CSI guy shot up the ladder like a monkey.

Despite a head start, Troy didn't stand a chance. Barefoot, and with Scott in pursuit, he had only reached the first-floor balcony before Scott's hand closed around his ankle and he toppled over, landing flat on his face on the metal platform.

'I've got him!' yelled Scott.

Becca pulled herself out of her inertia and climbed up to the balcony where Scott was now sitting astride the would-be escapee. Troy was putting up a token struggle, but must have known that the game was up.

Becca slapped a pair of handcuffs on him just as Dinsdale came lumbering up the lane, puffing and panting. 'Troy Woods,' he bellowed from below. 'I am arresting you on suspicion of murder.'

CHAPTER 16

'His name was Heinrich Meyer. He was a lovely boy. Tall, strong, and good-looking.'

At Becca's suggestion, Raven had driven straight to Larkmead, a great gothic mansion that looked like a haunted house, and had been met by the care home's manager, Judith Holden. Despite explaining that he was a police officer, there to interview a witness, she hadn't passed up the opportunity to extol the care home's many benefits – the well-kept grounds, the individualised care plans on offer, and the many stimulating activities available to residents. Raven wasn't sure if she thought he looked old enough to take up residence himself or whether she was hoping he might have an elderly relative stashed away somewhere in need of looking after. Either way, he was going to have to disappoint her.

After finishing the sales pitch she showed him into a wood-panelled lounge where comfortable chairs were arranged in small clusters around the room. Two elderly men were seated in front of the enormous fireplace, their heads bowed low over a game of chess, and a couple of other residents were reading or dozing in their chairs. It looked like a quiet place to spend the final days of your life.

Violet Armitage was sitting alone by the window,

looking out at the densely-packed trees and shrubs that adorned the grounds, a pot of tea and a plate of biscuits on the table beside her.

'She'll be glad to talk to you,' Judith assured him. 'Violet likes nothing better than a good natter about the old days. I should warn you that once she gets started, you'll find it difficult to escape.'

Judith hadn't been wrong. After she had introduced him and he had explained the reason for his visit, Violet had been keen to help.

Raven had taken off his black overcoat and slung it over the back of a nearby chair. The care home was dreadfully overheated and he would have liked to remove his jacket too, but Violet looked like she was turned out in her Sunday best – silk blouse, smart skirt, powdered face and lipstick – and Raven didn't want to appear too casual.

He had taken a liking to the old lady from the start. Despite her age and frailty, she was bright and chipper and the afternoon promised to be entertaining, as well as hopefully enlightening. It hadn't taken her long to start talking about her young days growing up in the town of Malton, and her friend Eileen who had become engaged to a German ex-POW.

Raven could hardly believe that he might finally have put a name to Forge Valley Man.

Heinrich Meyer.

The grubby old bones pulled out of the ground had suddenly become much more human.

'Tell me more about how Eileen and Heinrich met,' he said.

Violet finished her tea, returned the cup to its saucer and settled back in her chair, making herself comfortable. 'Eileen and I were best friends growing up. We were the same age and knew each other all the way through school. My father was the vicar of St Michael's and Eileen was the daughter of Dr Hunter, the local GP. Our families enjoyed a certain social standing in the town. I don't mean we thought we were better than other people, nothing like that. Just that we both knew a lot of people and they knew us.'

Raven nodded encouragingly to show that he understood, but there was really no need. Violet was in full flow now and was more than happy to continue with her reminiscences.

'When war broke out, the young men of the town went off to fight. Some joined the army, some the navy, and some the air force. Of course there were a few who worked in essential industries or failed the medical and stayed at home. Then in 1942 the government requisitioned a nearby plot of land and started turning it into a prisoner of war camp. It was practically on our doorstep.'

'That would be Eden Camp.'

'That's right. It was rather exciting to be honest. At first the people in the town were quite afraid. We thought the prisoners would be dangerous Nazis and fascists. We were worried they might escape. But it wasn't long before we realised that they were mostly young lads, just like our own boys who had gone off to war. They had no choice but to fight. Towards the end of the war, some of the prisoners were sent to work on nearby farms. They started to mingle with the locals and to learn some English. When the war ended, some chose to stay on.'

'Was that when Eileen first met Heinrich?'

'Yes, Heinrich was working as a farm labourer. As I said, he was a tall, strapping lad. Not unlike James Stewart in one of his early films.' Violet caught Raven's eye. 'Don't look at me that way, Inspector. I was a girl of seventeen. I was easily distracted by handsome young men.'

'And I'm sure they were distracted by you.'

She smiled. 'Well, there were one or two… but we were talking about Eileen.'

'Go on.'

She gazed wistfully out of the window for a moment before continuing. 'Heinrich was an airman, a navigator with the *Luftwaffe*. He came from the town of Köthen.'

Raven wrote down the name of the town, asking Violet

to spell it for him. He was impressed by the amount of detail that she could recall from such a long time ago. Her memory couldn't be faulted.

'Köthen was behind the Iron Curtain in the eastern half of the country which was occupied by the Soviets and later became communist East Germany. There was little incentive for Heinrich to return. Besides, his family had perished and he had already met Eileen.' She gave Raven a wink. 'In 1944, when Eileen was sixteen, she volunteered to work as a land girl on one of the local farms. She loved being outdoors, loved the fresh air and working with animals. Heinrich was sent to work on the same farm and they hit it off from the start. Sometimes, you just know when you've met the right person, don't you?'

'I suppose you do,' said Raven. An image of Chandice came to him, but he steered his attention back to what Violet was saying.

'Eileen was such a pretty lass. And it wasn't long before she and Heinrich started courting. One thing led to another... Eileen was soon in the family way. She and Heinrich got engaged and set a date for the wedding. My father even got as far as reading the banns for the first time. They were both in church that day and I remember how happy they looked.' Her face fell. 'I felt so sorry for Eileen when Heinrich left. They would have made the perfect couple.'

'What happened?'

'He suddenly decided to go back to Germany after all.' Violet shook her head as if she couldn't believe such a foolish decision. 'He just upped sticks and left.'

'What year was this?'

'1946.'

'Could Eileen not have gone with him?'

'How could she? She didn't speak a word of German. In any case, he didn't give her the chance. He just wrote her a letter with no forwarding address informing her of his decision and that was that. Poor Eileen was dreadfully upset, as you can imagine.'

'He just disappeared? Without saying goodbye?'

'Not a word.' Violet regarded Raven with a querying eye. 'All these years, I've never been able to understand it. It wasn't like Heinrich to do a thing like that. And it made no sense. He had so much to be thankful for here in Yorkshire. Why would he throw all that away?'

Why indeed? 'You said he wrote a letter,' prompted Raven. 'Do you know what happened to it?'

'No.'

'Is Eileen still alive? I'd like to talk to her if it's possible.'

Violet shook her head sadly. 'She died a few years back. But her brother Vincent may still be alive.'

'And what about her child?'

'His name is Joseph. Eileen gave him her own surname. Joseph Hunter.'

'What happened to him?'

'Well, he still lives in Malton, although he did spend many years travelling and living abroad. He was a troubled child and teenager. It wasn't easy for him growing up with no father. Everyone in the town knew he'd been born out of wedlock and his mother had been abandoned. You'd think that would have made people sympathetic, but instead they were quick to point the finger. As if any of that was Joseph's fault. But he seems to have made peace with his past now.'

'Is there anyone else who remembers that period of history?'

'There's Eric Roper,' said Violet doubtfully. She nodded at an old man who was fast asleep in a nearby chair. 'But you won't get much sense out of Eric these days, sad to say.'

Eric Roper.

Something stirred in Raven's mind.

Eric Roper. He had come across that name very recently. Then he remembered.

Jack Raven's best man.

So Eric had ended up here. The old man snoring in the armchair looked decrepit. It was hard to think of him as

Jack's sprightly young friend from the wedding album. Raven had assumed that everyone from that generation was long ago dead and buried. But his grandfather had died at a tragically young age, well before his contemporaries. Just thirty-five years old when he drowned, leaving behind a widow, Muriel, and son, Alan. How had Muriel managed to raise her young son in the face of such adversity, with no husband and no money? Raven knew the answer to that question well enough.

Badly.

Alan Raven had never risen above a life of poverty, drunkenness and violence.

Raven had hated his father, but perhaps Alan wasn't really to blame. His fate had been written in the stars long ago.

'I would have suggested you speak to Raymond Swindlehurst,' said Violet, 'but he died very suddenly last week. No doubt you're already aware of that?'

'Yes, I did hear about it.' Raven wasn't sure how much Violet knew about the circumstances of Raymond's death. He wouldn't be surprised if she had deduced more than what was public knowledge and was fishing for information. 'Was Raymond a friend of yours?'

'Another Malton resident.' Violet chuckled sadly. 'It's funny how all three of us ended up here. Me, Raymond and Eric. But then Scarborough does have a lot of care homes. It's that sort of place. It tends to attract those of us who don't have very long left for this world.'

'I'm sure you have many years left, Violet.' Raven reached into an inside pocket and took out a card. 'If you think of anything else, please call me on this number.'

'I will,' said Violet.

Raven stood up. 'Thank you again. It's been a pleasure talking to you.'

'It was no trouble, Inspector. I hope I've been able to help with your enquiry.'

'You certainly have.'

She gave him a shrewd look. 'Then perhaps you could

answer a question for me. Does your interest in Heinrich have anything to do with the skeleton that was discovered in Forge Valley Woods? It was all over the news.'

There seemed little point trying to conceal anything from the old lady. She had clearly put two and two together. 'We still need to confirm it, but I think it's likely that the human remains are those of Heinrich.'

She sighed. 'What a tragedy. It shouldn't really affect me after so many years, and yet it all seems so desperately sad. You will do your best to find out what happened to him, won't you?'

'I will.'

She suddenly shot out her frail arm and grasped his wrist. Her fingers were all bone, but her grip was surprisingly strong and she held on tightly. 'The truth still matters, you know. It matters to me, and it matters to Eileen's son.'

'I understand.' Raven bowed his head to her and she released him from her grip. He made his way out, passing the snoring Eric in his chair.

On his way back down the corridor he passed an open door. The room beyond was being cleared. Raven poked his head around and found two of the care home staff piling belongings into packing boxes. 'Is this Raymond Swindlehurst's room?' he asked.

The carers stopped and stared at him and he showed them his warrant card.

'Yes,' said one. 'We're just clearing out his stuff. Most of it will go to charity.'

'He had no family?'

'No.'

Raven swept his gaze across the room. It was a good-sized room with a high ceiling and a large window. But the glass let in little light at this time of year. Beyond the window, dark green conifers crowded in, almost close enough to touch. It reminded Raven of Quay Street, whose cobbled road was in places almost narrow enough to reach across to adjacent buildings.

Apart from the institutional furniture of bed, table and chairs, there wasn't a lot to show that a man had called this place his home. Soon all of Raymond's personal items would be packed away for removal. A lifetime's worth of baggage reduced to the contents of a few cardboard boxes.

Raven too travelled light. He doubted whether his own possessions would take up much more space than Raymond's. The place gave him a fleeting glimpse of how his own life might end.

A single room. An empty bed. A handful of boxes.

Would anyone miss him when he was gone?

His attention was caught by an old black-and-white photograph in a silver frame. The photo showed six young men leaning against some railings. Raven recognised the location as the promenade on Scarborough's South Bay. Behind them the sands stretched out to the distant sea. The men wore long trousers with vertical creases down the leg and turn-ups at the bottom. Several wore hats and one had a cigarette dangling from his lips. It must have been a hot day because their shirt sleeves were rolled up.

'Is Raymond in this photograph?' he asked.

'Let me see,' said the carer who had spoken earlier. She pointed to a tall man at the end of the row, standing slightly apart from the others. 'That's him there.'

'Would you mind if I borrowed this?'

'Help yourself. No one else will want it.'

Raven pocketed the photo and let himself out, deep in thought. He had never seen the photo before and didn't recognise Raymond. However, one of the other men in the photo looked decidedly familiar.

Oh yes. Raven knew that face all right.

CHAPTER 17

'**D**oes this hammer belong to you?' Becca slid a photograph of the hammer that had been recovered from the crime scene across the table of the interview room.

Troy Woods sat facing her, his forearms on the table, hands clasping and unclasping, one leg jiggling up and down. He was as jittery as when he'd attempted his foolhardy escape from the flat. But this time he was going nowhere. A uniformed constable stood guard in front of the door, and not even a guy like Troy would be stupid enough to try to break out of a police interview room.

Next to Becca sat DI Dinsdale, his face stony. And beside Troy sat the duty solicitor, a middle-aged woman whose expression was equally grim. It didn't look good for Troy, and not only because of his attempt to evade arrest. The evidence was steadily piling up against him.

He shrugged his shoulders. 'That could be any hammer.'

Dinsdale's eyes narrowed in annoyance. 'But it isn't just any hammer. It was found dumped in a wheelie bin a few yards from where your girlfriend was brutally murdered this morning. And it's smeared in what will almost certainly turn out to be her blood. So take a good look at it, son.'

Troy glanced at the photo a second time, turning it around as if that might make any difference, but it was already obvious to Becca from his body language that he recognised the tool. 'Never seen it before.'

Dinsdale gave a loud sigh.

The duty solicitor tapped her pen against the desk. 'My client says he doesn't recognise the hammer, Inspector.'

But Dinsdale wasn't that easily deflected. 'When we test it for prints, whose do you think we'll find all over it, Troy?'

The solicitor lowered her voice to speak to her client. 'You just have to say, "no comment".'

But the young lad looked more uncomfortable than ever. 'Well, now you mention it, it does look a bit like the hammer from the care home. Yeah, I think it might be that hammer.'

The solicitor glared at him, clearly dismayed that he had changed his story so quickly.

Dinsdale smiled. 'That would be Larkmead Nursing Home, where you work as a... what is your job exactly?'

'I look after the garden and do odd jobs around the place.'

'Odd jobs that might sometimes involve the use of a hammer,' suggested Dinsdale.

'Maybe.'

'Let's be clear about this,' snarled Dinsdale. 'Do you use a hammer in your job at the care home?'

'Sometimes.'

The DI jabbed his finger against the photo. '*This* hammer.'

'I think,' said the solicitor before Troy could say anything more to incriminate himself, 'that further evidence will be needed to establish whether or not this hammer was taken from the care home.'

Dinsdale regarded her with a look of loathing before

turning back to Troy. 'Let's assume for the sake of argument that this is the hammer you use in your work at the care home. How do you think it ended up in the wheelie bin?'

'Dunno.'

'Who has access to the hammer you use at work?'

'I keep it in the tool shed. Anyone could have taken it.'

'But who uses it?'

'Me.'

'Anyone else?'

'No.'

'My client means "no comment",' said the solicitor quickly.

'That's not what he said,' snapped Dinsdale. He snatched the photograph away from Troy before anyone could contradict him. He looked confident that he'd won the first round. 'All right, moving on now to the death of Raymond Swindlehurst.'

Troy's eyes widened in alarm. 'What? I thought this was about Natalia. I had nothing to do with Raymond's murder!'

Dinsdale eyed him slyly. 'I said "death". How did you know he was murdered?'

'Because I'm not stupid. And because you told Natalia it was murder.'

'Yes, well...' said Dinsdale, 'but what I want to know is where were you at the time of his death.'

'And when was that exactly?' demanded the solicitor.

Dinsdale looked to Becca for assistance.

'Perhaps,' she said to Troy, 'you could describe your movements last Monday evening?'

'Monday?' Troy wrinkled his brow in concentration. 'Well, normally I finish work at five, but on Monday, Judith asked me to stay on and bleed the radiators because some of the residents were complaining that their rooms were too cold.'

Becca wondered if that was why the care home had been so hot on her recent visits. Did the residents really think that it was cold? She dreaded to think how much the care home cost to heat. 'What time did you finish?'

Troy scratched the back of his head. ''Bout seven, I suppose.'

'And what did you do afterwards?'

'Went home. Natalia was working late that night.'

'You were alone?'

'Yeah.'

'So,' said Dinsdale, 'you bled the radiators. Did you go into Mr Swindlehurst's room?'

'I did.'

'At what time?'

'Dunno,' said Troy. 'But he wasn't alone when I went in. There was some guy with him.'

'Some guy,' repeated Dinsdale. 'Who?'

'No idea.'

'Can you describe him?' asked Becca.

Troy looked up at the ceiling as if the answer might be written there. 'Not really. I didn't pay any attention.'

'Young? Old?'

Troy shrugged helplessly.

Dinsdale was beginning to lose his patience. 'It's not a difficult question.'

'No comment,' said Troy.

Dinsdale leaned forwards, like an animal about to pounce on its prey. 'Did you kill Raymond Swindlehurst?'

'Of course not!'

The duty solicitor cleared her throat. 'Inspector, instead of listening to you making unfounded accusations about my client, I would like to discuss the circumstances of his unlawful arrest. From what Mr Woods has told me, he was assaulted and apprehended by someone who was not a serving police officer.'

The lawyer was obviously talking about Scott from CSI. As a crime scene investigator, Scott was a civilian, not a police officer. But Becca wasn't going to let Troy slip off the hook due to some technicality. 'I think you'll find,' she said, 'that the individual in question acted entirely lawfully, making a citizen's arrest of your client. Firstly, he had reasonable belief that Mr Woods had committed a crime. Secondly, he had reasonable belief that it was not possible for a police officer to make an arrest. And thirdly, in view of the fact that Mr Woods was climbing a ladder up to a rooftop, he believed that the arrest was necessary to prevent your client causing injury to himself or escaping before a police officer could assume responsibility for him.' The solicitor opened her mouth to protest, but Becca hadn't finished. 'And finally, we are considering charging your client with assault against Mrs Holly Chang, the head of CSI, and also with resisting arrest.'

The lawyer closed her mouth. Then, seemingly determined to make at least some token protest, she said, 'Well, then I suggest you either produce more evidence or bring this interview to a close.'

'More evidence, you want?' said Dinsdale, as if she had fallen into a carefully-prepared trap. 'I'll give you more evidence.'

Becca turned her gaze on her boss. Whatever additional evidence he had found or concocted, he had neglected to mention it to her. Troy and the solicitor also looked to Dinsdale, who was clearly enjoying this little piece of theatre.

The DI opened his file and removed a set of photographs. He spread them out across the table.

Becca could see photos of credit cards, driving licences and other documents.

'We found these in your flat,' said Dinsdale. 'Care to comment?'

Troy blanched, looking suddenly as if he were about to be sick. His solicitor studied the photos, her expression also becoming somewhat nauseous. 'What are these?' she asked.

'Good question,' said Dinsdale smugly. 'These are photos of bank cards and other documents recovered from your client's flat.'

Becca stared at the photos arrayed on the desk. One of

the bank cards displayed the name Eric Roper. What had Eric said to her that day she'd visited Violet? *What are you going to do about catching the person who nicked my money?* It looked like Eric hadn't imagined the theft at all. But why hadn't Dinsdale shared this information with Becca? He really was a terrible boss.

'So,' said Dinsdale, once he'd given everyone present sufficient time to ponder this latest revelation, 'did you steal money, bank cards or other documents from residents at Larkmead?'

Troy looked like he wanted to sink into the floor and vanish. 'It was just a bit of cash. A fiver here, a tenner there. No more than that.'

Dinsdale jabbed his thumb at the photographs. 'It was a lot more than that! This shows a highly organised activity. Theft of cash, cards and identity documents. We also recovered a laptop from your flat and have sent it away for our financial fraud team to examine. I bet they'll uncover a systematic operation involving all kinds of financial exploitation and identity theft.'

'No comment,' said Troy.

'Did you steal money or bank cards from Raymond Swindlehurst?' pressed Dinsdale. 'Did he catch you in the act? Is that why you murdered him?'

Troy shook his head. 'No comment.'

'And did Natalia find out what you'd done and threaten to go to the police? Is that why you killed her too?'

'No comment.'

Troy had retreated into himself, too terrified to face the appalling truth of what he'd done. They would get nothing more if Dinsdale continued to lay into him.

Becca leaned forwards. 'Troy?' He looked up, his lips quivering, a look of desperation on his face. He was hoping for some way out, some way of avoiding the consequences of his actions. 'If you say nothing, you'll be charged not only with theft and other financial crimes, but also with two counts of murder. Do you understand?'

He nodded mutely.

'So tell us everything you know about what happened to Natalia and Raymond. If you know anything, or suspect anyone, tell us now.'

All the fight had drained out of him. He put his head in his hands. For a moment, no one spoke. 'I didn't mean any harm,' he said at last. 'I didn't hurt anyone. I just helped myself to easy money when I saw it. You've seen how me and Natalia lived – we hardly had a thing. We were freezing to death in our flat while those old people in the home had their heating turned up full-blast like they were in the Bahamas.'

Becca nodded encouragingly, praying that Dinsdale wouldn't jump in and shut down Troy's confession, no matter how self-pitying and empty of remorse it might be.

'Old people are careless with their money, the way they leave it lying around,' he continued. 'And what have they got to spend it on, anyway? Half of them probably didn't even notice it had gone. I reckon, if people can't look after their own money they deserve to lose it.'

Dinsdale looked like he was about to blow his top, so Becca stepped in quickly. 'Troy, do you know anything about what happened to Raymond?'

Troy looked miserable. 'Raymond and Natalia were real close. She had a soft spot for him. In fact, she told me she was worried about him.'

'When was this?'

'It all started a few days before he died. He'd been watching the news and suddenly seemed very shaken by what he saw. Natalia said it was because of the flooding, but I reckon it was to do with that skeleton that was dug up.'

'At Forge Valley Woods?'

'That's the one,' said Troy. 'Anyway, the morning after the skeleton was on the news, Raymond wrote two letters and gave them to Natalia to post.'

'Did Raymond say what the letters were about?'

'No, just that they were very important and he wanted them sent straight away. A couple of days later he was dead. If that's not suspicious, I don't know what is.'

'Think carefully now, Troy,' said Becca. 'Did Natalia tell you who the letters were for?'

'She didn't have to. She gave them to me to post. She was busy that day, so I popped out in my lunch break to drop them in the letter box.'

Becca hardly dared breathe. 'Who were the letters addressed to, Troy?'

'I only noticed one of the names, the one on top. It was a Mr Vincent something. I didn't look at the other one. Sorry.'

Becca made a note of the name. 'Did you notice the address?'

'It was somewhere in Scarborough. I don't remember where exactly.'

'Probably because these letters never existed,' said Dinsdale, unable to hold back any longer. 'I've heard enough of you trying to save your skin. All this talk of skeletons and mysterious letters. Do you think I'm some sort of halfwit? Natalia found out that you'd murdered Raymond Swindlehurst. And that's why you had to silence her.'

'No!' Troy was horrified. 'That's not what happened. I'm telling the truth. I'm trying to help.'

Becca knew that her chance to get any more useful information from Troy was over. She leaned back in her chair as Dinsdale rose to his feet.

'I think we're done here,' he said, looking at his watch. 'Interview terminated at five thirty.'

'What's going to happen now?' asked Troy.

Dinsdale gave him a gloating look. 'You, my friend, are going to spend a night in the cells while we wait for forensics to confirm that the blood on the hammer is Natalia's and that your grubby little fingerprints are all over it. And then you'll be charged – with two counts of murder as well as a list of financial and other offences as long as your arm. Meanwhile, I'm off home to get my tea.'

CHAPTER 18

Raven was as sure as he could be that Detective Superintendent Gillian Ellis was not going to like what he had to say.

He'd returned from the care home following his chat with Violet, to find Becca at her desk looking uncharacteristically grumpy. 'Problems?' he asked.

She sighed. 'It's just that working with Dinsdale is trying my patience.'

He raised one inquisitive eyebrow, inviting her to continue. He supposed he ought not to be encouraging her to moan about a colleague, but he had a soft spot for Becca and there was no love lost between him and Dinsdale. The man was enough to try anyone's patience.

'It's these two deaths at the care home,' said Becca. 'Dinsdale's convinced that he's got his man. He's ready to lock up Troy Woods for both murders and throw away the key.'

'Troy Woods?'

'The gardener and handyman at the care home. The boyfriend of the murdered nurse.'

'A boyfriend's always a good place to start.'

'I know,' said Becca. 'And maybe Troy did murder Natalia… the evidence all points that way and I did see the two of them arguing together outside the care home… and I suppose it's possible he murdered Raymond too…'

'If two murders have taken place within a few days and both are connected to the care home, then it's extremely likely that the same person committed both crimes,' said Raven.

'I know that,' said Becca, 'and Troy was definitely involved in some kind of theft and financial scam at the home, so he had motive and opportunity…'

'But something doesn't sit right?'

Instinct was often hard to explain and even harder to justify, but Raven knew from experience that it was often to be trusted. Instinct was more than just a hunch, it was a signal from some deep part of the brain, some unconscious process that sifted all of the available facts, both the obvious ones and those less clearly connected, and arrived at a conclusion that was felt rather than understood. Becca had demonstrated good instincts on the previous case, and Raven was inclined to trust her.

She shrugged, struggling to put her thoughts into words. 'I just think there's more going on than we know about.'

'I agree,' said Raven.

'You do?'

'Definitely. If two murders connected to the care home are hard to explain away as coincidence, then three murders are impossible to ignore.'

'Three? You mean your skeleton?'

'I think I have a name for him now. Heinrich Meyer.'

'But hasn't he been dead and buried for years?'

'Exactly,' said Raven. 'Until the storm brought his bones to the surface. And within a fortnight, two more people have been killed.'

'But how are the three deaths linked?'

Raven gave her a wink. 'I'm still working on that. Wish me luck.'

He left the incident room and made his way along the corridor to the Super's office. The working day had already ended, but he was fairly certain that he would find Gillian Ellis still at her desk. Workaholics, perhaps like alcoholics, had a way of knowing each other. Sure enough, when he knocked on the door, he was answered with a 'Come in.'

Gillian was seated at her desk, wearing a cream blouse, her customary reading glasses perched on the end of her nose, giving her a stern appearance. 'Ah, Tom, you have some progress to report?'

'I have a name, or at least I think I do.' He summarised the information that he'd learned from his visit to Eden Camp and from speaking to Violet Armitage.

'A German ex-POW. You may well be right. So how are you going to proceed? You'll need to find a way to confirm the ID. And then what? I imagine that most potential witnesses are already dead, and quite possibly the murderer too.'

'That's what I thought, at first.'

Gillian removed her glasses and lifted her head to study him better. 'At first?'

'Until two more people ended up dead.'

'You think that the murders at the care home are connected to your historic murder?' There was more than a dash of scepticism in her voice.

'I do,' said Raven. 'As Violet said, it's funny how three Malton residents ended up living at the same care home.'

A look of consternation crossed Gillian's face. 'So what are you saying, Tom? That there's some kind of conspiracy or cover-up going on? Do you seriously think we're looking for a man in his nineties on a killing spree?'

'I'm saying that there may well be a link between the historic murder and the recent murders. I'm saying that I'd like to run all three investigations together.'

Gillian's features darkened to a quiet anger. 'You want to take over from Dinsdale?'

'With my experience, ma'am, I'm well placed to do so.'

'That may be so, but I need a better reason than that to

remove the current SIO from his role. Especially when he's just made an arrest. Just because I put you in charge of Derek's case once before, doesn't mean I'm in the habit of doing so.'

Raven knew that he had entered dangerous waters. Although he was more senior than Dinsdale, he was still the new boy in town. He and Dinsdale had tussled on a previous case, and he'd been warned by Gillian not to overstep the mark. And yet he knew that he needed to get involved. 'Raymond Swindlehurst lived in Malton at the time of Heinrich Meyer's murder. He knew the dead man, and now, immediately after the discovery of the skeleton in Forge Valley Woods appeared on the news, he too was murdered. I want to know why.'

Gillian watched him through her beady eyes. 'We all want to know why, Tom. Have you discussed the matter with DI Dinsdale?'

'He doesn't know about the possible connection yet.'

Ellis didn't like that. She gave him a stony stare. 'You should have gone to him first, Tom, whatever your personal feelings about him. A detective of your experience ought to know that.'

Raven bowed his head. She was right of course. He had hoped to avoid a fresh row with Dinsdale, but instead he had managed to engineer a confrontation with Gillian. And Gillian Ellis was a far more formidable opponent than Derek Dinsdale.

She squared her broad shoulders. 'I'm not happy about this, Tom. Not happy at all. You need to learn to become a better team player. On the other hand' – Raven looked up, hopeful – 'it does sound as if these cases need to be looked at together.'

'Ma'am?'

'I agree that there's every reason for you to work alongside DI Dinsdale and for the two of you to share your resources as you search for common ground. But I will not have you sowing discord in my station by taking over a case that has been assigned to someone else. So go home and think about how you're going to cooperate with DI Dinsdale and work together. I shall look forward to hearing the results of your combined wisdom. Do I make myself clear?'

'Yes,' said Raven. He left the office, frustrated and chastened.

★

'I chased a suspect today,' said Becca. 'I didn't have to chase him very far, but it was still quite exciting.'

Sam lay motionless, his hand in hers, his face devoid of expression.

'He's been arrested for murder, but I don't know if he did it. Dinsdale thinks he's been stealing money from the residents at the care home, and perhaps he has, but there's more to it than that. There's a bigger mystery behind it all, I'm sure of it. I wish I'd had more time in the interview room without Dinsdale. Then I'd have been able to ask more questions and maybe even get some answers. But I've told you what Dinsdale's like.'

She looked to Sam, hoping for a response. Just a tiny flutter of the eyelids or a parting of the lips. But there was nothing.

The contrast between how she'd spent her day and how Sam had spent his was stark. So too, were her own feelings compared with the blunt advice that Liam had given her when she'd returned home from work that evening. 'It's time to move on, sis. I don't mean that in a cold-hearted way. But it's not selfish to think of yourself for a change. You always put everyone else first. Not even Sam would have wanted that. If he could see you now, he'd be the first one to say, "Come on, stop clinging to the past. Go and live your life."'

Becca had shaken her head in fury. She knew Liam would never understand. 'I'm not clinging to the past,' she'd told him. 'I'm clinging to the future. A shared future. Sam would understand. He knew better than anyone that you have to stand up for what you believe in.'

She'd slammed the door and left the house, determined to escape from the voices, like Liam's, that insisted she needed to put herself first.

Didn't they get it? She *was* putting herself first. This was what she wanted.

'I thought we might listen to some music together,' she continued, pulling out her mobile phone. The doctors had told her that music could be a way of reaching someone in a comatose state. Especially familiar music. She lowered the volume on her phone and began to play a song.

'Do you remember this one, Sam? It was the first song we ever danced to together, at that party. Do you remember?'

The first few bars of Ed Sheeran's *Shape of You* began to play, the upbeat rhythm and catchy vocals transporting her back to happier times. Becca swayed back and forth in her seat, pressing the loudspeaker to Sam's ear, willing him to respond. She remembered what Judith Holden, the manager at Larkmead, had said about how music had the power to reach the part of the brain lost to ordinary speech and memory.

'Do you remember what happened afterwards?' she asked, recalling the sensual kiss they had enjoyed, but Sam's body remained resolutely inert.

The door behind her opened and the senior consultant in charge of treating Sam entered the room. Dr Kirtlington. He stopped when he saw her.

She quickly turned off the music. 'Sorry. Have you come to see Sam? Do you want me to go?'

Dr Kirtlington cleared his throat, perhaps unsure of what he wanted to say. Or afraid to say it. 'Actually, Becca, I'm not here to see Sam. I wanted to speak with you.'

'Okay.'

He glanced awkwardly in Sam's direction. 'Perhaps we could go through to the visitors' room.'

Becca could feel a sense of dread rising in her throat. She gripped Sam's hand tighter. 'Anything you have to say to me, you can say here. If Sam really is beyond help, then he won't be able to hear anything you say anyway.'

The doctor's mouth made a thin line. 'I just thought you might be more comfortable in there.'

'I'm perfectly comfortable here. And no one can overhear us. Except Sam, if he's listening.'

'Quite.' Dr Kirtlington pulled up a chair and sat down. 'I understand that Sam's parents have spoken to you about withdrawing life support?'

'About switching off his ventilator, you mean. Taking away his feeding and hydration. Leaving him to die.'

Dr Kirtlington winced. 'Becca, you really mustn't think that we're against you. My duty as Sam's doctor is to put his interests first.'

'But—'

He held up a hand. 'A doctor always puts his patient first. It's a given. You're a police officer, so perhaps you can understand it better than most. When you joined the police force, what was it that made you choose that career?'

Becca shook her head, afraid that she was being patronised. But the words came out of her mouth without her even needing to think. 'I wanted to help people, to protect the vulnerable, to make the world a better place.'

Dr Kirtlington nodded quietly. 'Was it police procedure that excited you, the intricate workings of the law, the science behind criminal investigations?'

'No. It was always about helping the victims.'

'Exactly. And for me, it wasn't medical science that made me want to become a doctor. Nor the hospital environment or bureaucracy of the NHS.' He smiled. 'It was patients. Patients like Sam.'

'In that case—'

He cut her off again. 'Becca, the reality is that sometimes medical science can't help. When that happens, doctors are unable to do any more for their patients. Even the good old NHS doesn't have the answers. When we get to that point, we need the wisdom and compassion to stop.' He paused and gazed directly at her. 'We've reached that point with Sam. In fact, we reached it some time ago.'

A tear came to Becca's eye and began to run down her cheek, but she ignored its sting. 'When Sam first came to the hospital you told me not to give up hope.'

'But that was almost a year ago,' said Dr Kirtlington. 'I told you that because you needed – then – to have some reason to keep believing in Sam. But the people who make a recovery from coma usually do so within a few weeks. Failure to show improvement after such a long period usually indicates severe brain damage. Even if, by some miracle, Sam were to show some change now, we would expect him to suffer from severely reduced brain function. Do you understand what I'm saying? Prolonging treatment is now, in my view, counterproductive.'

'I'm not ready to give up on him,' said Becca defiantly. 'Sam's a fighter. He wouldn't want me to walk away.'

'Of course he wouldn't. But sometimes we have to accept hard choices.' Dr Kirtlington looked at her, the compassion in his eyes now clearly evident. 'The thing is, Becca, Sam's parents have made their decision in agreement with clinical advice. You can't change that. The smart thing now is not to continue to deny it, or to fight it, but to accept it. Then you can enjoy your last few days with Sam in peace.'

★

Jess was about to leave the station when her phone buzzed to let her know that a message had arrived. She picked it up and thumbed through to see what was new.

She wondered if it might be her parents enquiring after her. She often went back to visit them at the weekend, but she'd spent this last Saturday with Scott instead. She would have to take Scott up to Rosedale one of these days and test him out on Ingleby Incline. Find out if he was as good a hillwalker as he claimed. But not for a little while. She didn't think she was ready to introduce her new boyfriend to her mum and dad just yet. And it would be totally unfair to parade Scott in front of them at such an early stage in the relationship. Jess's dad could be stern and forbidding when he wanted to be, even though he was a softie when you got to know him properly.

But as she read the message, her eyes clouded over and the hand that held the phone began to tremble.

The message wasn't from her parents. It was from Scott.

It was short, yet anything but sweet.

I can't see you again. When I saw you at the weekend, I told you a lie.

My mum wasn't murdered. She's still alive and well.

I don't know why I told you that. Perhaps I was trying to make you like me.

But I am a liar. So it's over between us.

I'm sorry.

Scott

Jess let the phone fall onto the desk, and the tears fall from her eyes.

*

Raven returned to Quay Street in a foul mood. He had hoped to be given free reign to run the combined investigation his way. Instead, Gillian had ordered him to work alongside Derek Dinsdale.

Raven had almost come to blows with Dinsdale during his previous murder investigation at Scarborough and didn't relish the prospect of working with his rival now. He didn't like the man's methods, he didn't care for his attitude towards junior staff, and he had little respect for his investigating ability. But he had no choice if he wanted to get involved in the murder cases at the care home. He would have to put aside his differences with Dinsdale and find a way to cooperate.

He wondered what the older DI was doing right now.

Perhaps he was at home, being looked after by the long-suffering Mrs Dinsdale, if such a creature existed. It was hard to picture Dinsdale having a wife, but it was equally difficult to conceive of him alone, living a carefree bachelor existence. Indeed, it was hard to imagine the detective inspector having any kind of inner life at all.

In any case, that was for tomorrow. For now, Raven had other concerns. The building work, or lack of it, at his house.

Barry had dropped in on Sunday evening, promising to get started "real soon now, mate", and Raven had handed him the spare key to the house in anticipation of seeing that promise become reality. Barry had followed up with a text message just this afternoon to say that he was "dropping some gear off". But when Raven opened the door to the front room, his hope turned to dismay.

The fireplace, with its seventies-era gas fire, which Raven hoped might soon be replaced by a trendy new log burner, was piled high with bags of cement and plaster. Next to the teetering tower of building materials stood a grey plastic bucket filled with an assortment of trowels, mixing paddles, pointing knives, measuring rules and set squares. A paint-spattered step ladder propped against the wall completed the collection.

Raven regarded the tools with horror. Was this how his life would be for the foreseeable future? He had, of course, accepted the notion that the building work would necessarily create a certain amount of mess. But until now that had remained an abstract proposition. He had been too fixated on the end goal – a new kitchen with a dishwasher and a big fridge freezer, fit for the twenty-first century, in which he might prepare romantic suppers for Chandice, or entertain Hannah when she visited him between university terms – that his imagination had selectively edited out the dirt and chaos that would come between then and now.

Raven's pathological dislike of disorder meant that he kept his desk, car and house meticulously clean and tidy.

How was he going to be able to cope with the mayhem that was about to be unleashed?

Pushing the thoughts to one side, he skirted around the disturbance in the front room and was wondering what to do about dinner when his phone rang. Chandice. He answered and was thrilled to hear her voice.

'Hi, I was going to call you,' he told her. 'I have news.'

'Good news?'

'Interesting news. Forge Valley Man has a name, or at least I'm pretty certain he does.' He filled her in on Violet's story, telling her about Eileen and her German fiancé who had so suddenly and mysteriously disappeared just before they were due to get married.

Chandice fell silent as she processed the information. 'It makes it all so much more real, doesn't it, when you begin to learn the dead man's story?'

'Yes.' It was the same in any murder investigation. As a police detective, Raven had to work with the evidence, which usually meant a corpse. But to the members of the public involved in the case, the victim had once been a real flesh-and-blood person. It was necessary always to keep that in mind. And equally necessary not to be distracted by that.

'I wonder what happened to Heinrich's family in Germany?' said Chandice. 'They would never have known the truth.'

'According to Violet they perished in the war.' Raven was more concerned about who else might have known the truth, and might still be alive. Someone who didn't want the truth to come out, and would take desperate measures to bury it.

After saying goodbye to Chandice, he took the photograph from Raymond's room at Larkmead, and set it down on the dining table beneath the dim light of the ceiling rose.

Six young men, frozen in time.

At one end of the row stood the man that the care home workers had identified as Raymond Swindlehurst. Next but one to him was a man that, after some careful study, Raven convinced himself was a young Eric Roper, the old man who had gently snored his way through Raven's chat with Violet. And next to him stood a man – a smile lighting his face, his trousers held up with a pair of wide braces – that Raven had no trouble at all recognising.

He retrieved the yellowed photo album of his grandparents' wedding and turned to the page where his grandfather was standing proud as punch with his new wife on his arm.

Jack Raven.

There was no doubt about it.

So Jack had known the two men at the care home. Had he also known Heinrich Meyer? Was Heinrich perhaps even in this very photograph? Raven wished he had a picture of the dead man.

He slid the photograph out of its frame and turned it over. On the back, in pencil, was the date it had been taken. Fifteenth of August, 1946. The year Heinrich had disappeared. One year after Raven's grandfather had married.

He turned another page in the wedding album. There was Jack again, that unmistakable cheeky grin on his face. And next to him was his best man.

Eric Roper.

It was strange to think that although Jack had died more than half a century ago, Eric was still alive and living nearby. Raven wondered what stories the old man could tell him about his grandfather, a man he had never known.

He studied the three other men in Raymond's photograph but no amount of peering at the black-and-white image revealed any further information.

Three known faces. And three unknown.

The young men gazed silently back at him, their whole lives ahead of them, although who knew what horrors they had already witnessed?

Six young men from a generation scarred by war.

Finally Raven reached for the cardboard box he had

recovered from the attic. Beneath the flat cap and carefully-folded pin-striped suit, the old tea towel and the object it concealed remained undisturbed. He drew it out and unwrapped it again, placing it carefully on the table.

The gun, which had at first seemed little more than a curious souvenir from his grandfather's past had now taken on a much more sinister significance.

Was this the gun that was used to kill Heinrich Meyer?

Raven stared at it for what seemed like an hour. But the weapon was in no hurry to give up its secrets. Eventually he wrapped it up again and replaced it in the box. Feeling the ache in his bones, he carried the box and photo album upstairs and hid them at the back of his old bedroom wardrobe.

CHAPTER 19

Becca felt as if she had a ringside seat at a boxing match. Not a fair fight, perhaps, but one that would be fought hard. In one corner of the office, DI Derek Dinsdale – brown suit, dandruff, sweat marks already staining his armpits and it was barely eight thirty in the morning. In the opposite corner, DCI Tom Raven – a heavyweight with his set jaw, dark stubble and black overcoat that he hadn't removed even though he'd been pacing his office for nearly twenty minutes.

Becca wasn't a betting person, but if pressed she would put her money on Raven.

Except that there was a third player in this match. Detective Superintendent Gillian Ellis – unseen, apart from a fleeting appearance when both men had first entered the ring, but whose muscular presence was still felt, and whose word here was law. Becca hadn't heard what Gillian had said to the two men, but she had seen their reactions and knew how unhappy they were about what they'd been told.

The two opponents circled each other warily, both seeming reluctant to make the first move.

Becca decided that perhaps that role fell to her. She went to fetch some tea and coffee from the machine in the corridor, then returned and placed one cup in front of each man. 'So,' she suggested, once she had their full attention, 'perhaps the three murders are connected in some way.'

'I believe so,' said Raven.

'Rubbish,' sneered Dinsdale.

The room fell into a deeper silence.

After a minute, Raven broke it. 'The skeleton discovered at Forge Valley Woods has been provisionally identified as Heinrich Meyer, a German airman from the prisoner of war camp at Malton. When he went missing in 1946, he was engaged to be married to Eileen Hunter, a doctor's daughter from the town. Raymond Swindlehurst was a contemporary of Eileen's from Malton. He must have known Heinrich. Fast-forward seventy-odd years and Raymond is found murdered immediately after the discovery of the skeleton hits the news. Coincidence? I don't think so.'

Becca sifted through the facts of Raven's case. She couldn't say she was entirely convinced by his argument. Maybe it was just a coincidence. Coincidences sometimes happened. There didn't always have to be a conspiracy.

Dinsdale levelled a meaty finger in Raven's direction. 'I don't see it. These two cases are decades apart. I've caught the man who killed Natalia Kamińska. He almost certainly killed Raymond Swindlehurst too. And his motive was simple – financial. There's no connection with some historic crime. You're clutching at straws because you have no hope of solving such an old case. Why not leave it, Raven?'

Raven gritted his teeth. When he spoke it was in a slow clear voice as if he were battling to control his temper. 'Because Detective Superintendent Ellis has asked that we merge our resources and work together. There are leads from the care home that could help with the investigation into Heinrich Meyer's death. And the murders of Raymond Swindlehurst and Natalia Kamińska may be more complicated than they at first appear.'

'Or they may be perfectly straightforward,' countered Dinsdale. 'Are you saying I haven't done my job properly?'

An ominous silence fell on the room.

Raven turned to Becca. 'What do you think?'

Becca wished she hadn't been asked. Dinsdale turned to look at her, his eyes narrowed. She felt like she was being forced to take sides and would be judged badly whichever man she backed. She wished that Detective Superintendent Ellis had simply put Raven in charge instead of expecting these two pig-headed men to cooperate.

'I think,' she began, 'that it might be worth seeing if the two investigations would benefit from a joint approach. We'll hold Troy Woods, since the case against him is strong' – she flashed a smile in Dinsdale's direction – 'but continue to gather evidence. Who knows, perhaps if we combine resources we'll make rapid progress on both fronts. And if there is a connection' – she nodded at Raven – 'then this will be the best way to make a breakthrough.'

She could see both men nodding in satisfaction, and knew that she'd managed to pull off a diplomatic feat.

'Good,' said Dinsdale, 'like I said, we've already caught the bastard who killed the nurse and the old man. Maybe we can find out who killed that German too.'

'Excellent,' said Raven. 'So that's agreed then. Becca, call everyone together for a combined team meeting.'

'Yes, sir,' said Becca, relieved that the match had ended with no blood spilled. She scuttled from the office before either contestant could change his mind and begin a new round of sparring.

★

Ten minutes later, Becca had assembled DC Tony Bairstow and DC Jess Barraclough in the incident room and explained what was going to happen.

'Sounds like a good idea to me,' said Jess. 'We could

use some more help on the Forge Valley case.'

'Now that we have a possible ID for the skeleton, we've got more to work with,' agreed Tony.

'I just hope there's no bickering,' said Becca. She didn't need to explain who might be doing the bickering.

When the two SIOs entered the room, it was clear that the uneasy truce Becca had brokered was just about holding. Raven took centre stage in front of the whiteboard while Dinsdale skulked at the side.

Despite all the wrangling that had been necessary to bring the two teams together, now that it was done, Becca found that she was quite excited. Both cases needed a fresh approach – despite all the evidence against Troy Woods, Becca didn't believe that the case was as watertight as Dinsdale maintained – and she was looking forward to getting involved in the investigation of the skeleton in Forge Valley Woods. She had never worked on such an old case before, and was intrigued. Or maybe she was just glad to be back working with Raven.

'Okay everyone,' said Raven. 'We have three ongoing murder investigations and it's become apparent that there could be connections that need following up. So from now on, the teams led by myself and DI Derek Dinsdale will be combined and we will share our information. Any questions?'

'Who do we report to?' asked Jess.

Raven hesitated for a moment before answering. 'This will be a joint operation, so DI Dinsdale and myself will be as one.' It sounded to Becca as if those words had cost him dearly. He looked to Dinsdale for confirmation.

Dinsdale grunted something that might have been, 'Yes.'

'Right then,' said Raven. 'We'll begin by laying out all the facts for both cases. Let's start with the murder weapon used to kill Natalia Kamińska.' He turned to Dinsdale, who stepped forwards.

Dinsdale fixed the photograph of the blood-stained hammer to the whiteboard and waited for everyone in the room to take a good look at it. When he spoke his voice was self-congratulatory. 'Troy Woods admitted that he used this hammer in his work at Larkmead. The hammer has now been analysed by forensics. The blood is Natalia's, and the post-mortem has confirmed that the head injury that killed her is consistent with a blow from a hammer of this type.' He glared sideways at Raven. 'There's no doubt that this is the weapon used to kill her.'

'No one's questioning that,' said Raven, 'but was the hammer wielded by Troy Woods, or someone else?'

'Fingerprints lifted from the handle match Troy's,' said Dinsdale with a smug nod.

'Okay,' said Raven. 'Although we should bear in mind that someone else wearing gloves could have struck the fatal blow.'

His remark won him an undisguised sneer from Dinsdale. 'Troy Woods has confessed to stealing cash and bank cards from the residents' rooms. That gives him a motive to have killed Raymond Swindlehurst, if Raymond caught him red-handed. We know that Troy stayed late at work on the evening Raymond was murdered, and he's admitted to being in Raymond's room. If Natalia discovered what he'd done, that gives him a clear motive to have killed her too.'

Raven turned over the information before responding. 'Becca?' he asked.

Becca groaned inwardly. It seemed as if Raven was determined to keep putting her in an awkward position. 'Troy's a petty, opportunistic thief. It's possible that he panicked when caught and so killed Raymond, trying to make his death look like suicide. And I did see him arguing with Natalia outside the care home. Natalia tried to contact me the day before her death. She was clearly frightened about something.'

'There you go,' said Dinsdale.

'All right then,' said Raven unperturbed. 'Now, moving on to the skeleton in Forge Valley Woods. The remains were found with a B-Uhr watch' – Raven stuck a photograph of a watch on the whiteboard – 'suggesting the victim was in the German *Luftwaffe*. There was a prisoner of war camp near Malton and some Germans stayed on after the war. Tony has looked into missing persons from that time, but the records are patchy at best, and possibly no one would have reported a missing German anyway. However, we do know about a German ex-POW who disappeared very suddenly, so there's a good chance that this could be our man.'

Becca saw how Jess and Tony listened with rapt attention while Raven related the story that Violet had told him. Eileen Hunter had been engaged to marry a German called Heinrich Meyer from Köthen. She was expecting his child, and the marriage would have made a happy end to the long years of war and misery.

There were a few details that Becca had been unaware of. For instance, she hadn't known that Violet's friend Eric Roper, the old man with dementia, had also lived in Malton.

'But then Heinrich disappeared,' said Raven. 'He wrote Eileen a letter, saying that he'd decided to go back to Germany and help rebuild his hometown. But according to Violet, there was no one waiting for him there, and he'd been very happy with Eileen. Eileen, of course, was devastated.'

'What happened to the baby?' asked Jess.

'Eileen had the baby,' said Raven. 'A boy, called Joseph. But it was a tough life as a single mother in those days.'

'Still is,' said Jess.

'But even more then,' said Becca, 'because of the social stigma and sense of shame.'

'Eileen died some time ago,' continued Raven, 'but her brother Vincent is still alive, as is her son, Joseph.'

Dinsdale interrupted. 'This is all fascinating, but what makes you so certain that this missing German is in any way connected to the recent events at Larkmead?'

It ought to have been Raven's chance to respond, but

to her surprise, Becca heard her own voice answering. 'It's because of what Natalia and Troy told us – that Raymond began acting strangely after news of the discovery of the skeleton appeared on TV. According to Natalia, he'd been really shaken up by what he saw. Why would he react like that unless he knew who was buried there?'

'There could be any number of reasons,' said Dinsdale.

Becca carried on, undaunted. 'And then, according to Troy, the morning after learning about the skeleton, Raymond handed two letters to Natalia to post. He told her they were very important. Fortunately for us, it was Troy who posted them and so he was able to tell us that one was addressed to somebody called Vincent living in Scarborough. Vincent is the name of Eileen Hunter's brother.'

Dinsdale folded his arms. 'Do you really believe a word that Troy Woods says?'

Nobody answered him.

'Who was the other letter addressed to?' asked Raven.

'Troy couldn't remember. But just a few days after writing the letters, Raymond was killed.'

Tony and Jess were busy scribbling notes.

'Oh, and another thing,' said Becca. 'On the day he died, Raymond received a visit from a writer, Craig Clarkson, who's writing a book about World War Two veterans. There may be no connection, but we shouldn't forget about him.'

'Thank you,' said Raven. 'Now, we need some actions to move this forward. I'm going to track down Vincent Hunter and see what he can tell us about Eileen and Heinrich. Becca and Jess, could you try to trace Joseph Hunter? If possible, I'd like to see if he'll agree to a DNA test. Then we'll know for sure if the skeleton is Heinrich Meyer. Tony, could you contact the German police and see if Heinrich Meyer ever did return to Germany after the war? His hometown was Köthen. And DI Dinsdale, I think we need to follow up the full extent of Troy Woods's criminal activities at the care home. Could I leave that in your hands?'

Becca was expecting Dinsdale to register some kind of protest at being told what to do, but he nodded his assent, picked up his jacket and stalked out of the room. She smiled at Raven to show she approved of his plan of action.

CHAPTER 20

The Osgodby area of Scarborough lay to the south of the main town. It was reached by following the Filey Road for a mile or so beyond Larkmead Nursing Home. Raven's BMW swallowed up the distance in no time, pushing past bungalows, detached houses and semis, all boasting a grand sea view. At least they would have done during the summer months. In November, the coast was shrouded in mist, the sea invisible in the murk, only greyness between here and infinity. Gulls appeared out of the sea fret, their shrieks biting the cold air like ghostly wraiths of drowned sailors.

Raven turned the M6 off the main road and pulled up alongside a dormer bungalow in one of those very quiet streets where nothing ever seemed to happen. He could almost feel the curtains twitching behind neighbouring houses as he opened a set of metal gates and walked past a black Volkswagen Golf parked on the short driveway.

A tall, elderly man was pruning and shaping the shrubs around the edge of the lawn. A neat pile of sticks and twigs was already heaped in a waiting wheelbarrow. Even at his great age he displayed the zeal of a man determined to bend nature to his will. At Raven's approach, he stopped what he was doing and studied him with hawkish eyes. 'Are you from the council? Is this about next door's planning application? If I've told you lot once, I've told you a hundred times, they can build that extension over my dead body. It'll block all the light to my garden. My home is all I have, and I'll fight for it to my dying breath.'

Clearly life wasn't all beer and skittles in bungalow land. Raven studied the man's features, trying to work out if his weathered, wrinkled face matched one of the fresh young men in Raymond's photo. He couldn't be sure. The photograph had been taken seventy-six years ago. People changed.

'DCI Tom Raven from Scarborough CID.' Raven showed his warrant card. He had the impression that this man would respect authority, but he could be wrong. After all, he had shown scant regard for the local council. 'Am I talking to Mr Vincent Hunter?'

'You are.'

'Brother of Eileen Hunter?' Raven had tracked down his quarry aided by Becca's tip-off, courtesy of Troy Woods, that one of the letters Raymond had sent just before his death was to "somebody called Vincent living in Scarborough". Raven would have preferred Troy's information to be more precise, but with the help of the police database he'd been able to put two and two together.

To make four, in this case.

Vincent narrowed his eyes suspiciously. 'What do you want?'

'I'd like to talk to you about a case I'm working on related to your sister. I think you might be able to help.'

'I doubt it. She's been dead twenty years.'

Raven stood his ground and eventually Vincent said they might as well go inside. It was starting to spot with rain.

He made Raven wait outside the back door while he unloaded the wheelbarrow and stowed his gardening tools away in the shed. Raven had the distinct impression that the old man was showing him who was boss around here. But eventually Vincent unlocked the door to the house and allowed him inside. But only as far as the kitchen. There, they sat down at a pine table. Coffee and tea were not on offer.

'What's this about then?' asked Vincent.

Raven took a moment to study the interior of the house, trying to get more of a feel for the man's character from the place where he lived. The kitchen was clean and tidy, a single plate and mug left to dry on a rack. The familiar sign of a man who lived alone, and who, like Raven, was fastidious in his habits.

Raven decided to plunge straight in, judging that small talk would be wasted on this man who clearly resented the presence of a detective in his home. 'Your sister was once engaged to a German called Heinrich Meyer.'

'Are you asking, or do you already know?'

'It would help if you could confirm the fact.'

'I won't deny it.' Vincent's face showed no emotion and he was giving away nothing more than the bare information.

'Could you tell me what happened to him?'

'That was a lifetime ago. Why are you asking?'

'If you could just answer the question, please.'

Vincent gave an exaggerated sigh of frustration. 'That German bastard buggered off home, that's what happened.'

'You sound bitter about it.'

'Do I? Perhaps I have a right to be. He left her with a child, and no one to look after her. So yes, I was angry about the way he treated her. Not that I ever expected much from a German.'

The words were delivered with surprising vehemence, as if the wound was still raw.

'Were you in the war, Mr Hunter?'

'Aye, I was. Right at the end. Proud to serve my country.'

'Can you tell me what you did?' Raven knew from personal experience that many veterans appreciated a willing audience.

'Rear gunner in a Lancaster at eighteen years old.' Spoken with pride.

Raven didn't need to feign admiration. He was genuinely impressed. 'That was a dangerous job.' As an ex-soldier himself, Raven knew his facts. The life expectancy of the crew of a World War Two heavy bomber had been measured in mere weeks, and the post of rear turret gunner was the most exposed of all to enemy fire. It was lonely too, and freezing cold, stuck at the back of the aircraft on your own at night, trying to protect the plane and the rest of the crew from enemy fighters. 'But you survived.'

'By the skin of my teeth.' Vincent was loosening up, becoming more voluble. 'You can't imagine what it was like up there, bouncing around through flak, explosions on all sides, planes erupting into fireballs before your eyes. It was the nearest thing to hell. We were on our fifth sortie over Munich in January 1945 when we were hit and had to bail out.'

'You parachuted into enemy territory?'

'It was either that or be incinerated in the aircraft. I got out in time, but I don't think the pilot made it.'

'What happened to you?'

'Four months in a Stalag. Conditions were atrocious, I can tell you. Thousands of prisoners crammed into overcrowded huts. British, French, Belgians, Dutch, Greek, Yugoslavs. But the Soviets had it worst of all – the Gestapo shot them.' He aimed two fingers at Raven's head in imitation of a gun. 'The rest of us were used as slave labour, or left to rot.'

Raven was getting a clear impression of a man whose experience of war had left him emotionally and psychologically scarred.

'How did you feel when you returned to Malton and discovered that Eileen was engaged to Heinrich?'

Vincent fell silent for a moment, pondering his reply. 'I'll tell you how I felt. I felt confused. I was pleased she'd found someone, but dismayed that he was one of them – the enemy. Although once I got to know him a bit, I realised he was just a lad like one of us. He'd never killed anyone. The war wasn't his fault. I made my peace with him... until he abandoned Eileen.' Vincent's face darkened. 'That just confirmed my worst beliefs. I swear that if I'd seen him again after that, I'd have let my fists do the talking.'

'Did you see him again?'

'Of course not. He went back to Germany. I told you that.'

'How can you be certain Heinrich returned to Germany?'

'That's what his letter said. Anyway, where else could he have gone?'

'Did you know a Mr Raymond Swindlehurst who lived at Larkmead Nursing Home?'

'I did.' Vincent's guarded tone was back.

'When did you last see him?'

'I used to meet up with him regularly, every week or so. But over the years things slipped. It's a good two months since I last saw him.'

'Are you aware that Mr Swindlehurst passed away recently?'

'Yes.' It was impossible to detect any trace of emotion in Vincent's response. The word might have expressed sorrow, or regret, or anger. There was no way of knowing.

'Shortly before Mr Swindlehurst died, he wrote two letters. One was addressed to you.'

'It was a private matter,' said Vincent, confirming to Raven that he had been right about Vincent receiving the letter but at the same time firmly closing off any discussion of its contents. 'Nothing of any consequence now.'

'And yet Raymond told his carer that the letter was important and urgent. Do you still have it?'

Vincent shook his head. 'I threw it on the fire when I

was burning leaves.'

'Why did you do that?'

'A dead man's words. No business of the living.'

Raven decided not to push the matter. If the letter was gone, it was gone. 'Mr Swindlehurst also sent a letter to another person. Do you know who that might have been?'

'No idea.'

'Could I show you a photograph?'

'If you must.'

Raven retrieved the photo he'd found in Raymond's room and placed it on the table. 'Are you in this picture?'

Vincent fished a pair of reading glasses out of his breast pocket and perched them on his nose. It was clear that the photograph had roused his curiosity, despite his best efforts to appear uninterested. 'That's me.' He pointed to a tall, languid man at the opposite end of the line-up from Raymond. 'Where did you get this?'

'It belonged to Mr Swindlehurst. Can you tell me who the other people in the photograph are?'

Vincent scanned the row of faces. 'That's Raymond on the left, but I assume you already knew that. That one is Cyril Stubbs. Died forty years ago. Lung cancer.' He indicated a short man with dark hair standing next to Raymond, the one with the cigarette in his mouth. 'And that's Eric. He's still going, but might as well not be.'

'That would be Eric Roper from Larkmead.'

'You've met him, then? Poor Eric. He was sharp as a pin once. Now his brain's gone to mush. He wouldn't recognise his own face in the mirror.' Vincent's attention returned to the photograph. His finger skipped over Jack Raven and landed on the man standing next to himself wearing a pair of round glasses. 'That's Donald Cartwright.'

'Is he still alive?'

'Old Donald? He's still kicking around, as far as I know.'

'Where can I find him?'

'Last I heard, he was still in Malton, but I haven't seen

him for years.' Vincent's finger had drifted back to Jack Raven. 'This one was new to our group. Eric introduced him – they'd fought together in Italy during the war. What was his name?'

He looked up, and Raven had the distinct impression that Vincent Hunter knew precisely what Jack Raven's name was. 'Was it John? Jim? No wait, I remember now. It was Jack. Jack Raven. That was his name. A relation by any chance?' His piercing stare rested on Raven's face, as if searching for a family resemblance.

'Common surname,' said Raven.

'You reckon? Not that common, I'd say. Pretty damn uncommon.'

Raven slid the photograph back into his folder and rose to his feet. 'Thank you for your time, Mr Hunter. No need to get up.' Vincent hadn't made any effort to rise to his feet. 'I'll see myself out.'

★

Vincent Hunter watched from his living room window as Raven drove away in his swanky silver car. Although the DCI had been careful not to mention the discovery at Forge Valley Woods, there was no doubt what he was up to.

There was only one thing for it.

Vincent went into the hallway and picked up the phone. The number he wanted was in his address book. He flipped to the right page, dialled and waited. The call was answered after three rings.

'The police have just been,' said Vincent. 'A DCI Tom Raven. He's some relation of Jack Raven's – a grandson most likely. We need to talk.'

CHAPTER 21

'Everything okay?' asked Jess.

They were in Becca's car, heading towards the town of Malton, once the home of Eileen Hunter.

'Why do you ask?' said Becca, trying to keep her voice light.

'Tell me if it's none of my business, but you don't seem to have been yourself these last few days.'

Becca gripped the steering wheel and stared straight ahead at the car in front. She thought she'd done a pretty good job of carrying on as normal, but Jess was clearly an astute observer of people's moods. Over the past year, Becca had tried to leave her heartache at the hospital. Work was an escape, a place where she could pretend that the world was as it should be. She had done her best to place her worries about Sam in a separate compartment in her mind, safely walled off to prevent them filling every waking moment with anguish.

But the walls that protected her were breaking down.

'I've had a few things on my mind,' she said to Jess.

How she would have loved to unburden herself to her

junior officer. Jess would have listened sympathetically and wouldn't judge or offer an ill-thought-out opinion. But Becca knew that if she started talking about Sam, she would be overwhelmed by emotion and wouldn't be able to do her job. Now that she was working for Raven – Dinsdale had been effectively side-lined this morning – she was more determined than ever to keep it together.

The walls would have to hold for a while longer.

'I can't talk about it. Sorry.'

'I understand,' said Jess. 'But any time you want a friend, I'm here.'

'Thanks.'

They drove in silence for the next few miles until Becca realised with a start what she ought to have said in response. 'What about you, Jess? Are you okay?' Becca had been so wrapped up in her own troubles that she hadn't been paying attention to her colleagues. But now she thought about it, Jess wasn't quite her usual self either. The young detective constable was normally bubbly and cheerful, but had been unusually subdued since the weekend.

'I had a nasty shock,' said Jess. 'I thought I'd met someone really special. We got off to a good start, but then... well, I'm still trying to understand what went wrong.'

'I'm sorry to hear that. If you want to talk, I'm here for you too.'

A few miles further along the A64, they came to a sign for Malton and turned off the main road. The satnav began directing them through the quiet streets of the old market town.

They were on the hunt for Eileen and Heinrich's son, and the electoral register had a record for a Joseph Hunter living at Sheepfoot Hill close to the River Derwent. Becca drove past an old church and parked the Honda outside a terraced stone cottage overlooking a small green. It looked like a pleasant place to live.

The man who answered the door wore loose-fitting

jogging pants and a bright green T-shirt. He was barefoot, his shoulder-length hair tied in a ponytail. He wasn't quite what Becca had been expecting. If this was the right man, he must be about seventy-five, but he looked at least ten years younger.

'Joseph Hunter?'

He smiled and welcomed them into his front room.

An orange yoga mat was rolled out on the wooden floorboards, some new age music was playing, and a joss stick burned in the hearth, filling the room with the heady smell of incense. There was little furniture in the room except for a small sofa and a well-stocked bookcase. Becca stole a quick glance at the books. They were all about healing and spirituality as far as she could see. Slatted wooden blinds covered the windows and an Indian Mandala tapestry hung above the sofa. An onyx Buddha sat on the mantelpiece, flanked by a pair of candles.

The room looked like it was auditioning hard for a role as a yoga studio.

'I'm sorry we've interrupted your practice,' said Becca, indicating the orange mat stretched out on the floor.

'No worries. I'd finished anyway. Would you like some tea? I was just going to make a pot.'

'Lovely,' said Becca. 'Milk and two sugars, please.'

Joseph grinned at her. 'It's green tea, so I wouldn't recommend adding milk. And you know that sugar's the silent poison, don't you? I don't actually have any in the house.'

'I love green tea,' said Jess.

'Maybe I'll skip it,' said Becca.

Joseph invited them to take a seat on the sofa while he went to boil the kettle.

'I tried yoga once,' confided Becca, 'but I wasn't flexible enough.'

'It's not all about flexibility,' said Jess. 'That's the mistake everyone makes. It's also about strength and balance. And finding inner harmony and peace of mind.'

'Maybe I'll give it another go,' said Becca, knowing that

she wouldn't. When was there time in her life for sitting on a mat, twisting herself into funny positions?

Joseph returned with the tea in two hand-painted mugs and passed one to Jess who accepted it gladly. Becca wondered where he was going to sit but he dropped down onto a yoga block and sat cross-legged on the floor without even spilling a drop of tea. 'So, how can I help you?'

'Is it correct that your mother was Eileen Hunter and your father was a German called Heinrich Meyer?' asked Jess.

'Yes, that's right.' Joseph put his mug down on the floor and sat with his hands gently resting on his knees. With his relaxed but upright posture, he looked like a thinner version of the Buddha sitting on the mantelpiece behind him. 'But I never knew my father. He went missing before I was born.'

Becca noted the curious choice of words that he used. *Went missing.* 'Do you mean that he returned to Germany?'

'That's what some people say.'

'You don't believe that?'

'People can believe whatever they like.'

'You may have heard on the news that human remains were recently unearthed at Forge Valley Woods in Scarborough,' said Jess.

'I have.' Joseph remained outwardly calm, but Becca sensed a heightened alertness in his demeanour, as if he was waiting for her to tell him something he had already guessed.

'We have reason to believe,' she said, 'that the remains are those of a former German prisoner of war, possibly your father, Heinrich Meyer.'

Joseph picked up his tea and sipped. 'I see.'

'You don't seem surprised,' said Becca.

'No. I always thought that Heinrich would turn up one day.' He breathed out deeply, as if releasing a lifetime of forbearance. 'How certain are you that it's him?'

'We wanted to ask if you would be willing to submit to a DNA test in order to verify it.'

'Of course.'

'What do you know about your father?' asked Becca.

'Only what I've been told. My uncle always said that Heinrich ran off back to Germany. Uncle Vincent was very angry with Heinrich for deserting my mother. But she maintained that Heinrich would never have abandoned us.'

'What did she think happened to him?'

'Something bad, but no one would listen to her. She was a young, unmarried mother. People looked down on her. No one was interested in what she had to say.'

'Did she bring you up on her own?'

'Yes. It was a struggle for her. She had a series of part-time jobs but they never paid very much. Her brother gave her money from time to time, but they never really got on after the war. I think their experiences of life drove them apart. He'd been in a German prisoner of war camp, and she was engaged to a German. Besides, Uncle Vincent likes respectability, and his sister wasn't seen as respectable in those days.'

'Are you still in touch with your uncle?' asked Becca.

'Not really. I "dropped out", you see.' Joseph smiled self-deprecatingly. 'I left home in the sixties and went to India to "find myself". I know it's a cliché, but having grown up without a father, I needed to find something that would give me a sense of self-worth.'

'And you found that in yoga?'

'Yoga, meditation, travel. And various worthy causes over the years – CND marches, protesting against the Vietnam war, the war in Iraq. Now I do what I can to support environmental issues.' He laughed. 'I'm one of those annoying people that governments and other authorities wish would keep quiet.'

Becca was growing to like Joseph, despite his terrible taste in tea. She admired the fact that he exuded an inner calm. His responses to questions were thoughtful. She envied the simplicity of his life.

How good it would be to find such peace and certainty,

instead of the turmoil that was threatening to engulf her right now.

Joseph smiled at her. 'I always knew that my father would be found eventually. I wish it could have been when he was still alive. But if this skeleton in the woods really is my father, then he deserves to rest in peace next to my mother in the churchyard here in Malton.'

'I'm sure that will be possible,' said Becca, 'once the coroner has released the remains for burial. But the investigation will need to be completed first.'

Joseph nodded. 'Of course. Then shall we get on and do that DNA test?'

CHAPTER 22

When Raven returned to the station after visiting Vincent Hunter, Becca and Jess weren't yet back from Malton, and Dinsdale was nowhere to be seen. Tony Bairstow was busy on the phone. Raven pulled his office door closed and dialled Chandice's mobile number. She answered straight away.

'I'm not disturbing you, am I?' he asked.

'Not at all, Chief Inspector!' She sounded pleased to hear from him. 'Any news on the Heinrich Meyer case?'

'Possibly.'

'Sounds intriguing. Is that all you're going to tell me?'

Raven hesitated. The investigation was confidential, but he felt he owed her something after all the work she'd put in. 'The son is still alive.'

'Heinrich and Eileen's son?'

'He lives in Malton.'

'I bet he has a story to tell.' She was inviting him to continue.

'We're hoping to use a DNA test to confirm the identity of the remains.'

'Yes, that makes sense. Anything else?'

'I really can't go into details.'

There was a pause at the end of the line. 'I understand,' she said at last. But it didn't really sound like she did.

'You know–'

'It'll always be like this, won't it?' she interrupted.

'Like what?'

'Secrets.'

Raven didn't know what to say. He had lived the whole of his working life this way, self-censoring, editing the truth, being deliberately evasive. He no longer even realised that he was doing it. No wonder Lisa had left him.

'I do understand,' said Chandice quietly. 'Really, I do. For me, this is just an interesting side project, but for you it's your job. The case is confidential.'

'I can tell you more perhaps, next time we meet.'

He waited, almost too afraid to hear how she would respond. Was there going to be a next time? Could a woman like Chandice ever stay with a man like him for longer than a single weekend?

'You can tell me more,' she said after a beat, 'when you take me out for a posh dinner. I assume they have expensive restaurants in Scarborough and not just fish and chips?'

'Very expensive,' Raven assured her. 'Far too expensive for a poor policeman like me.'

'That's where you can take me then,' she said. 'And then you can show me where you live.'

Raven grimaced, thinking of the bags of plaster and cement in his front room and wondering what other horrors Barry might have brought to the house in his absence. 'I don't think you want to see that. My house really isn't fit for human habitation at the moment.'

'But you live there.'

'If you can call it living.'

'Then I want to see it too. I want to know everything about you, Tom, and that includes your house. Anyway, it can't possibly be worse than an archaeological dig.'

'Don't be too sure,' said Raven. But his heart leapt at

the thought of seeing her again, even if he would have to show her the domestic disaster that was his home. 'I'll call you again to confirm.'

He was still grinning like an infatuated teenager when DC Tony Bairstow knocked on the door.

'Sir, I've just been speaking to the German police in Köthen. They've done a search.'

Raven hastily adjusted his expression to one more suitably serious. 'That was quick.'

'They're very efficient over there. They have a system called' – he frowned at his notes – '*Anmeldung*, if that's how you pronounce it, that requires people to register their address at the local citizens' office. They have no record of a Heinrich Meyer returning to Köthen after the war.'

'Thanks, Tony,' said Raven. 'Good work there.'

Raven was now more convinced than ever that the Forge Valley Woods skeleton was Heinrich Meyer. A DNA test would prove it once and for all. Then the only question would be how he had ended up shot in the back of the head and buried in the woods, and Raven was already formulating a working theory about who might have done that and why. If he was right, it would also explain the murders of Raymond Swindlehurst and Natalia Kamińska.

Through the glass window of the office, the rotund form of Derek Dinsdale appeared briefly in the incident room and Raven went to intercept him before he could vanish again. Dinsdale looked up as Raven bore down on him. 'Ah, Raven, I was just heading off.'

Raven resisted the urge to check his watch. He was sure it was still early in the day, but he was determined to avoid antagonising Dinsdale if at all possible. 'How did you get on with Troy Woods?'

Dinsdale gave a self-satisfied smile. 'I think it's safe to say that we've wrapped things up there. I visited the care home and spoke to the manager, Judith Holden. She tried to cover it up, but I eventually got her to admit that several of the residents had made complaints about missing money and bank cards.'

'It hadn't been reported to the police?'

'She'd managed to persuade the residents and their relatives that it was just absent-mindedness. She obviously didn't want anyone to know that there was a thief at large.'

'Did that take all day?' asked Raven, instantly regretting it.

Dinsdale's face darkened. 'Not at all. I've also spoken to the financial forensics team. They're working their way through Troy Woods's laptop. He may not be the brightest of cyber-criminals, but he certainly knows how to fleece vulnerable old people of their savings. When I sent the evidence through to the CPS they had no problem authorising me to charge him on two accounts of murder and several others of theft and related crimes.'

'What?' Raven was taken aback. 'But we agreed this morning that it might not be that simple.'

'Did we? I don't believe in looking for complications where there aren't any. Haven't you ever heard of Occam's bloody razor?'

Damn the man. Raven took a breath to calm himself down. How could Gillian expect him to work with someone like this? And what was the Crown Prosecution Service thinking of, authorising a suspect to be charged on evidence that was largely circumstantial? Whatever Troy Woods was guilty of, Raven doubted that a double murder charge would stick in court. 'This is still an ongoing investigation,' he told Dinsdale. 'A joint operation, tied to the skeleton in Forge Valley Woods. You should have spoken to me before charging a suspect.'

Dinsdale puffed indignantly, his cheeks colouring. 'Is that so? Well, may I remind you that whatever Gillian may have said about working together, I'm still the SIO on the Raymond Swindlehurst and Natalia Kamińska case. So I get to decide what happens there, not you. The skeleton in the woods is your problem,' he continued, jabbing his finger at Raven's chest in that annoying habit he had. 'And I don't intend to stand in the way of any arrests you make there. If you ever make any, that is.' The glint in his eye revealed precisely how unlikely he thought that to be.

So this was how it was. Dinsdale had only ever been going through the motions of cooperating. He had carried on running his own investigation his way, making no effort to consult or share information. If Raven hadn't happened to run into him now, Dinsdale wouldn't even have informed him that Troy Woods had been charged. As far as Dinsdale was concerned, his job was done and Raven could take a running jump if he expected any help from the DI.

Raven felt his anger boiling. Once before he'd had a run-in with Dinsdale, and that had resulted in him losing his temper and very nearly his job. He was damned if that was going to happen a second time.

He pushed his face up close to Dinsdale's and was gratified to see the older man draw back in fear. 'You're not worth it,' growled Raven. 'But get out of my sight before I change my mind.' He lifted his hand and watched as Dinsdale turned and scarpered out of the office as quickly as his legs would take him.

Out of the corner of his eye Raven noticed Tony observing the altercation from the other side of the office. He did his best to give the DC a reassuring look, but it was hard to tell if Tony was convinced. He scuttled away, busying himself in the contents of a filing cabinet.

Raven returned to his office, furious at himself for having lost control once again. A memory from childhood pushed its way unbidden into his mind. His father, drunk, fist raised, his mother cowering in fright. He felt the bile rise in his throat, sickened by the possibility that he might become the man he had spent his life fearing and hating.

I am not my father.

But the declaration sounded hollow, even to his own ears.

The office phone rang loudly, breaking through the memory, and he snatched up the receiver. 'DCI Raven speaking.'

'Just the man I was hoping to catch,' said a male voice.

'It's Andy here, from ballistics.'

Andy from ballistics was a hitherto unknown figure in Raven's universe, but he latched onto the newcomer's cheerful tone, grateful for a distraction. 'What have you got for me, Andy?'

'We've analysed the bullet you sent us. From that skull. Forge Valley Woods, wasn't it?'

'That's the one. What do you make of it?'

'Interesting. It's a 9mm parabellum from a semi-automatic pistol. Common enough, except that this isn't your run-of-the-mill variety of ammo.'

Raven sensed that Andy was a man who enjoyed telling a good story. He leaned back in his chair. 'I'm listening.'

'This is an old one. The characteristics and condition point to it being many decades old, most likely even dating back to wartime. You don't see many of these around.' Andy sounded as if he'd made a rare archaeological find, which in a sense he had. 'At that time, when lead was in short supply, instead of a lead core, an iron core encased with lead was used, just like in this one. And if that's the case, it was most likely fired from a Walther P-38 or a Luger P-08. They were the most common semi-automatics issued to the German army in World War Two. Mostly used by the *Wehrmacht*, the *Luftwaffe* and the SS.'

Raven pictured the gun hidden at the back of his wardrobe, but said nothing.

'Here's an interesting story,' continued Andy. 'The word "parabellum". Do you know what it means?'

Raven did, but decided to indulge Andy's storytelling a bit further. Who knew what nuggets of information the ballistics expert might impart? 'Go on, tell me.'

He had obviously said the right thing. The eagerness in Andy's voice rose a notch higher. 'Parabellum. It comes from the Latin phrase, *Si vis pacem, para bellum.* "If you want peace, prepare for war." It was the motto of the German weapons maker Deutsche Waffen- und Munitionsfabriken.'

'Okay, Andy. Thanks for the info.'

'Delighted to help. Do you have any idea what happened to the gun that fired the round?'

'Sorry. No.'

'Oh, well,' said Andy, obviously disappointed. 'I was just curious. Thanks, anyway.' He hung up.

Self-censorship, editing the truth, deliberate evasion.

Lies.

It was Raven's job. Or had it become a way of life?

★

When Becca returned to the guest house that evening she found her grandparents in the breakfast room talking in low conspiratorial voices with Sue.

Discussing me and Sam, I bet.

They all looked up as she entered, guilty looks on their faces.

They could hardly make it more obvious.

Sue rose hurriedly to her feet. 'Well, it's been lovely to chat to you both, but I've got loads of jobs to be getting on with. Becca, I'll leave you to sit with your grandparents, shall I?'

Her grandparents smiled at her expectantly, and Becca realised that this was no unplanned visit. Whatever it was her grandparents were supposedly doing here, the real reason for dropping by was to talk to her and try to cheer her up.

'Come and sit next to me,' said her grandmother, patting the chair that Sue had just vacated.

Becca knew she had no choice in the matter. She could protest if she wanted but what would that achieve? Besides, she was grateful to them for calling round. She needed all the support she could get at the moment and knew she could count on them to take her side.

Her grandfather poured a cup of tea from the pot and passed it to her on a saucer. 'Get this down you, love. A nice strong cup of Yorkshire tea. There's nothing like it after a hard day's work.'

'Thanks.' Becca accepted the tea and sank gratefully into the chair. Her lack of sleep combined with the stress of working with Dinsdale had left her exhausted. It would be nice to sit down for a while and just relax. The Yorkshire tea was very welcome after the green stuff that Joseph had offered her. And what was wrong with milk and two sugars anyway?

'Your mother says you're working on a case dating back to the Second World War,' said her grandmother. 'We have fond memories of the war.'

'Fond?' The idea seemed strange to Becca. There was nothing good about war as far as she could tell from the coverage of foreign conflicts she was familiar with on the news. But Violet Armitage had also reminisced about her wartime experiences as if they were the best days of her life.

'Oh yes,' said her grandmother. 'Of course, your grandfather and I were just children during the war years. It was all a great adventure for us.'

'Did much happen in Scarborough during the war?' asked Becca. She recalled a school history lesson in which they'd learned about the so-called Scarborough Blitz of 1941, during which German planes had dropped bombs on the town one night. A number of people had been killed and hundreds injured. But that had been a single air raid. It wasn't like the London Blitz which had lasted for months and claimed the lives of tens of thousands of civilians.

'I should say so,' said her grandfather. 'Scarborough was very much involved in the conflict. The trawler fleet was one of the first targets. German planes attacked and sunk several boats and others were hit by mines.' He turned to his wife. 'Do you remember Mr Dunwell and his mine?'

'Oh yes.' Becca's grandmother chuckled and took over the storytelling. 'The mine was caught in the nets of a trawler and brought to shore along with the day's catch. Mr Dunwell loaded it into the back of his van and drove it through town to the depot to get it weighed. The folk there sent him packing, so he took it to the scrapyard instead. It was only after they sent him away too that he took it down to the sands and dropped it off.'

Becca looked from one elderly face to the other, unable to tell if her grandparents were teasing her.

'It's true!' said her grandfather. 'And did you know that all the hotels in town were closed for business for the duration of the war and that troops were billeted there? The RAF took over the Grand Hotel and placed anti-aircraft guns on each of its four turrets.'

Becca tried to imagine the town's biggest landmark turned into a military base, but couldn't. It was equally impossible to imagine enemy ships and aircraft coming to attack the peaceful seaside town.

'I remember them getting up at the crack of dawn and doing exercises in singlets and shorts on the prom,' said her grandmother.

'I bet you do!' replied her grandfather with a wry smile. 'And they used to practise shooting up at the castle. Do you remember when the RAF dropped a bomb on the Dog and Duck?'

Her grandmother looked askance at her husband. 'Get away with you! It wasn't a bomb, it was part of the wing that fell off.'

'It was a bomb, I'm telling you!'

Becca decided to intervene before a full-blown row could develop. 'Where is the Dog and Duck?' She was aware of a Dog and Duck Lane, a stepped passageway leading down the castle hill to Quay Street, but no pub or inn by that name.

'Well it's not there anymore,' said her grandfather. 'On account of the bomb.'

'The wing,' interrupted her grandmother. 'It was a piece of the wing that came off. It fell right on top of the old pub and brought it crashing down. Bricks, timbers, tiles, the lot! It was just opposite the house where the Raven family lived. They had a narrow escape, I can tell you.'

'Raven?' said Becca, intrigued. 'You knew the Raven

family?'

'Of course,' said her grandmother. 'The old town's not such a big place. Everyone knew everyone in those days.'

It sometimes seemed to Becca that her mum still knew everything about everyone. And Liam too had all kinds of sources of information – the kind it was best not to ask many questions about. 'What do you remember about them?'

'Let's see. Back in those days it was Jack Raven who lived in the house. Jack was a fisherman like his father before him. They were seafaring folk, the Ravens. Had been for as long as anyone could remember. Jack went away to war, then after he returned he married Muriel and they had a son called Alan. But Jack drowned at a young age. Such bad luck. The Ravens were always an unlucky family.'

'Why do you say that?' asked Becca.

'Tragedy followed them,' said her grandfather darkly. 'Jack's father died young and so did Jack. Jack's son Alan lived long enough, but his wife was killed at a young age and his son ran away.'

'That would be Tom?' Becca refrained from explaining that Alan's son had returned to Scarborough after an interval of thirty years and was now her boss.

'Aye, Tom, that's right. They say that bad luck follows father to son, don't they? And that the raven's a bird of ill omen. That's what they say.'

His wife tapped him on the back of the hand. 'Only if they're superstitious old fishermen. Now stop talking nonsense. We're supposed to be here to cheer Becca up.'

★

Raven called in at the fish and chip shop on his way home and ordered a large haddock and chips with curry sauce. He carried his supper back to Quay Street and ate it with his fingers, sitting on the sofa in the living room. The mound of building materials piled up around the fireplace had grown since the morning, indicating that Barry had called round again. But there was still no sign of any actual work taking place.

Raven regarded the latest bags of cement and building sand with a sense of unease. The resemblance to wartime sandbags was uncanny and it was hard to shake off the notion that he was gradually being entombed inside a bunker.

Prepare for war.

Was it too late to phone Barry and cancel the job? He shook away the idea as soon as it came to him. It would only make him look like a tit, and he would be further away than ever from his dream home. But at the same time he had no desire to see his front room turned into a foxhole. Would work on the house ever begin?

He finished the last of the chips, licked his fingers clean and scrunched the fish and chip paper into the bin. He knew that all this gloomy introspection was simply a ruse for putting off what he had to do. Eventually he pushed himself up from the sofa and clambered up the steep staircase to the top floor.

The cardboard box was where he had stashed it in the wardrobe, partially hidden beneath the old photo album. Raven drew it out and carried it over to the bed. There he unpacked it, removed the tea towel that concealed the gun and laid it carefully on the mattress.

A Walther P-38. The *Pistole 38*, to call it by its correct name.

It had been no surprise at all when Andy informed him that the bullet that killed Heinrich Meyer had come from a Walther or a Luger. He'd known it all along, like some sixth sense. A whisper in his ear. Instinct.

He picked up the gun, weighing it in his hand. Made from forged steel, it was heavy by modern standards. The handgun had an elegant design, built to the demanding specifications of the German *Wehrmacht*. The P-38 was a classic, whose design had heavily influenced modern combat handgun development. To Raven's way of thinking, it was an object of deadly beauty.

The pin above the hammer showed that the gun was unloaded. Raven pulled the slide all the way back and removed the empty magazine, laying it to one side. He released the hammer and removed the slide completely from its rails. Finally he eased the barrel from the front of the slide.

When the P-38 was broken down into its four constituent parts he sat back in contemplation. Although there was no ammunition with the gun, the weapon appeared to be in perfect working order.

Was this the gun that killed a German prisoner of war?

And if so, could his own grandfather, Jack Raven, have fired that fatal shot?

Execution-style, in the back of the head.

Raven winced. He had never known his paternal grandfather. Jack had died in a fishing accident in 1955, twenty years before he was born. His boat had capsized in a storm. Raven remembered crusty old sailors from his childhood who had hailed Jack as a hero, raising their glasses to him at every opportunity. Raven had been proud to have a grandfather who was so admired.

But what if Jack was a murderer?

He opened the wedding album and looked again at the picture of Jack and Muriel on their big day. They had married in June 1945, straight after the war. They looked so happy. Two years earlier, Jack had been sent to North Africa from where he'd taken part in the invasion of Sicily. He'd battled his way up the spine of Italy and fought at Monte Cassino. Jack had survived, but must have witnessed terrible losses among his friends.

War changed people. Raven knew that from his own experience. Even if it didn't change their outside appearance, it changed them inside.

And rarely for the better. Raven considered himself lucky to have survived Bosnia with nothing worse than a bullet wound to his leg. Psychological damage was much harder to deal with.

What had the war done to Jack Raven? Had it transformed him from a happy chap into a vengeful killer who had taken the life of a young German freed from a prisoner of war camp?

Raven had known neither Jack nor Heinrich, but they had come to occupy his thoughts almost as much as the living.

The right and proper thing would be to take the P-38 to ballistics. Andy would be delighted to get his hands on a genuine German war artifact. He would check it against the bullet and confirm whether this was the gun that had fired the fatal shot.

Yes, that would be the correct course of action, exactly what any law-abiding citizen should do. Let alone one whose job it was to enforce the law.

But this was personal.

Raven reassembled the gun, then wrapped it back up and returned it to its box. Wincing slightly as he rose from the bed, he hid the box once more at the back of the wardrobe, tossing an old shirt over it to better conceal it.

Jack was long dead. What good would come of branding him a murderer now?

The truth, whispered the voice in his ear. *Don't you want to know the truth?*

He did. But that didn't mean he wanted to share it with the rest of the world.

CHAPTER 23

Dr Chandice Jones dismissed her morning tutorial class by setting her students an essay on identifying and diagnosing the seven types of pathologies affecting the skeletal system. It was to be handed in before the end of term to give her chance to mark it. Her second-year students were a bright group and she had high hopes for them.

She made herself a glass of espresso and returned to her desk where she tried to focus on the pile of first-year essays on Archaeological Theory she was supposed to be grading. But her thoughts kept drifting as they so often did at the moment to DCI Tom Raven.

Raven, to his friends.

Tom.

An enigma.

He wasn't like other men she'd dated who were so keen to impress you with their accomplishments. In fact, apart from one or two details which had slipped out when she had pushed him or he had dropped his guard, he had hardly told her a thing about himself.

Yet Raven intrigued her.

He was a dark horse, not ready to reveal all just yet. She understood that she needed to gain his trust, and for that she would have to exercise patience. That was fine, she was used to being patient. It came with the job. Often people made the mistake of thinking that being an archaeologist was like living in an *Indiana Jones* movie. *How exciting,* they would say, when she told them what she did for a living. Did they think she spent her days outrunning giant boulders or being lowered into pits full of writhing snakes? She would smile and politely change the subject. She knew they didn't really want to hear about mass graves in Bosnia. Or grieving mothers and widows searching for their children and husbands. And they certainly didn't want to be told of long hours spent clearing away sand or brushing off dirt until you were so stiff you could barely stand. But the rewards at the end of the day were tangible: a valuable discovery that would be displayed in a museum, or a positive identification that would allow a family to finally lay their loved one to rest.

If she continued to "chip away" at Raven, dusting off the layers of sediment, scraping away the surface covering that had been steadily accumulated by a man determined to hide himself from view, what would she find underneath?

He was a man clearly passionate about his work, and this was a trait they had in common. They were both obsessives perhaps, dedicated to their respective jobs. Appropriately, it was work that had brought them together. Forge Valley Man – Heinrich Meyer – had begun their relationship, and she was as keen as Raven to unearth the identity of his killer.

A knock at the door interrupted her thoughts.

'Come in.' She expected to see one of her students come back to ask a question. Instead, a man aged about thirty-five with dark hair in need of a trim put his head around the door.

'Dr Jones? I hope I'm not disturbing you.'

'No, not at all.' She was glad of an excuse to put the

first-year essays aside. As she'd anticipated, they were derivative at best. 'What can I do for you?'

The man entered the room and held out his hand. 'Craig Clarkson. You probably haven't heard of me. I write history books, mainly about World War Two and those who served in it.'

Intrigued, Chandice invited him to take a seat. He clearly already knew who she was. She wondered why he was there. Might it be related to the Heinrich Meyer case?

'I understand,' said Clarkson, 'that you're involved in the identification of a skeleton that was discovered recently in Forge Valley Woods.'

'I am, but who told you that?'

'It was reported in the Scarborough News,' said Clarkson.

'Was it?' Chandice was surprised to learn that. She knew that the discovery had been covered by the media but Raven hadn't asked her permission to release her name to the press. And given his mania for secrecy she didn't think he would have mentioned her name to a reporter without first asking her if it was okay.

'Well,' said Clarkson, backtracking, 'strictly speaking, it wasn't made public. But a journalist mate of mine told me your name.'

'Did he indeed?' Already Chandice was regretting having welcomed this stranger into her office. 'What else did your mate tell you?'

'That you're working alongside DCI Tom Raven. He's leading the investigation. Is that right?'

At the mention of Raven's name, Chandice shifted in embarrassment and hoped that she wouldn't give away her feelings. She had no idea what Craig Clarkson wanted from her, but she was determined not to tell him anything.

'I take it from your reaction that you do know DCI Raven,' said Clarkson. 'So, I was wondering what you could tell me about the skeleton. Has it been identified yet?'

'Not as far as I know.' Chandice made no effort to keep

the irritation from her voice, but Clarkson didn't appear to be discouraged.

'What about its age? Is it pre- or post-war, for instance? The bones must have been carbon dated by now. Is that what you've been doing here at York?'

Chandice was starting to thoroughly dislike Craig Clarkson with his intrusive questions. 'If the police haven't disclosed any information, then presumably they feel it's not appropriate to do so at this time.'

'Is there anything else you can tell me about the remains?'

'It's not my place to tell you anything, Mr Clarkson. But let me ask you a question instead.'

'Craig, please.' He gave her a disarming smile, but she refused to be drawn by it.

'Craig, then. Why are you so interested in this skeleton? What relevance does it have to the books you claim to write?'

'I really do write history books,' he said defensively. 'You can look me up online if you don't believe me.'

'Perhaps I will. But you haven't answered my question. Why are you so interested in what the police know or don't know about Forge Valley Man?'

Craig smiled and Chandice immediately realised she'd given away more than she intended. 'Forge Valley Man? That's a good name. Let's just say that I have a personal interest in the case.'

'Well,' said Chandice, endeavouring to bring the interview to a close and get rid of Craig as quickly as she could, 'I suggest that you speak to DCI Raven and put your questions about the murder investigation to him.'

Craig smiled again. 'So Raven is in charge. And the police are treating it as murder. That's very useful to know.'

Chandice grimaced at her latest blunder. Unlike Raven, she had no experience at this kind of subterfuge. She was used to sweeping away mysteries, not creating them. She looked pointedly at her watch. 'Now if you don't mind, I have somewhere I need to be in five minutes.'

Craig studied her face for a moment, as if gauging how she measured up. There was something in his expression that made her suddenly fearful. Would he leave, now that he'd been asked to? And if he didn't, would someone come to her aid if she screamed? She began to wonder how many other people were in the building and how loudly she'd have to scream to make them hear her. But eventually Craig nodded. 'All right. Thanks for your time. You've been most helpful.'

She watched him go, breathing a sigh of relief as he left the office, pulling the door quietly closed behind him. But even though he'd gone, she felt a residual uneasiness that she couldn't shake off. Who was this Craig Clarkson and what was the purpose of his visit? More worryingly, had she given away something she ought to have kept secret?

CHAPTER 24

Raven stood in front of Gillian's desk, bracing himself for further confrontation. It wasn't too late for him to turn around and leave, but he knew he wasn't going to do that. Some things needed to be said.

He seemed to be making a habit of this, but it was better to get these kinds of professional disagreements out into the open so they could be dealt with. Sweeping problems under the carpet wasn't his style.

Unless he was dealing with personal problems, that is. Then his instinct was always to sweep them away.

'You want something, Tom?' Gillian's voice was borderline hostile. Understandable, given the way that he had barged into her office unannounced.

'You ordered me and Dinsdale to work together,' he told her, 'but he deliberately undermined the joint investigation by bringing charges against Troy Woods even though there are still unanswered questions about the case.'

Gillian removed her reading glasses to study him better. She was clearly annoyed by his unscheduled interruption, but was holding her anger in check. 'From what I understand, Tom, he was simply acting on the instructions of the CPS.'

'Yes,' conceded Raven, 'but only because he'd presented them with the case for the prosecution and requested permission to proceed. He didn't tell me he was going to do that. He went behind my back.'

'He was just doing his job, Tom.'

'But he should have come to me first,' insisted Raven. 'That was what you told him, wasn't it?'

Gillian regarded him as if he were a petulant child complaining about some playground squabble. 'Derek played it by the book. He was just following procedures.'

Raven shook his head in mute dissent. So the truth was starting to emerge. Despite everything Gillian had said, she still thought Dinsdale was right about the care home murders. She had just been humouring Raven all along. When she'd instructed the two detectives to work together, she hadn't really expected the joint investigation to bear fruit. She still doubted Raven's line of enquiry. Probably she would give him another day or so before informing him with regret that it was time to bring it to a close and file the death of Heinrich Meyer as an unsolved cold case. He wanted to protest, but what was the point?

'How about you, Tom?' she asked. 'Are you following procedures?'

'To the letter.'

'I'm pleased to hear it. So how is the Forge Valley murder case progressing?'

He resisted the urge to say how much better it would have been going if Dinsdale had been kept well out of it, and if Raven had been given free rein to investigate the care home murders too. 'The thing about Forge Valley,' he told Gillian, 'is that many of the people involved are already dead. That tends to narrow the field of suspects.'

'I'd have thought that was your biggest problem.' Her face registered a degree of scepticism. 'Do you expect to make an arrest?'

'I'll make one,' he promised. 'Just give me a little more

time.'

★

'Let's start with an easy question,' said Raven, leaning against the door of the interview room. 'What were you and Natalia Kamińska arguing about, the day DS Shawcross visited Larkmead and saw the two of you rowing in the garden?'

Troy Woods regarded him sullenly from across the room, where he was seated behind the table. It was the first time for Raven to see the lad face to face. His assessment confirmed the impression he had already formed – that Troy Woods was a small-time crook, potentially capable of murder if forced into a corner, but very unlikely to have killed twice. 'My lawyer says I don't have to answer any more of your questions now that I've been charged.'

'That's correct,' said Raven. 'But if you've got nothing to hide, then perhaps you wouldn't mind indulging my curiosity.'

A sneer spread across Troy's face. 'You're trying to trick me. You just want me to say something that you can use to pin Natalia's death on me.'

'Not at all,' said Raven. 'You see, I don't think you murdered Natalia.'

'What?'

'Nor Raymond Swindlehurst, for that matter.'

Troy's eyes narrowed. 'Why do you say that?'

'Because I'm convinced that Raymond was killed for reasons entirely unconnected with your criminal activities at the care home.'

'Like what?'

'I can't really tell you. Let's just say that it all started a very long time ago, even before you were born.'

Troy fell silent. He seemed to be making a calculation about whether he could trust Raven, and whether anything he said now might land him in further trouble. 'I already told that other detective, Dinsdale, everything I know.'

'Dinsdale maintains that you killed Raymond after he caught you stealing from him. Natalia found out, and that's what you were arguing about. When you discovered that she planned to talk to the police, you killed her too.'

'No!' yelled Troy in frustration. 'That's not what happened.'

'Then tell me what you were arguing about.'

Troy sighed. 'Natalia said she'd seen someone sneaking out of Raymond's room. On the evening he died, I mean. She was convinced that the person she'd seen was Raymond's killer. She wanted to go to the police and tell them what she knew. But I said no. I didn't want the police to start taking an interest in me and Natalia. Not with all the bank cards and other stuff I'd been taking. I told her to keep her mouth shut, that's all.'

Raven nodded. So this was what Natalia had wanted to tell Becca. 'Did Natalia tell you who she'd seen leaving Raymond's room?'

'No,' said Troy miserably. 'I wish I knew, so that I could tell you who the murderer is. But you know, I never even asked.'

★

The old man who opened the door peered at Raven with eyes filmy with cataracts.

'Donald Cartwright?' Raven introduced himself and held up his warrant card. The old man squinted at it briefly then looked away none the wiser. Raven could have been anyone claiming to be a police officer.

'Do come in,' he said. 'Just through here.'

Donald – the sixth man in Raymond's photograph – lived in a modest bungalow on a twisty cul-de-sac at the edge of Malton, right next to an electricity pylon that some thoughtless planning department had allowed to be positioned on the roadside. Raven doubted that such an eyesore would have been given the go-ahead if Vincent Hunter had been living there instead.

He followed Donald inside, taking in the details of the house. The telephone in the hallway was equipped with an extra-large keypad. Next to the phone was a set of house keys. No sign of car keys. Nor had there been any car on the driveway outside. Clearly the ninety-something-year-old man who could hardly see was no longer able to drive.

Donald led him into a small but comfortable sitting room furnished with a three-piece suite in brown velour. On the wall above the mantlepiece hung a painting of a typical Yorkshire landscape – all dry stone walls, grassy hills and sheep. 'Would you like anything to drink, Chief Inspector? Tea? Coffee?'

Raven had no wish to put Donald to any trouble, so he politely declined the offer of refreshments.

'So what can I do for you?' asked Donald once they were seated.

Donald Cartwright was certainly a lot more amenable than his old friend Vincent Hunter.

'I'm investigating the death of Raymond Swindlehurst. He died recently at Larkmead Nursing Home. You were a friend of Raymond's, I believe?'

'I was,' said Donald. 'We grew up in Malton together. But I hadn't seen him for years. I don't get out much.'

'May I show you a photograph?' Raven extracted the photo of the six men on the promenade on Scarborough's South Bay and handed it over.

Donald reached for a magnifying glass that he kept on a side table and peered through it at the picture. 'Goodness me, this picture takes me back. I can't see it so well now, but I remember it being taken.'

'Who took it?'

'Oh, just some jobbing photographer on the seafront trying to earn a living after the war.'

'Which one is you?' Even though Raven already knew the answer.

'That's me there.' Donald pointed to the man standing next to Vincent Hunter, confirming what Vincent had said.

'And the others in the picture?'

Donald took his time, but eventually he named them all: Raymond Swindlehurst, Cyril Stubbs, Eric Roper, Vincent Hunter, Jack Raven.

'How did you know them?' asked Raven.

'We were all Malton men. We'd known each other since childhood. Apart from Jack, that is. He was a newcomer to the group. It was Eric who introduced him to the rest of us. They'd got to know each other in Italy.'

Raven waited to see if Donald would enquire about any possible family connection to Raven himself, but he handed the photo back without further comment.

'Do you remember a German prisoner who stayed on in Malton after the war?' asked Raven. 'His name was Heinrich Meyer.'

'Heinrich? Oh yes, I remember him well. Tall, blond chap.'

'He was engaged to Vincent's sister, Eileen.'

'That's right. The two of them met on one of the local farms. They hit it off. Eileen didn't look twice at any of the local lads after she met Heinrich. So sad that he left her.'

'Do you remember what happened?'

Donald stared into the middle distance, lost in thought. 'I remember it well. It was the strangest thing. One day he was there, and they were engaged to be married. The next, he'd gone.' He clicked his fingers. 'Just like that.'

'Was there any explanation for why he'd gone?'

'He sent Eileen a letter saying that he'd decided to go back to Germany.'

'Did the letter explain why?'

'I never saw the letter myself, but I can tell you that Eileen didn't entirely believe it.'

'What did she believe?'

Donald leaned forwards, as if about to impart some great secret. 'Eileen thought that if Heinrich had gone back to Germany, it was because Vincent had scared him off.'

'Why would Vincent want to scare off his sister's fiancé?'

'He hated them,' said Donald, shaking his head. 'The

Germans, I mean. He spent time in a Stalag over there, you know. Came back a bitter man. So you can imagine what he felt when he realised his sister was going to marry a German. Of course, I don't think he knew then that she was expecting a child. That didn't come out until Heinrich had gone.'

'Did you fight in the war?' asked Raven.

The old man's face became as clouded as his eyes. 'No. They wouldn't have me. Bad eyesight, you see. Even then I was short-sighted. It's just got worse ever since. They sent me to work on the farms instead. I did my bit, even though I'd much rather have gone off to do some real fighting.'

'Did you receive a letter from Raymond Swindlehurst before he died?' asked Raven.

'I did,' said Donald. 'But I have trouble reading.' He indicated his eyes. 'I had to wait for my daughter to come and read it to me. She visits me most weekends. She does my shopping and helps with letters and so on. I'm not really able to do much for myself anymore, I'm afraid to say.'

'So she read the letter to you?'

'That's right.'

'Do you still have it?'

'No. My daughter put it out with the rubbish. I'm sorry. I didn't realise that it was important.'

Raven kept his voice level as he asked, 'What did Raymond say in the letter?'

'He'd written it after seeing reports of the discovery of the skeleton on the news. Raymond seemed to be having doubts about whether Heinrich had really returned to Germany all those years ago. He suggested that perhaps this skeleton might be Heinrich's.'

There was a questioning tone in Donald's voice, but Raven chose to ignore it. 'Why would Raymond think that?'

'I don't know, except for what I told you – that Eileen had expressed doubts about whether Heinrich had really returned to Germany.'

'Any other reason?'

'None that I can think of.'

'What did Raymond propose that you do about the skeleton?'

'I really don't know,' said Donald. 'I think he just wanted to see if I agreed with him that the skeleton might be Heinrich's.'

'Did you write back to him, or phone him?'

'And say what? That skeleton could have been anyone. What reason was there to suspect it was Heinrich? I thought it best to say nothing.'

'The six men in the photo,' said Raven. 'What were you all doing together at Scarborough?'

Donald smiled. 'A visit to the seaside. What young people today might call a "lads' day out".'

'The other men,' said Raven. 'Apart from Raymond, when did you last see any of them?'

'Not for a long time, I'm afraid. Friends have a tendency to move apart over the years. Two of them are dead now – three counting Raymond – and Eric's barely got any of his wits remaining from what I hear. That only leaves me and Vincent.'

'And when did you last see Vincent?'

'I really can't remember. But it must have been years ago. Vincent's not the best company, I'm afraid. Besides, these days I mostly stay in Malton. I no longer have a car so I depend on my daughter if I want to go anywhere.' Donald cocked his head to one side. 'Is there any truth in what Raymond said in his letter? Is the skeleton in the woods Heinrich?'

'I'm afraid I can't comment.' Raven wondered if he was going to get anything useful out of his visit to Malton. Everything Donald had told him simply confirmed what he had already known or guessed.

But the facts still didn't make sense.

How had Jack Raven come into possession of a German pistol? Prisoners of war wouldn't have been allowed to keep their weapons, so the gun couldn't have belonged to

Heinrich Meyer. Raven felt as if he was trying to do a jigsaw with only half the pieces in the box and no picture to guide him.

He decided to push the boat out and take a gamble. 'Did any of the men in the photo I showed you ever own a gun?'

Donald's eyebrows rose up to meet the wispy hair that sprouted from his mottled scalp. 'A gun? Well, I suppose they all had guns when they served in the war. But do you mean afterwards?'

Raven nodded.

'Not to my knowledge. But you never know. This is a rural part of the county. Some farmers keep shotguns. People who go hunting might own rifles.'

'I was thinking of a handgun.'

'I thought they were illegal in this country.'

'They are.'

'Then I really don't know what you're getting at, Chief Inspector.'

Donald suddenly looked very tired and Raven remembered that the man was in his nineties. 'I'll leave you in peace now,' he said, standing up. 'Please don't get up. I'll show myself out.'

CHAPTER 25

Raven had been out all morning, visiting an old man in Malton for no clear reason that Becca could discern. Now he was back, and she found him deep in thought in front of the whiteboard in the incident room. Pinned to the board was the black-and-white photograph that she'd first spotted in Raymond's room. Beneath it he had written six names.

Raymond, Cyril, Eric, Vincent, Donald, Jack.

Some of the names she knew. Raymond was obviously Raymond Swindlehurst, the first murder victim at Larkmead. Eric must be Eric Roper, Violet's old friend from Malton, the one suffering from dementia. Vincent was Vincent Hunter, Eileen's brother. And Donald was presumably the man Raven had just been to visit, Donald Cartwright.

But who was Cyril, and who was Jack?

'Who are these people?' she asked. 'What are you doing with this photo?'

Raven didn't answer her questions directly. Instead he tapped the whiteboard with a marker pen. 'One of these men killed Heinrich Meyer. They took him to Forge Valley

Woods, shot him and buried him in a place where they thought he would never be found. Or perhaps he was killed somewhere else and was taken to the woods afterwards. The other men knew what had happened but kept quiet about it. Maybe they were all in on it together and spent a lifetime covering it up.'

Becca gritted her teeth. Raven could be infuriating at times, perhaps even worse than Dinsdale. 'How do you know that?'

Raven turned to look at her. 'The photo was taken in 1946 at the South Bay. Vincent Hunter gave me the names of the men, and Donald Cartwright confirmed them when I spoke to him this morning.'

His explanation sounded reasonable enough. But Raven had only half answered her questions. 'Okay, but how do you know that one of them shot Heinrich?'

Instead of telling her, Raven turned back to the board and drew a thick black line through three of the names – Raymond, Cyril, Jack. 'These three are dead. That leaves three alive. Eric, Vincent and Donald. Raymond sent letters to two of them immediately before his death. In his letters he suggested that the skeleton found at Forge Valley Woods was Heinrich's.'

'That doesn't prove one of them killed him.'

'Proof?' said Raven, almost to himself. 'No. We still need proof.'

'And who were Cyril and Jack?'

Raven pointed at one of the men in the photo. 'Cyril Stubbs. Born in Malton, 1926. Served in Burma from 1944 to 1945 with the York and Lancaster Regiment. Died from lung cancer in 1982.'

'And Jack?'

But Raven said nothing to that, seeming not to hear her.

Becca shook her head in frustration. Beneath the names of the six men, Raven had also written down "Walther P-38". 'I thought ballistics said the gun that killed Heinrich could have been a Walther or a Luger?'

189

'It was a Walther,' said Raven without further explanation.

'Sir,' said Becca stiffly, 'I don't think you're being straight with me.'

Much as she hated to admit it, Dinsdale's theory that Troy Woods had murdered Raymond and Natalia was much easier to believe than Raven's assertion that the modern-day murders were connected to what happened over seventy years ago and that a nonagenarian serial killer was on the loose, desperately covering up all traces of the historic crime. Dinsdale may be lazy and narrow-minded, but his explanation had the advantage of simplicity. Whereas the fantastical threads of the story Raven was spinning were looking less likely to lead anywhere with each passing day. And Raven wasn't doing himself any favours by refusing to explain his reasoning.

'Are you following the facts, sir?' Becca challenged. 'Or is this just guesswork?'

Raven was only half listening to her. 'Of course I'm following the facts.'

'Then is there something you're not telling me?'

'No, there's nothing.'

But there was of course. There was always something Raven wasn't telling her.

He dragged his eyes away from the whiteboard at last and turned to face her full on. 'So next we need to speak to Eric Roper. Are you up for that?'

'Eric?' Becca pictured the frail old man who had demanded to know if she was going to catch the thief who'd stolen his money. She felt she owed Eric something, if only because she had dismissed his concerns as the ravings of a crazed old man. But whether they would get any useful info from him was another matter.

Still, she was getting so little sense from Raven, she had nothing to lose.

★

In the lounge at Larkmead, a music therapy session was in full swing. A cheerful-looking woman with grey hair sat at the upright piano, gamely bashing out the kind of tunes popularised by Vera Lynn during and after the war. From what Raven could hear, the pianist was an accomplished musician and led the singing in a rich contralto voice. The old folk who had gathered for the session joined in with mixed results. But everyone seemed to be enjoying themselves, and surely that was all that mattered.

'Eric loves singing along to the old songs,' said Judith, who had shown Raven and Becca into the lounge. 'He's always more lucid after one of these sessions. There's another ten minutes left if you don't mind waiting.'

Raven and Becca took seats at the back of the room. *A Nightingale Sang in Berkeley Square* was just coming to an end. The pianist then launched into *The White Cliffs of Dover*, which was clearly a popular choice because the volume in the room doubled.

Raven spotted Violet singing along merrily. She gave them a wave. Eric was sitting at the back of the group and appeared to be asleep, despite Judith's assertion that he loved to join in.

Raven hoped this wasn't going to be a waste of time. Eric Roper almost certainly held the key to unlocking the mystery of who had killed Heinrich Meyer, but whether he would be able to remember any of it or communicate it was another matter entirely.

The final song was the poignant *We'll Meet Again,* which never failed to touch a nerve, and the music even managed to rouse Eric from his slumber. The lyrics of the song spoke of the loss of loved ones. Raven felt a lump fill his throat. There were people in his own life that he would never see again. His mother for one. The song went on to promise reunion in some unspecified time of sunny days and blue skies. Unbridled optimism in the face of stark adversity. It was a good sentiment for wartime. But Raven couldn't bring himself to believe in an afterlife. A second chance at life was too much to hope for.

He glanced across at Becca who was sitting with her head bowed. She'd been unusually quiet in the car. He knew that he'd frustrated her by refusing to answer her questions. But how could he admit that his own grandfather might have been the killer of Heinrich Meyer?

The pianist rose from the piano stool and took a bow. Raven and Becca joined in the applause. After that there was a general moving around. Some people got up and left, others stayed behind to chat. A couple of carers appeared and started rearranging some of the furniture.

Violet came over to say hello. 'Back again?' She nodded at Raven and smiled at Becca.

'We've actually come to see Eric this time,' said Raven.

'Eric? Well, you've come at a good time. The music always perks him up, but you'd better be quick. In half an hour he'll be back in his own little world.'

Raven rose from his seat. 'Then we'd better get started. Maybe you'd like to introduce us?'

'I'd be delighted.'

Eric was sitting in the corner of the room close to a window. Violet took a chair next to him and beckoned for Raven and Becca to join them. 'Eric, Chief Inspector Raven is here to see you. And Sergeant Shawcross too. They have some questions for you.'

Eric lifted his head to peer at his visitors, regarding them through rheumy eyes. It was the first time Raven had studied him close up. The man appeared ancient, his eyes dim, his head bald and spotted. Tufts of grey bristly hair sprouted from his ears and nose, and his eyebrows grew wild and unkempt.

Yet the fine young man captured in black and white at the South Bay so many years earlier was still recognisable, and when he spoke his voice was surprisingly strong and clear. 'Police? What do the police want with me?' He leaned forward, craning his neck. 'What are you going to do about catching the person who nicked my money? Eh?'

'Actually, we've caught him,' said Becca. 'We arrested the man who stole your money, and we'll make sure that it's returned.'

Eric swung round to stare at her. 'Good. It's about time too.'

'Mr Roper?' Raven had the photograph to hand. 'Could I show you an old photo?'

Eric took the photograph in trembling fingers. He frowned at it, as if he had never seen such a thing before. Then he smiled and pointed to the third man from the left. 'That's me.' His finger quivered, then slid to the end of the row. 'And that's Raymond.' Eric looked to Violet. 'Where is Raymond today?'

'Raymond's not here. Concentrate on the photo, Eric.'

'Do you recognise any of the others?' asked Raven.

Eric's gaze returned to the picture. His finger slid across the photo, lingering briefly on Raven's grandfather before settling on Vincent Hunter. 'I know this one. Vincent, that's it.'

'He was Eileen's brother,' remarked Violet.

'Eileen, that's right. Never liked him much. Too angry.'

'What else can you tell us about Vincent?' Raven asked, but Eric's finger was already roaming the photo once more. 'Cyril,' he announced, stabbing at the figure of Cyril Stubbs. 'Whatever happened to Cyril?'

'He's dead,' said Violet. 'He died years ago, Eric. Don't you remember?'

Eric shook his head. His finger was on the move again. It hovered for a second time over Jack Raven and Eric seemed to be mouthing something silently to himself. But then he pointed at the fifth man in the image. 'That's Donald Cartwright. Poor old Donald. I always felt sorry for him.'

'Why do you say that, Eric?' asked Violet.

'He had to stay home during the war, didn't he? There was something wrong with him.'

'His eyesight,' said Violet.

'That's it. Couldn't see to fight. Had to grow potatoes instead.'

Becca leaned in, stretching out her arm to point at the

face of Jack Raven. 'Who's this man, Eric? The one standing next to you?'

This time Eric had no trouble remembering. 'That's Jack. Good old Jack Raven.'

Violet seemed puzzled. 'I don't know him. He's not from Malton. How do you know him, Eric?'

'Jack and I were with the Green Howards. We fought together in Italy. Monte Cassino.'

Raven could feel Becca looking at him, but didn't dare catch her eye.

Eric chuckled. 'He was a right one, was Jack.'

Violet was giving Raven suspicious looks. She had obviously picked up on Jack's surname and realised there was a family connection between the two men. 'What did he do?' she prompted. 'Can you tell us about Jack?'

Eric grinned, his mouth wide and toothless. 'He was always up to something. What we called a spiv. Cigarettes, chocolate... if you wanted something you went to Jack.' He nodded to himself, remembering.

Then suddenly his face changed and he turned to stare at Raven. 'He found a gun!'

'What?' said Violet. 'What are you talking about, Eric?'

'In the monastery, after the Germans fled.'

Raven's mouth felt dry. It was always so unbearably hot in this damn place.

Eric's lower lip hung open, but he had stopped talking.

'What did Jack do with the gun?' asked Becca.

'Kept it. Hid it. Brought it home with him. Like a souvenir. He kept it in his house.'

Raven couldn't stand the heat any longer. He undid his top button and loosened his tie. 'Did you know a German called Heinrich Meyer?'

The old man flinched at the name. He became agitated and started jabbing his finger all over the photograph.

'He shot him!' he shouted. 'He shot Heinrich!' Eric was stabbing the photograph at random. It was impossible to tell who he was pointing at.

'Who shot Heinrich?' asked Raven. If this was going to

be the moment when his grandfather was revealed as a murderer, then he wanted to get it over as quickly as possible. He could sense Violet and Becca also waiting with bated breath.

'Shot him!' repeated Eric. He flung the photograph away and started banging the arms of the chair with his fists. Then he rose to his feet and lunged at Raven. His arms were as thin as sticks but there was strength in his hands. He locked them around Raven's throat and began to squeeze.

Raven grasped hold of Eric's fingers and prised them away. The old man put up some resistance then slumped back into his chair, his head hanging down, exhausted.

'What's going on here?' Judith Holden appeared in front of them, her face a mask of concern. She looked from Eric to Raven. 'Really, this is quite unacceptable. You told me you had some questions for Eric. You didn't tell me how upsetting they might be. I'm going to have to get one of the staff to give him a sedative. And I'm going to have to ask you to leave.'

'I'm very sorry,' said Raven. 'We didn't mean to upset him.'

'Yes, well, you can see the result of your questioning.'

Raven rose from his seat and turned to Violet. 'Thank you for your help.'

The old lady nodded curtly in reply but was distinctly less friendly than she'd been at the start of the visit. Did she think he was the grandson of a murderer? And did she somehow blame Raven for the death of Heinrich, her best friend's fiancé? The sins of the father, or in this case the grandfather, being passed down through the generations.

Becca retrieved the photograph from the floor and handed it to him. 'Sir? We should go.'

Raven nodded reluctantly. He had come here hoping to learn the truth, but was leaving without it, although at least he now knew how his grandfather had got hold of the Walther.

And one further fact was clear. Eric knew exactly what

had happened.

The old man was being restrained by a nurse who was putting an injection into his arm. Violet did her best to soothe him while shooting angry looks Raven's way. And Judith stood with folded arms, waiting for him to go.

Becca was already leaving. Raven followed.

★

Jess had spent an entire day and a night trying to make sense of Scott's message. She had turned it over in her mind, examining it from all angles. She had lain awake in the dark, unable to find solace in sleep. And she had cried for the ending of a relationship that had barely begun. But she was still no nearer to finding an answer. She'd tried contacting him but he had refused to take her calls or respond to any of her messages.

She hadn't known Scott for long, but from what she did know of him, this behaviour seemed totally out of character. More than that, it was plain weird. Jess was no stranger to creepy boyfriends, but nothing she'd experienced had ever prepared her for this.

Lying about a murdered mother in order to get a date.

Scott didn't come across as a guy who would tell lies, even about trivial things, let alone this. And in any case there had been no need for him to invent such an unlikely story. They had already been out on a date – if a walk across a beach could be considered a date – when he told her. No, it made no sense.

I am a liar. My mum wasn't murdered. She's still alive and well.

Well, Jess was a detective and had been trained not to accept statements at face value. If Scott was lying about inventing the story it surely wouldn't take long to find out the truth. He had given her more than enough information to work with.

A woman murdered seven years ago. In Scarborough.

Jess logged into the police national database and

entered the relevant date range together with Scott's surname: Newhouse. Amongst other data the system held records from all the police forces in the country of every person reported as an offender, victim or suspect. She narrowed the search to murder victims in the Scarborough district and hit the search button.

She waited.

The results appeared on the screen and she began to read. There it was in black and white. The body of Caitlin Newhouse, aged thirty, had been found seven years ago with her throat cut. Caitlin was a single mother, and her only son, Scott, then aged fourteen, had been taken into local authority care and sent to live in a children's home. The murder had never been solved.

Jess leaned back in her chair, more confused than ever.

Scott's story was completely true. So why had he lied about making it up?

*

Raven returned home, no longer expecting to find any sign of a start to construction work. He wasn't disappointed. There was none.

By the look of it, Barry hadn't even popped in that day to add more bags of cement to the wall of building materials that was steadily sealing off his front room.

Raven was too tired to care.

He flopped onto the old sofa and stared at the mound of bags and tools that filled the fireplace. He hadn't really known how Eric would react to his questions, but he couldn't say he was too surprised at the outcome. The old man had revealed a few nuggets of information but ultimately the visit had ended in disaster.

Had Raven pushed him too hard? Quite probably.

Eric had been happy until Raven had mentioned the name of Heinrich Meyer. That had been the trigger. He should have left the questioning to Becca. With Violet's gentle assistance, perhaps Eric could have been coaxed into revealing more.

Now it was too late. Judith Holden wouldn't easily be persuaded to let him talk to Eric again, and he had lost Violet as an ally too. He could hardly bring Eric into the police station and interview him under caution. No lawyer would allow it.

Raven mulled over the few facts that he had learned. The Walther P-38 was a war trophy from the Battle of Monte Cassino. Jack had brought it back with him and Eric had known all about it. From what Eric had said about it being a souvenir, it was reasonable to suppose that the four other men in Raymond's photograph had also known of the weapon's existence.

But it wasn't clear what Eric had meant by his outburst. Had Jack fired the shot that killed Heinrich? If so, why? Or had Eric been talking about someone else entirely?

The truth remained tantalisingly out of reach.

Perhaps, as Gillian clearly believed, it would never be uncovered.

Yet there was still a glimmer of hope. If Eric knew what had happened, Raven was pretty sure that Vincent Hunter and Donald Cartwright also knew.

And there was more at stake here than a historic crime. Two more people had lost their lives in recent days. Someone was killing in order to cover up the events of over half a century earlier.

Raven really wanted to talk it all over with someone. He reached for his phone, ready to call Chandice, then stopped. What was he going to say to her? That at last he had a suspect for Heinrich's killer, and it was his own grandfather? That wasn't a conversation that could possibly go well. But if he didn't tell her that, what could he tell her?

Nothing. He had nothing to say to her.

He checked his emails to see if Hannah had replied to his invitation, but there was nothing from his daughter.

There was no one for him to talk to.

He put the phone down and stared once more at the

bags of building materials opposite. The walls were going up all right, and not just walls of sand and cement. The walls were going up in his head.

*

Becca sat at Sam's bedside, unable to get the tune of *We'll Meet Again* out of her head. If only it were true! If only Sam would stir and open his eyes. If only he would talk to her again. A proper conversation, instead of what they had now. Her words falling on deaf ears. Her fingers clutching his unfeeling hand.

Still, she held onto it for all she was worth. If she let go now, she knew she'd be lost.

'You won't believe what Eric said,' she told him. 'He all but accused Raven's grandfather of firing the gun. Or at least I think he did. He was very confused.'

Had Eric really meant Jack Raven was the killer? He'd certainly been in no doubt when he said that Jack found a gun and brought it home from Italy.

Becca wondered how much Raven had already known about the gun. When she'd spoken to him in the incident room, he'd seemed remarkably certain that the gun that killed Heinrich was a Walther. What exactly did he know, and what was he still keeping from her?

Raven had been typically reticent in the car on the drive back to the station and Becca hadn't needed to ask him what he was thinking about. But she'd been reluctant to push him on the matter. How must he have been feeling, learning that his own grandfather had likely shot and killed a man?

If only they could be sure, one way or the other.

But Eric had become too agitated to continue and it would have been cruel and pointless to push him. Besides, Jack Raven couldn't have murdered Raymond Swindlehurst or Natalia Kamińska, and those were the deaths that primarily concerned Becca.

She felt the tears begin as she spoke to Sam. 'So much

pointless killing. Heinrich. Raymond. Natalia. Not to mention the countless millions lost to the war.'

And you, my love, a living death.

She yearned for Sam to respond. Just a flicker of the eyelids. A stirring of the lips.

Anything.

'Sam,' she begged, 'you have to wake up.'

But the only response was the murmur of the machines that were keeping him alive.

She gripped his hand and let the tears fall freely.

CHAPTER 26

There was no doubt anymore. The DNA results had come in that morning. They confirmed that the skeleton found at Forge Valley Woods was indeed that of Heinrich Meyer, former prisoner of war, fiancé of Eileen Hunter, and father of Joseph Hunter. Heinrich had not returned to Germany. He had been shot and his body buried in the woodland on the edge of Scarborough.

Becca and Jess returned to Malton to break the news to Joseph.

Becca was still upset after her visit to the hospital the previous evening. The worst thing was that she felt so alone. At a time when she needed Sam more than ever, he wasn't able to speak to her.

The last time she and Jess had driven to Malton, Jess had invited her to share her concerns. Becca knew that Jess meant well, but she didn't feel able to talk. What was the point of reiterating what she had already said a dozen times to her grandparents, her mum and dad, Liam, and Sam's parents? That the love of her life was lost to her and she was all alone in the world. That she didn't know how she could go on without him.

It was easier to say nothing.

Jess too seemed lost in her own thoughts and they passed the journey in silence. On arrival they parked on Sheepfoot Hill and knocked at Joseph's door.

He invited them inside. 'Would you like a drink?'

Becca hesitated, remembering the green tea incident.

Joseph smiled. 'I've got black tea this time, but only soya milk, and no sugar.'

Becca decided to meet him halfway. 'I'll try that then. Thanks.' She offered him a weak smile in return. She and Jess sat down to wait. There was no joss stick burning today but the scent of incense still lingered in the house. The stone Buddha regarded them inscrutably from the mantelpiece.

Joseph returned after a minute bearing a tray with three mugs. 'I expect you've come about the DNA results?'

'Yes,' said Becca. 'The results came back from the lab this morning.'

He handed out the mugs and sank cross-legged onto his yoga blocks. 'So is it true? Is the skeleton in Forge Valley Woods my father?'

'I'm afraid so,' said Becca. 'I'm very sorry.'

'Thank you for coming all this way to tell me.' Joseph's demeanour didn't change as he digested the news. Maybe this was what a lifetime of yoga and meditation did for you – made you more resilient and able to withstand the knocks life threw at you. 'My mother always said Heinrich would never have willingly abandoned us. She thought he'd been put under pressure to leave. But I don't think she ever imagined that he might have been murdered. At least she was spared that knowledge.'

They all sipped their tea in silence. After a mouthful Becca set hers aside. It really was disgusting.

'Just a moment.' Joseph sprang to his feet with the agility of a much younger man. 'I have something to show you.'

He returned with a yellowed envelope and handed it to Becca. The stamp bore the head of King George VI and the paper was brittle and spotted with age. She thought she knew what this was, but she waited for Joseph to explain.

'This is the letter my mother received, supposedly from Heinrich, explaining that he was returning to Germany. I always wondered if it was a forgery.'

Becca slid open the flap and drew out a single piece of writing paper. She unfolded the letter and read the opening words. *My Dearest Eileen*. The letter went on to express Heinrich's fondness for Eileen and his regrets at leaving. *I must return to Germany. My country needs me*.

'I'm afraid we'll need to take this with us,' said Becca. 'It's now evidence in a murder enquiry.'

'I understand,' said Joseph. A single tear fell from his eyes.

★

'There are three possibilities,' said Raven once Becca had presented him with the letter and explained to him and Tony what Joseph had told them. 'First, this is a genuine letter from Heinrich, written by him and expressing a real intention to return to Germany. And that he was murdered after he sent it.'

'But you can't possibly believe that,' said Becca.

Raven grinned. 'I consider it to be extremely unlikely.'

'So what are the other two options?'

'Second, that Heinrich was forced to write the letter before he was shot. And third, that it's a forgery.'

'So how can we tell which it is?' asked Jess.

'I have an idea,' said Tony. 'Can you show me the letter?'

Becca handed it over and he studied it closely. 'Yes, it's like I thought. Look, there's a reference here to Heinrich's hometown of Köthen, and another one here, but in both cases the writer failed to use the *umlaut* above the "o". No German would make that mistake.'

'So the letter was forged,' said Raven. 'Can you read it again? Aloud.'

He paced up and down while Tony read the letter a second time.

'Wait – read that bit again.'

'*"My country is all I have"*'

Raven snapped his fingers. 'That's it!'

'What?' said Becca.

'I heard something similar very recently. When I visited Vincent Hunter at his bungalow, he was up in arms about his neighbour's plans to build an extension. He practically shooed me off his land with a pitchfork when he thought I was from the council. He said *"My home is all I have"*. For a moment I thought he was going to start spurting nonsense about Englishmen and their castles.'

Becca eyed Raven sceptically. It seemed like a stretch, picking on a single phrase. But if, as Tony said, the letter had not been written by Heinrich, then Vincent Hunter was the obvious candidate. He was Eileen's brother. He hated Germans. He was the most likely person to have wanted Heinrich gone.

Raven was already grabbing his coat from the stand. 'Come on, we're going back to bungalow-city to see what Vincent Hunter has to say for himself now.'

CHAPTER 27

Vincent Hunter did not look pleased when he opened the door to Raven and Becca. 'Now is not a convenient time.' He started to close the door.

Raven put a hand out to stop him. 'Maybe it would be more convenient for you to come down to the station. I can send a police car round to pick you up.' That would certainly get the net curtains twitching. And it would give the neighbours plenty to talk about in between plotting their next moves on the planning application.

Vincent gave Raven a cold stare before making up his mind. 'Very well,' he grumbled. 'You'd better come inside.'

He stepped aside to allow them to enter before closing the door firmly behind them. Whether that was to keep out the weather or prying glances was anyone's guess.

'This way.'

Raven and Becca followed him through to the living room. There, Raven immediately lighted upon a black-and-white photograph that had pride of place on a glass shelf. The image showed seven young men standing in front of a Lancaster bomber. It didn't take Raven long to pick out a very young Vincent Hunter at the end of the line-up. The rear gunner in last place.

'This must be your RAF crew.'

'Aye,' said Hunter. 'From left to right, the pilot, the navigator, the wireless operator, the bomb aimer, the flight engineer, the air gunner, and the youngest – me, the rear gunner.'

'You must have been a strong-knit group.'

Vincent was unable to keep the pride from his voice. 'When you're flying through flak, being shot at from all sides, your life is in the hands of your crew members, and theirs is in yours.' He sneered at Raven. 'But your generation doesn't understand the first thing about war.'

Behind Vincent's back, Becca raised her eyebrows. She was the only person at the station who knew about Raven's time in Bosnia. He'd kept his military service a secret from the others, reluctant to take credit for his war medal, worried that if they knew he'd been a soldier it would worsen his reputation for being strict and difficult to work with.

'Actually,' he told Vincent, wondering if in this case he could use his time with the army to his advantage in breaking through the old man's hostility, 'I'm ex-military myself. I served with the Duke of Wellington's regiment.'

'The Dukes,' said Vincent, a look of grudging respect entering his eyes. 'So you were a soldier?'

'I spent two years in Bosnia and Herzegovina.'

'Then you understand about war.'

'Understand what?'

'That it never truly leaves you.'

The old man was right about that. But if he thought Raven was on his side, or was willing to turn a blind eye to the past, he was wrong.

Murder was murder, no matter who had done it or how long ago.

'Do you mind if we sit down?' Raven didn't wait for Vincent to reply but took one end of the sofa. Becca sat at the other end. Vincent had no choice but to take the armchair opposite.

'So what do you want this time?' The old man's antagonism was back with a vengeance.

'Let me show you something.' Raven opened a black folder and took out the letter that Joseph had given to Becca. It was sealed in a clear plastic wallet. 'Does this mean anything to you?'

Vincent reached for his reading glasses. 'If I'm not mistaken, this looks like the letter Eileen received after Heinrich had run back to Germany.' He peered at Raven over the top of his glasses. 'How did you get hold of it?'

'Your nephew gave it to us.'

'Joseph? He kept it then, did he? All these years. What was he expecting? For his father to come crawling back begging for forgiveness?'

'I think he kept it as evidence.'

'Evidence? Of what?'

'That Heinrich Meyer didn't write the letter.'

Vincent's face screwed itself into a scowl. 'What rot! Of course he wrote it.'

'I don't think so,' said Raven. 'In fact, I think you know who did.'

Vincent tossed the letter onto a side table. 'Nonsense!' But for the first time there was a hint of fear in his eyes.

'How did you feel about your sister being engaged to Heinrich Meyer?' asked Raven.

'How was I supposed to feel?'

'Well, weren't you happy for her? It was presumably what she wanted.'

'I wanted *her* to be happy,' said Vincent. 'Our parents both died in the war, so she was all I had. But no, I wasn't happy she was marrying a German. And neither would you have been if you'd spent time in a German Stalag.'

'Perhaps not,' said Raven. 'But that doesn't justify you killing Heinrich and forging this letter.'

Vincent snorted with derision. 'Killing Heinrich? Forging a letter?'

'We know the letter is forged,' said Raven, 'because of

the missing *umlaut* above the word Köthen.'

Vincent looked puzzled. 'A spelling mistake? That's proof of nothing.'

'The error occurs twice in the letter. No German speaker would make such a simple mistake, especially not Heinrich. Köthen was his hometown. And do you see that phrase about "my country is all I have"? You said something very similar to me the first time I came here – "my home is all I have". And just a moment ago when you spoke about your sister, you said that "she was all I had".'

'Is that your evidence?' Vincent's tone was derisive. 'It proves nothing. What I said was just a figure of speech. Anyone could have said it. The fact is I didn't write this letter and I didn't shoot Heinrich.'

Becca leaned forward, breaking her silence since entering the house. 'Mr Hunter, no one has said anything about Heinrich being shot.'

Vincent turned to look at her, directing as much malevolence as he could muster. 'Shot? Strangled? Drowned? Who cares what happened to him!' He took a deep breath, trying visibly to calm himself down. When he spoke again, his emotions were back in check. 'It doesn't take a genius to work out that the reason you're here is because of the skeleton you found in the woods. You think it's Heinrich Meyer. Maybe you've even done a DNA test and proved it. Fine. But now you come here brandishing a letter, accusing me of forgery, and goodness knows what. Murder? Try proving that I killed Heinrich! Try proving that I owned a gun!'

Vincent swung round in his chair to face Raven. 'But I know who did own one. Eric's friend, Jack. He had a gun, a German pistol from the war. Showed it to us, he did. If you want a murderer, look no further. Jack Raven – he's your killer!'

Raven felt that Vincent was playing him like a pawn. It was hard to sit here listening to the rantings of a bitter old man accusing his grandfather of murder. Raven was glad he'd brought Becca along. If it wasn't for her, he wondered if he'd be able to restrain himself from grabbing Vincent by his scrawny neck and shaking the truth out of him.

As it was, her presence kept him calm. 'Where were you last Monday evening, Mr Hunter?'

'Why do you want to know?'

'Because that was when someone visited Raymond Swindlehurst and decided to end his life by smothering him.'

'You think I did that? I'm flattered you think I have the strength.'

'From what I've seen of you, I think you're more than capable.'

Vincent shook his head. 'Raymond was an old friend of mine. I would never have killed him.'

'Then where were you?'

'I was here watching TV, like I always do in the evening.'

'Is there anyone who can confirm that?'

'My wife would, if she was still alive. But no, it was just me alone. So you'll have to take my word for it.'

'And did you know Natalia Kamińska?' asked Becca.

Vincent thought for a moment. 'That's the Polish nurse who looked after Raymond. What about her?'

'She was killed too. In the early hours of this Monday morning. Where were you at that time, Mr Hunter?'

'Asleep in bed, where do you think?' Vincent rose to his feet, standing straight and tall for a man in his nineties. 'I think we're done here, now.'

'Not quite, Mr Hunter.' Becca passed him a pad of paper and a pen. 'It would be helpful if you could provide us with a sample of your handwriting. If you don't mind, I'd like you to copy out the first few lines of Heinrich's letter. That would help us confirm whether or not you wrote it.'

Vincent scowled at her. But he had no choice. Returning to his seated position, he lifted the pen and began to write.

CHAPTER 28

It was already dark when Raven and Becca left Vincent Hunter's bungalow. In these closing days of November the daylight didn't last long. A steady rain was starting to fall. Raven drove to the rhythmic swish of the windscreen wipers.

Beside him, Becca was unusually quiet, almost withdrawn. He'd expected her to challenge him about Jack Raven and ask awkward questions. He'd already made up his mind that if she did ask, he would tell her. About his own worries and suspicions. About the pistol in the attic. About everything.

Becca of all people deserved to know the truth.

She would be perfectly within her rights to suggest he should step down from the case. Maybe she was planning to speak to Detective Superintendent Gillian Ellis about him. Gillian would not be impressed if she discovered that Raven's grandfather was implicated in a murder that Raven himself was investigating. It was a clear conflict of interest. The best thing would be to raise the subject himself.

'Listen,' he began. 'There's something I should–' His

phone started to ring, cutting him off. He answered it handsfree. 'Hello?'

'Is that Detective Chief Inspector Raven?' A quavery voice filled the car.

'Speaking. Who is this, please?'

'It's Violet Armitage from Larkmead. I hope this isn't a bad time, but you said to call if there was anything...'

'No, not a bad time at all.' Raven was relieved to hear that Violet was still willing to speak to him after the revelations at the care home when Eric had as good as accused Jack Raven of shooting Heinrich. 'I'm in the car with DS Becca Shawcross. What can we do for you?'

'It's Eric.' Violet sounded distressed, nothing like her usual cheerful self. 'He's gone.'

'Gone? Gone where?'

'He's wandered off. Disappeared.'

Raven pulled over to the roadside so he could focus on the call. 'When did this happen?'

'I don't know. He wasn't in the lounge this afternoon, but that's nothing unusual. Sometimes he has a nap in his room. But then he wasn't at tea, which isn't like him because Eric likes his food. I asked Judith where he was and she sent one of the carers to check on him. I overheard the carer telling Judith that he wasn't in his room and she didn't know where he was.'

'What did Judith say to that?'

'She said she would deal with it. I asked her if she was going to call the police and she promised she would, but I don't know if she has. The trouble with Judith is that she never wants to admit when things go wrong. That's why she didn't tell anyone what really happened when Raymond was found dead. And she tried to keep Natalia's death quiet too. Sorry, I know I'm rambling, but I'm just so worried about Eric. After everything that's been going on here...' Her voice trailed away.

'You did the right thing in calling,' said Raven. 'Do you have any idea where he might have gone?'

'Well, when he goes on days out he likes to visit the spa

and also the harbour.'

The harbour! It was well over a mile from the care home to the harbour. Raven exchanged worried glances with Becca.

'Leave it with us, Violet. We're on our way to the police station now. We'll look into it and get back to you.'

'Oh, thank you, Inspector!'

Raven drove off, his mind in turmoil. He was very much aware that he had potentially contributed to this latest development by his questioning of Eric. He had upset a vulnerable man whose state of mind was clearly fragile. And he had stirred the hornet's nest by visiting the other two surviving Malton men, Vincent and Donald. Who knew what train of events he had set in motion?

Was Eric in danger? Where could he have gone, and why? Had someone taken him?

The priority was to find him, and find him fast.

Raven pulled up in front of the station and got out of the car. An icy wind hit him, driving drops of rain like thin needles into his face. This was no weather for an elderly man with dementia to be out. Whenever Raven had seen Eric, he had always been wearing slippers and a thin cardigan. If he'd gone out dressed like that he could die of hypothermia.

Raven and Becca entered the station and found the duty sergeant at his desk. 'Has there been a report of a missing person from Larkmead Nursing Home? A chap in his nineties. Eric Roper.'

'Aye,' said the officer. 'I took the report myself about an hour ago. There's a patrol car out looking for him, but no luck so far.'

It didn't sound to Raven as if the police were pulling out all the stops. A man's life was at stake here.

Becca was clearly of the same opinion. 'The best place to start is at the care home itself. I suggest we drive over and search the grounds, then move out from there.'

Raven nodded his agreement. 'What about the harbour and the spa?'

'It's worth a look, but he could be anywhere.'

Raven turned back to the duty sergeant. 'Can you get us a couple of uniforms to help with the search?'

'No probs, boss.'

'And radio the patrol car that's already out there and tell them to try the harbour. If Eric's not there, go to the spa.'

'Will do.'

'Come on then.' Raven turned to Becca. 'Let's go.'

★

Larkmead was a different place at night. The yews and laurels that enclosed it in a shroud of shadows during daytime now stood like prison walls, an almost impenetrable barrier that blocked all view from the outside. The only light was glimpsed through the cracks between curtains or from the occasional open windows that gazed out into the darkness like glowing eyes.

But if those eyes had seen Eric they were keeping it to themselves.

On arrival, Raven strode through the entrance, Becca in his wake. His leg protested at the sudden turn of speed, but he ignored it, just as he ignored the nurse who insisted that he and Becca sign their names in the visitors' book. 'We're here on urgent police business,' he told her.

Inside too, the character of the home seemed altogether gloomier and spookier at night. The grand staircase that led to the upper floors was mired in shadows. Floorboards creaked as Raven swept along the corridor, Becca scuttling after him, and the very walls and fabric of the building seemed to have come alive, rasping and rattling as the wind outside blew at the window panes and shook the doors in their frames.

They found Judith in her office. 'Chief Inspector? Sergeant? How can I help you?'

'We're here about Eric Roper. We understand he's gone missing.'

Judith seemed reluctant to admit it. '"Missing" is the wrong word. I have someone searching the building right now. I don't think he can have gone far. It's quite possible that Eric's still inside somewhere.'

'Possible, but unlikely. When was he last seen?'

Judith wrung her hands together. 'The last reliable sighting was at lunchtime.'

Becca checked her watch. 'That's over six hours ago. He could be anywhere now.'

'I'm sure he'll turn up.'

'We're not leaving it to chance,' said Raven. 'We're organising a search. We have uniformed officers with us. If you have people searching the building, we'll start outside.' He was already striding away down the corridor. When he reached the exit, he organised the two waiting officers to start looking in the streets around the care home.

'What about us?' asked Becca.

'We'll carry out a thorough search of the grounds. Eric could be far away by now, but we need to start in the most obvious location.'

Outside the main entrance, Raven lifted his chin and looked up at the gothic tower of the home. Raindrops fell freely, soaking his face. If Eric was out there, he would be soaked to the skin by now.

And if someone had taken him… Raven didn't want to dwell on that. He set off across the black carpet of the lawn, sweeping the ground with the beam of a flashlight.

Becca followed, six feet to his side, the light of her torch criss-crossing his.

The earth was sodden and the water seeped into his shoes, soaking his socks and freezing his feet. His leg was always worse in these kinds of conditions. Deep shrubs and tall trees threw long shadows across the grass, and there were plenty of places where an old man might have fallen, but together they scoured the entire grounds, completing a circular lap of the building.

'He's not here,' said Raven. 'He could be anywhere.'

'Perhaps.' Becca was looking up, and Raven followed

her gaze. The grounds of the care home sloped steeply uphill. Beyond them loomed the dark mass of Oliver's Mount, its summit just visible as a black mound beneath a blanket of grey cloud.

'I've got an idea where Eric might be.'

'Oliver's Mount?' queried Raven. 'Why there?'

'I was at the cenotaph on Sunday for the Act of Remembrance. There were several residents from the care home taking part, including Eric.'

Raven had no better ideas. The various search parties would bump into Eric if he was still in the vicinity of the care home, and the patrol car would pick him up if he'd made his way as far as the spa or the harbour. But if Eric wasn't at any of those places, they would need luck or inspiration to find him.

'Get in the car, then. We're going for a spin.'

CHAPTER 29

You could say one thing for Raven. He didn't hang about. No sooner had Becca made her suggestion that Eric might have gone to the war memorial than Raven was driving them up Oliver's Mount at breakneck speed, taking the hairpin bends like a racing driver. Becca clung on tightly to the door handle, hardly able to look. It seemed impossible for her boss to drive anywhere slowly.

'Be careful, you might hit him if he's in the road.'

'I won't hit anyone. Trust me.' Raven stamped his foot on the brake as the BMW swung around another bend. The wheels squealed in protest, but the car clung to the road like a limpet. Becca didn't know how he did it. She would have taken the journey at half the speed, even in good driving conditions. And at night, with rainwater running down the tarmac, the conditions were anything but good.

'Can't you slow down a little?'

Raven took his eyes off the road for just a second. 'Where would be the fun in that?'

Tall trees leaned in on either side as the gradient steepened, shutting out the grey of the sky and making an

216

arch overhead. The car accelerated up the final stretch, the pitch of its engine drowning out the drumming of the rain.

What had Raven told her about the car's engine? Ten cylinders. Five litres. Crazy. The BMW may have been hopelessly impractical on the narrow cobbled streets of the old town, but out here it roared and leaped like a tiger released from its cage. Raven swung it around a one-eighty-degree corner bringing them onto the crest of the hill.

They were on the flat summit now and the faint lights of the town twinkled in the distance far below. After a last race along flat road, Raven braked sharply as the dark needle of the war memorial came into view. He jumped out of the car, Becca close on his heels.

The wind was stronger here, coming in from the sea and driving the weather before it. Lightning forked, and a thunderclap followed immediately afterwards.

Horizontal rain whipped Becca's face.

Raven's black coat flapped around him.

The cenotaph rose before them like a lightning rod, almost touching the ribbon of clouds that streamed overhead. The headlights of the car picked out the base of the column in white relief, the names of the fallen standing out in ranks on a stone plaque. And beneath the steps that led up to the column, a figure moved.

At first Becca couldn't make out what she was seeing. She wondered if her eyes were playing tricks on her.

A man lay prostrate on the grass, his arms and legs moving like a swimmer's.

She took a step closer.

'Mr Roper?' The wind stole her voice away.

Raven shouted too. 'Eric?'

The old man took no notice. He continued to scrape at the ground, muttering something to himself. His fingernails were black with mud.

Becca crouched down beside him, straining to catch his voice above the roaring of the wind.

'Buried,' he murmured. 'Dead and buried.' He turned

to her, his face white with anguish. 'Buried and forgotten.'

'Who's buried, Eric?'

He shook his head violently. 'We should remember the dead, not forget them.'

Raven unbuttoned his coat and draped it over the old man's shoulders, but Eric continued to tear at the grass, oblivious.

'Buried,' he repeated. 'Dead, buried, forgotten. We should have remembered him. We should remember them all.'

Raven took Eric gently by the hand. 'It's time to go.'

At his touch, Eric seemed to give up on whatever it was he was trying to do. His body fell limp and Raven lifted him in his arms. Cradling him like a baby he carried him to the car.

'Sit in the back with him,' said Raven. 'We'll take him to the hospital.'

Becca did as he said, sitting beside Eric and wrapping the coat around his frail body. His hands and arms were shaking with the cold.

'We have to remember the dead,' he insisted as she buckled his seat belt, but Becca didn't know if he was speaking to her. His gaze lingered forlornly in the direction of the war memorial.

She strapped him in and Raven set off, taking the road at a more sedate pace than on the drive up. Eric was asleep by the time they reached the first bend.

CHAPTER 30

Visiting hours were well over by the time Becca and Raven had delivered Eric to the emergency department and waited with him while he was checked over. But for once Becca felt no regret at missing an opportunity to see Sam. Much as she ached to tell him all about her adventure with Raven and hear the concern in his voice, to see him smile or laugh once he knew that Eric had been rescued and was safe, she knew that there was no possibility of those things happening. Instead he would lie there as he always did.

What was the point in relating her story to him, knowing full well that he would make no reply, offer no opinion, not even register the fact of her presence at his bedside?

Instead she asked Raven to drop her at home, glad to be returning to her family.

Sue was waiting anxiously for her in the hallway. 'Becca, where on earth have you been? You look half drowned.'

Becca stole a glance at herself in the mirror and saw that she did look somewhat bedraggled. Her hair was still damp from the encounter with Eric, and her coat was caked in mud. As for her shoes... she slipped them off her feet and left them by the front door to dry.

'I've been up to the war memorial again. But this time to rescue an old man who escaped from the care home.'

Sue's eyes went wide. 'Rescue him? Whatever do you mean?'

But Becca was too exhausted to explain everything that had happened. 'I'll tell you in the morning,' she said, heading up the stairs.

On the top landing she bumped into her dad. He regarded her with a face full of concern. 'Becca, how are you?'

She knew he wasn't only referring to her current dishevelled state. Of all the members of her family, her father had always shown the most understanding about her feelings for Sam. More even than her grandparents.

She lifted her face to his and suddenly it was all too much. A cry escaped her throat, and the next thing she knew she had her head buried in his chest, heaving with great sobs while he wrapped his arms around her.

She cried for ten minutes or more until she felt there was nothing left inside. All that time he held her close, making soothing sounds, never once asking what was wrong. When it was over, she felt oddly calm. A weight that had been bearing down on her for so long, quietly crushing her, had finally been lifted and she felt she could breathe again.

Might she now be finally able to move on from the accident, and place Sam where he must surely remain – in the past?

Dead. Buried. But never forgotten.

At the going down of the sun and in the morning
We will remember them.

The Sam that she had loved before the accident – caring, intelligent, funny, kind, admittedly a bit untidy and chaotic, but generous to a fault – was gone and she knew she had to leave him behind so that she could walk forwards without him. If she tried to carry him with her, he would eventually drag both of them down.

Strangely, the thought no longer aroused feelings of guilt.

Was it even possible that she had clung to Sam not out of selflessness, but because of her own selfish wants?

Because Dr Kirtlington was right. Even if by some miracle Sam woke up, he might be damaged beyond all recognition. Would he remember the things they'd enjoyed together – watching their favourite films, relaxing at music festivals, or eating fish and chips on the seafront? Would he even remember *her*? People were made of their memories, and without them, they were nothing.

Becca held on tightly to her father. 'I have to go and say goodbye to him, Dad. Not tonight, but soon.'

He nodded his understanding. 'When do they plan to turn his machines off?'

'Tomorrow. It'll be one year since the accident.'

'You did your best, love. No one could have done more. If love could have brought him back, he'd be awake right now.'

'I know.'

'Do you want me to come with you?'

She shook her head. Much as she would have liked her father's strong hand to hold onto, she knew that this was something she must face alone. 'Thanks, Dad, but I have to do this on my own. Just me and Sam.'

★

Raven hated hospitals.

Perhaps his antipathy dated from his experience in the field hospital in Bosnia, carried in on a stretcher from the battlefield, his leg bound to staunch the flow of blood, the looks of concern on the faces of the professionals, just one question ricocheting around his head – would he walk again? It wasn't a memory he cared to relive, although PTSD had sent him back to that moment night after night before he had finally made peace with his past.

Then again, maybe his dislike of medical environments had been acquired during his years with the Met, visiting victims of stabbings, gunshot wounds, domestic and sexual violence and good old-fashioned punch-ups.

Or maybe it was simply a perfectly rational fear of sickness, death and human suffering. Not to mention the interminable waiting.

Whatever the reason, Raven hated hospitals. Hell, what sane person liked them?

He was relieved to make his escape after learning from the doctor in charge that Eric would be okay. Shaken after his excursion to the top of the Mount, and more confused than ever, but he would live. For a man in his nineties, who by Raven's reckoning was mostly skin and bone, it seemed that Eric was a lot more robust than his appearance suggested.

It was late when Raven returned home, having dropped Becca off on the way. But it wasn't too late to give Barry a call and demand to know what the hell was going on. Because while chatting to Becca at the hospital, Raven had picked up an interesting snippet of information: Barry was currently working on a job for Liam.

Standing in his front room, in front of the teetering mound of sand and cement, the streetlight leaking in through the window, Raven dialled Barry's number and waited for the builder to pick up.

He didn't have long to wait.

'Raven, mate, how's it going?' Barry was his usual cheery self. Which wasn't surprising, given the outrageous amount Raven had agreed to pay for the work on the house.

But Raven didn't have patience for small talk or pleasantries. 'What part of "real soon now" did I fail to understand?'

'Sorry?' said Barry. 'I'm not quite following you.'

'"Real soon now" is when you promised you'd start work. It's nearly two weeks since you first came to see me. What's keeping you?'

There was a delay before Barry replied. Although not as much of a delay as there had been since his promise to begin work on Raven's house. 'Yeah, don't worry about that. I've very nearly finished the job I'm currently working on. You'll be absolutely next on my list of priorities, I promise. Very near to the top of the list in any case. There's just this one job that—'

Raven cut him off. 'I don't care about your other jobs, Barry. You promised to get the work done for me. I want to see progress by tomorrow at the latest. Not just more stuff delivered' – he eyed the bags of building materials and tools with a furious eye – 'but some actual work happening. Got it?'

'Hey, squire, keep your shirt on. No need to get heavy.'

'Trust me, my shirt is firmly on and I haven't started to get anywhere near heavy. Yet. If that happens, you'll know about it.'

Barry started to say something, but Raven ended the call. If the builder hadn't shown up by Monday at the latest, Raven would be dumping the bags of cement in the road outside. And it would be the very last time he asked Becca for advice or accepted one of her brother's recommendations.

He held onto his phone, needing to hear a friendly voice. His fingers quickly found the person he wanted to hear most, dialling the number that was now at the top of his contacts list.

Chandice's warm tones soothed him almost as soon as she answered. 'Tom, hi. How was your day?'

'Eventful,' said Raven drily. He gave her a brief resumé of the hunt for Eric, culminating in Becca's flash of inspiration, the race up the Mount and the visit to the hospital.

'You've been a hero again,' said Chandice. 'My hero.'

Raven wallowed in the praise. God dammit, it was good

that one person in the world appreciated him. 'It was nothing,' he told her. 'So what about you?'

'I had a slightly creepy visit, actually.'

Raven was back in police mode in a flash. 'What kind of creepy? Who from?'

'From a writer who was very interested in the Heinrich Meyer case.'

Raven's fingers tightened around the phone. 'What did he want to know?'

'He said his name was Craig Clarkson, and he asked all kinds of questions about the identity of the skeleton, the cause of death, who was in charge of the investigation, and so on.'

Raven knew the name. Clarkson was the local historian who Becca had interviewed at the very beginning of the investigation. He was the last known person to see Raymond Swindlehurst alive. Apart from the killer, of course.

'I hope you didn't tell him anything.'

Chandice hesitated. 'I didn't mean to. But I'm used to answering questions, not avoiding them. I may have let something slip.'

'What?'

'That you were the SIO on the case.'

'He knew my name?'

'He did.'

'I hope he didn't threaten you in any way.'

'No, nothing like that,' Chandice assured him. 'The most interesting thing he said was that he had a personal interest in the case.'

'I see. Did he say what?'

'No. I think he enjoyed being mysterious.'

'Well if he shows up again, don't talk to him. And give me a call.'

'Okay. Any news on the case at your end?'

Raven considered carefully what he could tell Chandice. He ought not to reveal more than was necessary. In other words, he should keep his lips firmly shut. Chandice didn't strictly need to know anything. And the less she knew the less she could inadvertently reveal if Clarkson did make a return appearance. But he wanted to give her something. She was invested just as heavily as him in the Heinrich Meyer case.

'I've narrowed down Heinrich's murderer to a list of six men.' He reeled off the first five names of the men in Raymond's photo, then stopped, keeping Jack's name to himself.

Chandice wasn't that easy to fool, however. 'Who's the sixth suspect?'

'I can't tell you. Sorry.'

She paused before responding. 'Okay, I suppose I should be grateful that you've given me five out of six. It's good you're making progress. How confident are you that one of these six is the killer?'

'A hundred percent.'

'Wow. So all you need to do now is narrow it down…'

'Three of the men are dead,' said Raven. 'But Vincent Hunter is very much alive, and he's the brother of Eileen.'

'Heinrich's fiancée?'

'That's right.'

'So is Vincent your prime suspect?'

Raven hesitated. Chandice deserved better than his usual evasive replies. But he couldn't tell her everything he knew. Nor could he mention the ongoing investigation into the two recent murders – of Raymond and Natalia. 'It's complicated.'

'Hmm. Well, here's an easier question. When am I going to see you again?'

Raven smiled. Now he could be open and honest. 'As soon as possible.'

Chandice's laughter danced down the phone. 'What are you doing this weekend?'

Raven didn't need to think. 'My diary is clear at the moment.'

'Well, book a slot,' she told him. 'Book the entire weekend. I want you all to myself.'

'Your place or mine?'

'I thought your place was out of action?'

He glanced glumly at Barry's gear again. For a minute, he'd been able to forget the state of the house and the lack of progress at fixing it. But he'd promised Chandice a night out at the best restaurant in Scarborough and he always kept his promises. He didn't know where the best restaurant in town might be, but he could always ask Becca for a recommendation. On second thoughts, if he asked her, he would probably end up at some joint owned by a mate of Liam's. 'I'll think of something,' he told Chandice.

She laughed again. 'Friday evening, then?'

'Friday. Don't be late. Not if you want me all to yourself.'

CHAPTER 31

Becca woke the next morning with a feeling of dread in the pit of her stomach.

The day had come at last. The anniversary of Sam's accident. The day his life support would be turned off.

Although she had made her peace with the idea, it still filled her with terror. She knew she had to let Sam go, but that didn't mean his passing would be any easier, any less painful. She would feel his loss acutely. He would always be a part of her.

She was due at the hospital later. First she had to get through the day.

When she went downstairs, Sue and David were waiting for her in the kitchen. The looks on their faces told her that Sam was firmly at the front of their minds too.

She was so grateful for their presence she could hardly speak.

'Come and sit down, love.' Sue was clearly prepared to face the impending crisis the way she met every calamity – with food. 'I've cooked a full English for you. All your favourites.'

Becca stared at the huge array of food her mother had produced. 'There's enough for three people here, Mum.'

'Well, just eat as much as you want.'

'Maybe Liam will want some, if he drops in.'

Sue and David exchanged glances. 'We thought it best if Liam didn't call in this morning,' said David.

'We asked him not to come,' added Sue.

'There was no need for that.' Becca would have quite enjoyed her brother's cheeky presence at the breakfast table. It would have taken her mind off everything. But perhaps her mum and dad were right. Liam hadn't always been totally supportive during Sam's long decline. Nor was he the most diplomatic person to have around. Perhaps it was best that he wasn't here.

But how was she supposed to eat this mountain of food? She barely had any appetite.

Sue looked at her hopefully. 'Try a mouthful. A sausage. Some egg, at least. Or I could make you some porridge if you prefer.'

'Let the poor girl make up her own mind,' said David.

Becca pushed the plate away. 'I'm sorry, Mum. I really can't face a thing.'

Sue's face fell, but she rallied quickly. 'Of course, I understand.' She came to Becca and gave her a hug. 'Just look after yourself today. Wrap up warm. Don't work too hard. We'll be thinking about you.'

★

Becca's first stop before going into the station was to call at Larkmead and check on Violet. The old lady had been so upset after Eric went missing, Becca wanted to make sure she was all right.

She was pleased to discover Violet in the lounge sipping a cup of tea.

'DS Shawcross, how nice to see you.'

'Becca, please. How are you?'

'I'm fine. And I hear that Eric is doing well too. Thank

you so much for finding him last night.'

'All part of the job.' Becca smiled. At times like this she sometimes wished she could be back in uniform. Detectives rarely got a chance to do anything as useful as bringing an old man in from the cold and wet. Usually they weren't called upon until after a crime had been committed and their role was simply to find out who had done it. Perhaps she could become a bobby on the beat again and do something to prevent crime as well as catch the criminals.

'I do hope Eric stays put from now on,' said Violet. 'He's not safe to be left on his own. He's like a child, you see.'

'I understand.'

'He sleeps most of the day and wanders about at night. He's like a ghost haunting the corridors. Sometimes he even goes into people's rooms and watches them. It can be terrifying waking up and finding him there. Between you and me, I think Judith finds him a real handful. Well, you've seen for yourself what he's like. I've spoken to her about this before. If you ask me, there should be better security here, but she insists Larkmead is a home, not a prison.'

Becca recalled the manager saying something similar when she'd first visited the care home after the report of Raymond's death. 'I suppose there's some truth in that. And of course it's good that residents can get out and about easily. I've seen the minibus that takes residents into town. It was up at the war memorial on Sunday.'

'Yes, I saw you there. But that's not the problem, you see. Eric has a habit of slipping out by himself.'

'Wait,' said Becca. 'Eric has done this before?'

Violet peered at Becca through her glasses. 'Didn't you know? Why yes, my dear, this certainly isn't the first time Eric has gone out on his own. It's happened at least two or three times before. But as always Judith is in denial. The last time he went missing was on Remembrance Sunday, quite late.'

'At night? What time did he return?'

'Sunday was one of his late ones. I don't think he came back until the early hours.'

Becca could hardly believe what she was hearing. 'An elderly man suffering from dementia is allowed to wander around outside for hours?'

Violet nodded. 'I see that you agree with me. It shouldn't be allowed to happen.'

Becca certainly agreed with Violet on that. But what worried her even more was that Sunday night or Monday morning was the time that Natalia Kamińska had been bludgeoned to death.

★

Raven was looking forward to the weekend. Two whole days together with Chandice, starting this evening. All he had to do was find an expensive restaurant to take her to, and somehow make the house habitable. Not an easy mission, but one he was sure he could manage somehow.

And in the meantime he had another challenge on his hands. To find whoever was responsible for three murders – one historic and two present-day.

Raven gathered his team in front of the whiteboard for a briefing. They were a good bunch. Becca, always dependable, good with people, and not afraid to criticise him. Tony, a stalwart, willing to muck in with the most tedious task, and often making a breakthrough thanks to his close attention to detail. And Jess, the youngest and most enthusiastic member, always keen to get going. Fortunately there was no sign of Dinsdale, the ball and chain around Raven's ankle, always slowing him down and getting in the way. With Dinsdale absent, the job would get done in half the time and with far less aggravation.

'So, let's review all the facts. We'll start with the murder of Heinrich Meyer.' Raven indicated the list of six names on the board. Since his session with Becca, he'd added surnames and pinned a black-and-white portrait, enlarged from Raymond's photograph, above each man's name. 'These six were close friends at the time of Heinrich's death. Five lived in Malton, one in Scarborough. It's my belief that one of them shot and killed Heinrich, and the others helped to dispose of his body and conceal the fact that he was dead.'

The six names were there for all to see.

Raymond Swindlehurst, Cyril Stubbs, Eric Roper, Vincent Hunter, Donald Cartwright, Jack Raven.

Tony and Jess glanced from Raven to the board and then at each other. They had obviously seen Jack's surname and made the obvious connection. But neither made any comment, and nor did Raven or Becca. The silence stretched out, running the risk of becoming awkward, so Raven broke it.

'Raymond Swindlehurst was the second murder victim. I think he saw the news about the discovery of the skeleton at Forge Valley Woods and became concerned that the truth would emerge. The following day he sent letters to his two surviving conspirators – Vincent Hunter and Donald Cartwright – in which he expressed his concerns. Both men destroyed their letters, so we don't know exactly what he wrote, but perhaps he suggested going to the police and making a confession. A couple of days later he was dead. A case of asphyxiation, dressed as suicide.'

Raven pointed to the second name on the board. 'Cyril Stubbs died of natural causes in 1982.' His finger moved to the third name on the list. 'Eric Roper is a resident at Larkmead Nursing Home, where Raymond was found dead. He suffers from dementia, and nothing he says would make a convincing statement in court. In fact he probably wouldn't be allowed to give evidence. However, he clearly knows what happened to Heinrich. When questioned, he stated, "He shot him! He shot Heinrich!" But it was unclear who he was referring to.'

Becca shuffled in her seat and raised a hand to make a comment but Raven waved her question away. 'Let me finish running through the suspects, then you can ask questions and make suggestions later. Now, next on the list is Vincent Hunter. In contrast to Eric, Vincent still very much has his wits about him. He's fit and healthy and lives alone on the edge of Scarborough. Vincent was the brother of Eileen, Hienrich's fiancée, and was opposed to their marriage. During the war he was captured and spent time in a German Stalag. He made no secret of the fact that he hated Germans. I believe that Vincent forged the letter that was supposedly sent to Eileen by Heinrich explaining that he was returning to Germany. A sample of Vincent's handwriting has gone to a graphology expert, but to a casual observer the writing appears very similar to that in the letter. That fact alone suggests culpability for Heinrich's murder.'

Raven pinned both a copy of the letter and a copy of the handwriting sample that he and Becca had obtained onto the board. He was sure that the rest of the team would agree that they had been penned by the same hand, albeit one that had aged many decades between the two documents.

'Vincent is the most likely person to have shot Heinrich. He also had opportunity and motive to kill Raymond and Natalia, and has no alibi for either murder.

'Moving on next to Donald Cartwright, Donald was the only one of the group not to have served in the war. He failed the army medical due to poor eyesight and now has very limited vision. He lives in Malton and depends on his daughter to drive him around and read letters to him. I would say that he's incapable of killing Raymond or Natalia.'

Raven took a deep breath before plunging into the deepest, murkiest water. 'Finally, Jack Raven. Out of all the men listed, Jack was the only one not to have lived in Malton. He was a Scarborough resident but served in the army with Eric. According to Eric, Jack acquired a German pistol during the war and brought it home with him afterwards. It seems likely that this was the weapon used to shoot Heinrich. But needless to say, as Jack drowned in a fishing accident in 1955, he can't possibly be a suspect in the present-day murders.'

Raven breathed out. He'd said what he needed to. Now it was up to the others to see what they made of the facts.

Becca was the first to speak. 'You seem to have decided that Vincent Hunter is the most likely suspect, but I don't think we can rule out Eric. I visited Violet Armitage at the care home this morning and she told me that Eric has disappeared before, at night, and that he often wanders around the care home after hours. Moreover, he was out the night that Natalia was killed.'

Raven frowned at the news. Violet hadn't said anything about that to him. But if true, this certainly changed the situation. 'Then Eric could have murdered Raymond, and also attacked Natalia.'

'We saw him become violent when you questioned him,' said Becca. 'If Raymond spoke to him about confessing to Heinrich's murder, he might have lost his temper and smothered him with a pillow.'

'Yet whoever killed Raymond had the presence of mind to make it look like suicide.'

'It wasn't very convincing though.'

'True.' Raven turned back to the whiteboard and drew a red circle around Eric's name. He also circled Vincent's name. 'So we have two suspects. Anyone else?'

Tony raised a hand. 'Sir, what about Heinrich and Eileen's son, Joseph Hunter?'

Again Raven frowned. 'What about him?'

'Well, obviously Joseph wasn't responsible for his father's murder – he wasn't even born at the time. But the discovery of the skeleton provided him with proof that his father had been murdered. He might then have sought vengeance.'

'And murdered Raymond? That would imply that Raymond shot Heinrich.'

'Or that Joseph suspected him.'

Raven shook his head. 'This seems very hypothetical, Tony. And how could Joseph have got into the care home to murder Raymond?'

Tony wasn't deterred by Raven's criticism. 'I spent some time going through the visitors' book for Larkmead, sir. The day that Raymond Swindlehurst died, Joseph went to visit Violet Armitage. That would have given him the opportunity to slip into Raymond's room before leaving.'

Now Jess spoke up. 'But Joseph seemed really nice when Becca and I went to see him. He took the news of his father's death quite calmly. He didn't talk about vengeance. Quite the opposite. He was all about peace and love.'

Raven considered Tony's theory and the supporting evidence that he'd uncovered. It was typical of Tony to have dug out a detail that everyone else had missed. 'I'm sorry, Jess, but being nice doesn't rule him out as a suspect. We have to consider it a possibility.'

He added Joseph's name to the board and drew a third red circle around it. The number of suspects was growing alarmingly. He might as well see if there was anyone else he'd missed. 'Any other suggestions?'

'Well,' said Becca, 'we have to consider the possibility that the present-day murders are not connected to Heinrich's death.'

'You mean Dinsdale's theory? That Troy Woods killed Raymond and Natalia to conceal his financial crimes?'

'We don't have enough evidence to prove he didn't.'

Raven nodded glumly. Up went the name of Troy Woods encircled in red. He waited to see if any more names would come out of the woodwork, but they seemed to have exhausted all possibilities at last.

'Okay, four suspects to consider, one of them already in custody. Here's what we'll do. I'd like to speak to Eric at the hospital. I'll try not to upset him this time. Becca, Jess, can you go and see Joseph again? We need to pin down his movements and see if he has an alibi for the time of Natalia's death. Tony, you stay here and man the fort. Any questions?'

But for once everyone seemed happy just to do what he

told them. On balance, Raven much preferred it that way.

CHAPTER 32

Chandice Jones loved Fridays. She had no lectures to give and no teaching duties. There were a handful of essays to mark ready for the following Monday, but she could probably squeeze them into Sunday evening, leaving a whole weekend free for her visit to Tom. She was looking forward to finding out which restaurant he considered to be the best in Scarborough, half expecting it to be a fish and chip shop on the seafront. And she was very much looking forward to seeing him in person once again. Phone calls were better than nothing, but they could only take you so far.

She wondered, not for the first time, if she had made a smart move, taking on Raven as a boyfriend. She had done long-distance relationships before, and while York to Scarborough was only an hour's drive – probably less, the way Raven handled his car – it wasn't exactly next door. Besides, he was quite a few years older than her, and while she found him extremely attractive, already there had been a number of occasions when the age gap had led to misunderstandings. Their tastes in music were poles apart, their cultural backgrounds had zero overlap, and their experiences of life were drastically different.

But while these were good rational reasons for breaking off the fledgeling relationship, her heart was governed by feelings, not reasons. She couldn't deny the emotional tug she experienced whenever he walked into a room. Nor the pain she felt when he left.

He had asked her to meet him at his house that evening, and that left her a whole day for reading and research. But before she dived into her work, she decided to check out the writer who had paid her that unexpected and somewhat unwelcome visit the other day.

Craig Clarkson, he had called himself. He'd invited her to look him up online, and so she made herself a cup of coffee, kicked off her shoes and fired up her laptop.

It didn't take long to establish that Craig was a genuine historian. He'd written quite a few books, and some of them looked quite interesting. The format was the same in each case – edited interviews with veterans and civilians who remembered life during wartime. Judging from the number of reviews on Amazon, there was certainly a demand for books of that kind. War memoirs, you might call them, although Clarkson – or his publisher – had eschewed the word *memoir* and chosen titles that were far more attention-grabbing – *True Grit: Real War Heroes of 1945*; *One Woman's War on the Home Front: A Heart-Wrenching Story of Sacrifice and Courage*; *Tank Commander: The Battle of Arras*.

They did actually sound like page-turners.

She clicked on a sample of one of his books and began to read. It didn't take long for her to arrive at the author's bio. Craig Clarkson, born in Scarborough. A graduate of Durham University, who had always dreamed of being a writer. His passion for history and his particular interest in World War Two he attributed to his grandfather, Vincent Hunter, to whom the book was dedicated.

Chandice stopped.

Vincent Hunter was the brother of Eileen, Heinrich's fiancée. Vincent was one of the six men that Raven had identified as suspects.

So this was the personal connection Clarkson had claimed with the Heinrich Meyer case. He was the grandson of one of the key murder suspects. No wonder he was poking his nose into the investigation. Did he know who the guilty party was? Was he afraid that the police were closing in on them?

Chandice reached for her phone and dialled Raven's number.

*

On a good day he could see for miles. Just like that day on Welham Hill, looking back at Malton, the fields stretched out green and yellow and brown like a patchwork quilt. He could recall every splash of colour from that day, every flower in the meadows, every leaf on every tree and hedgerow. The summers had been grand back then, not like now. Real summers, long and hot, and a sky that stretched out as big as heaven, filled with birdsong. This day had been in August of '39, just before the war. The longest, hottest summer of all.

He'd been walking out with a lass that year. What was her name? He couldn't remember now. He would never forget her face though, and that was what mattered. Pretty as peaches, she was. Especially that day, dressed in her cotton frock. And him, in his Sunday best, for it must have been a Sunday, otherwise he'd have been out in the fields himself, working on the harvest.

Ah yes, the summer of '39, all blue skies and cotton dresses. It had been a grand year for butterflies too. He'd known the names of all of them. Peacock, Painted Lady, Red Admiral... a Small Tortoiseshell had fluttered up the hill and landed on her sleeve, making her squeal. 'Don't brush it away,' he'd told her. 'It means no harm.' They'd watched it together, quivering gently beneath the sun, and he'd leaned in and stolen a kiss while she'd been distracted.

She'd shoved him away – 'Get off with you, Eric

Roper!' – but he knew that secretly she'd been chuffed. June, that was her name. A pretty name for a pretty girl. He wondered where she was now.

One of the lads from the town had been sweet on the doctor's daughter. He'd dreamed of wedding her after the war. But she'd chosen another lad instead. Eric told him, 'Lasses are like butterflies, they have wings. They can fly. That's what makes them so beautiful.' But the lad was a fool and hadn't listened to him. That was the thing about fools, they never listened.

It was funny that he could remember so much about so long ago, and so little about what happened yesterday. It was like looking at the world through a telescope. Distant objects clear; close-up all blurry. He had no idea what he'd had for breakfast for instance, although it was probably the same he had for breakfast every day.

Except that something was different about today. He wasn't at home. Where was he?

This place was even noisier than the care home, all hustle and bustle. People dashing about like they had no time for anything. That was the trouble with folk these days. They never took the time to stop and stare. Not like that summer up on Welham Hill.

'Where am I?' he called out to one of the lasses rushing past. 'What is this place? What am I doing here?'

She came over to his bed. 'Mr Roper? Eric? You're in hospital. Do you remember being brought in last night?'

Eric frowned. He could remember nothing. 'In hospital? Whatever for?'

'You were ill last night. You were found out in the cold and the wet.'

He had no idea what she was talking about. 'Well, there's nowt wrong with me now, so you can send me home.'

She seemed unconvinced. 'I'll ask the doctor to come and see you.'

'You do that,' said Eric. 'You do that right away.'

Eric didn't like the home much, but it was better than

being in hospital. He liked it best at night, when the lights were dimmed and the visitors were shooed away. That's when he felt most alive, and he could think. In the daytime he felt so sleepy and confused. Sometimes at night he would go walking and stop in to visit his friends. He would watch over them and check they were safe. Seeing them helped him remember. Sometimes he even remembered their names.

When the doctor came, Eric looked him up and down with dismay. He was far too young to be a doctor, little more than a lad. But he had the look of a doctor about him, that "I know better than you" expression that all doctors wore on their faces. Well, Eric would see about that. He repeated what he'd told the lass, that there was nowt wrong with him and he wanted to go home.

The doctor made some notes on a clipboard. 'Before we send you home, Mr Roper, I'd just like to ask you a few questions.'

'Ask away.'

'Can you tell me what day it is?'

Eric shook his head, making a guess. 'Tuesday.'

The doctor made a note. 'And what's the name of the prime minister?'

'Winston Churchill.'

The doctor's eyebrows climbed halfway up his head and Eric chuckled.

'I know it's not really Churchill. I'm just pulling your leg. But I dare say we'd be better off if he was still in charge. I don't know the name of the current one, they change every five minutes. What does it matter anyway? They're one as bad as another.'

He thought the doctor would make another note on his clipboard, but instead he set it aside and smiled. 'You might well be right there, Mr Roper. Anyway, you seem to have regained your strength after your little excursion yesterday. Mrs Holden has said she's happy for you to return to the care home, and to be honest I think you'd be better off there. There's nothing more we can do for you here.'

Eric nodded. This doctor wasn't as much of a fool as he looked. 'There's nowt wrong with me,' he said. 'I don't know what I'm doing here anyway.'

The doctor went away, and soon another lass came to help him out of bed. Or it could have been the same lass as before. He looked up at her face and smiled. Pretty as peaches, just like that girl he'd known so many years ago, that long, hot summer. What was her name again? He couldn't remember.

★

It was the third time for Becca to drive to Malton with Jess as company, and the oppressive sense of gloom inside the car seemed to have grown with each journey. The imminent switching off of Sam's life support was all Becca could think of.

Fields, trees and houses flashed past in a blur, but she took nothing in.

She was pulling onto a roundabout when a car came at her from the right, its horn blaring, its headlights flashing. Becca stamped her foot on the brake and the Jazz skidded to a halt. The car on the roundabout blasted its horn one more time, the driver shaking his fist and making a rude gesture before driving off.

The Jazz had stalled. Becca gripped the steering wheel, her foot still on the brake, her shoulders shaking with shock.

'You all right?' Jess's voice was gentle and soothing, full of concern.

'I think I'll pull over for a minute.'

She drew the car into a nearby layby and switched off the ignition. She sat there, staring into the distance. More fields, more trees. Some distant houses huddled together against the November cold. What did any of it matter? What was a world without Sam? She thought she had come to terms with a life without him, but the truth had been brought home with a vengeance.

'Do you want to talk about it?' asked Jess.

And Becca found that she did. After a year of keeping it all to herself, the words came tumbling out, faster than she could make sense of them. All her emotions, all her bottled-up feelings. Her vain hopes, her shattered dreams. Now she had started, she couldn't stop.

She knew she had stepped over an invisible line, opening up like this to a junior colleague, putting her vulnerability on display. But in doing so, she understood that Jess was no longer just a colleague. She was a friend.

Perhaps the only friend Becca really had.

Jess held her hand as the words finally came to an end. And instead of offering trite sympathies and platitudes, she sat in silence, giving Becca the time she needed to pull herself together.

'So that's my story,' said Becca at last. 'Now you can tell me yours.'

She listened as Jess told her about Scott. Becca had seen the young CSI guy at work a few times, had noticed his tall, athletic build and tanned skin. But she'd barely ever spoken to him. Scott seemed shy, and when Holly was around, she tended to do most of the talking.

'So he told me the truth,' concluded Jess, 'and then he lied. It doesn't make any sense.'

'It doesn't,' said Becca. 'So there must be more to it. You know what you have to do, don't you?'

'Talk to him again,' said Jess. 'I know.'

The gloom of earlier seemed to have been dispelled. Becca checked her appearance in the mirror, wiping away the tear stains, glad that she didn't wear make-up. If she had, her eyes would have been a right mess by now.

'Do you want me to drive?' asked Jess.

'No, I'll be fine now.'

Becca signalled, checked her side mirror, and carefully pulled back onto the road. It was still another quarter of an hour to Malton.

★

Raven arrived at the hospital wondering how best to tackle Eric. It was clear that conventional questioning wouldn't work on the old man. Although he was convinced that the truth was locked inside Eric's mind somewhere, getting to it would require a more subtle approach than asking outright. The photo had worked before, encouraging him to start talking about the men he had once known so well, but it had also led to the old man's outburst and subsequent breakdown. It was quite probably why Eric had wandered off to the cenotaph at night in the middle of a thunderstorm.

Raven couldn't risk another incident like that.

And yet this might be his best chance of finally finding out what he needed to know. Who had fired that fatal shot? And who was acting so ruthlessly to prevent the truth from getting out? Three deaths already. Raven couldn't afford a fourth.

He showed his warrant card at the front desk and waited to find out which ward Eric had been taken to. 'Eric Roper. Echo Romeo India Charlie. Romeo Oscar Papa Echo Romeo,' he clarified when his initial enquiry yielded no results. 'He was brought to the emergency department last night. I brought him here myself.'

A long battle with the keyboard and mouse ensued before the receptionist admitted defeat. 'I'm sorry. Mr Roper doesn't appear to be on a ward right now.'

Raven fixed her with a hard stare. 'What do you mean?'

After a few more key strokes and an interminable wait – 'The system's really slow this morning' – he was finally given an explanation. 'Mr Roper was discharged twenty-five minutes ago.'

'Discharged? Was he sent back to Larkmead?'

The receptionist bashed at her keyboard for another minute before nodding confirmation. 'That's right. Is there anything else I can help you with?'

But Raven was already stalking back towards the exit.

Outside, he checked his phone and found a notification of a missed call. *Chandice.* Presumably she was phoning about the arrangements for the weekend. It was tempting to call her back immediately and luxuriate in the sound of her warm, soothing voice. But whatever she needed to discuss there was still plenty of time until the evening. He could catch up with her later. Right now, he had more pressing matters on his mind.

Instead he dialled Tony's number and filled him in on what was happening. 'I'm heading over to Larkmead straight away to speak to Eric. If you hear anything from Becca and Jess, get them to give me a call and fill me in.'

CHAPTER 33

The stone cottage on Sheepfoot Hill looked just as peaceful and pretty as before, and the man who answered the door to Becca and Jess had the same serene face as he always did. But was there just a hint of a shadow behind those clear blue eyes?

Becca looked Joseph Hunter up and down, reappraising what she saw. Yes, the kind and gentle expression she had noticed on her previous visits to Malton was still present, but now she also saw the tall, broad-shouldered man who wore it. He was dressed in exercise pants, this time with a vest that showed off his physique to good effect. Muscular despite his years, Joseph moved with an easy agility.

He tilted his head to one side. 'Another visit? To what do I owe the pleasure this time?'

'Do you mind if we come inside?'

'Of course not.' Joseph stood aside, making way for Becca and Jess to go through into the room beyond. There they took their seats on the sofa, the Buddha watching them from its usual position on the mantelpiece. Joseph had been practising his yoga again, judging from the strong smell of incense and the light sheen of sweat on his supple arms. 'Tea?' he enquired.

'Not this time,' said Becca.

Joseph remained standing, perhaps thrown off kilter by the change in tone. He was no longer an innocent in this case, but a suspect. 'So what is it you want? Do you have more news for me?'

'More questions, I'm afraid,' said Jess. 'We understand that you visited Larkmead Nursing Home approximately two weeks ago?'

Joseph didn't seem at all perturbed by the question. 'That's right. I went to see a friend of my mother's. Violet Armitage.'

'Are you a regular visitor?'

'Not really. I've kept in touch with Violet by letter over the years. When I returned to live in Malton I started visiting her. But I've only been to see her a few times. I ought to go more often. She's good company, and I'm sure she appreciates my visits.'

Becca could easily imagine Violet and Joseph sitting down with tea and biscuits together in Larkmead's oak-panelled lounge. 'Do you mind if we ask what you talked about?'

Joseph shrugged. 'A bit about the old days, about people we knew. We talked about Malton as it used to be, and how it's changed. But we also swapped stories about the latest news in our lives. One can't live in the past. It's not good for your mental health. Violet understands that. It's what keeps her outlook youthful and it's why she enjoys seeing people from outside the home.'

'Did you discuss your father?'

Joseph hesitated. 'I don't really understand why you're asking me these questions, but now you mention it, yes we did broach the subject. You see, it was just after the news about the skeleton being found at Forge Valley Woods. Violet had seen the news reports on TV, as had I. It was only natural for us to discuss it.'

'But at that stage you didn't know it was your father's

skeleton.'

'No, I didn't. But I... is *hoped* the right word? I don't know. I hoped for closure after such a long time, although I also feared the worst.'

Jess leaned forwards. 'You feared discovering that Heinrich had been murdered?'

'Exactly. It's a horrible thought, isn't it?' He shuddered.

'So,' said Becca, 'when you visited Violet, you already believed that your father had been the victim of a murder.'

Joseph shook his head, making his long loose hair swing from side to side. 'That's a bit too strong. I *suspected* that he had been murdered.'

'And who did you suspect?'

He fell silent.

'Did you suspect Raymond Swindlehurst of killing your father?'

'Raymond? Is he one of Violet's friends at Larkmead?'

'He was,' said Jess. 'But he was murdered on the day that you visited Violet.'

Joseph's blue eyes widened in horror. 'Murdered? But you can't possibly think that I have something to do with that!'

'Help us rule it out,' said Becca.

'But how can I? How can I prove I didn't do something?'

'Can you provide us with an account of your movements after you left Violet?'

Joseph's eyes were moving rapidly from Becca to Jess. 'I left her about six o'clock, but I don't know if anyone saw me go. I can't prove that I left at that time. Then I drove home. Nobody saw me that evening. As you know, I live alone.'

'When we spoke to you before,' said Jess, 'you told us that you "dropped out" as a youngster. What exactly did you mean by that?'

'I did what lots of young people did in the sixties. You've heard about the Summer of Love, surely? 1967.

We were hippies, we called ourselves flower children.'

'You took drugs?'

'Lots of people used psychedelic substances. It was part of the counterculture of the time.'

Becca stepped in with a piece of information she had uncovered by running Joseph's name through the police database before setting off. 'You were arrested and charged with assaulting a police officer whilst on an anti-war march.'

'I didn't mean to hit anyone.'

'But you're capable of violence.'

He leaned forward earnestly. 'Anyone is capable of violence, but suggesting that I killed someone is abhorrent. I always knew that something had happened to my father. But if you think I spent my life yearning for vengeance, you couldn't be more wrong. I admit there was a period when I hated the town I'd grown up in, I hated the narrow-minded people who persecuted me and my mother, and I swore that I would one day find out what had happened to my father. At that time, if I'd known for certain that my father had been murdered, then I might have done something stupid. But after I went away, my anger quickly cooled. I found peace, and learned to love those who hated me. When I returned, I even went to see my Uncle Vincent and told him that I forgave him for writing that fake letter. He denied writing it of course and threw me out of his house, but I didn't mind. People like him aren't really capable of accepting their faults and admitting that they did wrong.'

'Then who do you think murdered your father?'

At that he gave a wry smile. 'There are two important lessons that life has taught me. One is never to hold onto grudges. Don't allow the past to suck the joy out of the present. Choose love, not hate.'

'And the second?' queried Jess.

'You can never know anything with absolute certainty. So it's pointless for me to try and guess who might have killed Heinrich. I gave up on that hope many years ago.'

*

Chandice hadn't realised that she was capable of driving so fast. It must be Raven's influence rubbing off on her. Fortunately, the road from York had been mostly clear of traffic. On the few occasions when another vehicle had slowed her progress, she had thought of Tom, put her foot to the floor, and pulled out to overtake. She wasn't usually an impetuous driver, but her discovery that Craig Clarkson was Vincent Hunter's grandson had galvanised her into action.

If Craig was digging into the case of Heinrich's murder, it must be because he suspected his own grandfather of being involved. Maybe he even had proof that Vincent had shot Heinrich. And if so, might he try to disrupt the investigation to prevent his grandfather from being arrested? Her mind was caught in a whirl of ideas and hypotheses.

She needed to tell Tom what she had discovered.

Where was he? And why wasn't he answering his phone? She wasn't so reckless as to try and call him while driving, but she had tried three times before setting off and was still waiting for a reply.

She reached the outskirts of Scarborough and slowed down. The town was old, full of Victorian terraced streets that were not built for cars. The police station was located right in the centre, and as she grew closer the traffic slowed to a snarl. She honked her horn in frustration, inching through the jam. Finding herself at a traffic light turning red, she jammed her foot on the accelerator and shot out across the junction, provoking a cacophony of angry beeps. She ignored them, keeping her eyes firmly on the road in front.

She must have broken more traffic rules in the past half hour than in the previous five years. Never mind, she had now reached the police station. She pulled in at the side of the road behind a marked police car. Two uniformed officers were just emerging from the vehicle.

'I'm sorry, ma'am, you can't park here. This is for emergency vehicles only.'

Chandice hurried past them. 'I'm sorry. This *is* an emergency.'

She ducked inside the building before they could arrest her, and found herself at a desk. A duty sergeant was busy with some paperwork. He seemed in no particular hurry to finish what he was doing.

Chandice slapped her hand against the bell on the desktop, making it ring out. 'Excuse me, this is an emergency!'

The sergeant looked up, a resigned expression on his face. 'Yes, ma'am? How can I help?'

'I need to speak to Detective Chief Inspector Tom Raven. It's a matter of great urgency. I'm a forensic anthropologist from the University of York assisting him with a murder enquiry.'

The mention of Raven's name, together with her own credentials and the word "murder" seemed to have the desired effect. The sergeant quickened his pace. 'I'll see if I can find him.' He lifted a receiver.

After a quick phone conversation he asked her to wait, saying that one of Raven's colleagues would be along soon.

Chandice was too agitated to take a seat. Instead, she waited by the desk while the sergeant resumed his paperwork. After a couple of minutes a plain-clothes officer appeared. He was clean-shaven, wore glasses, and offered her a tentative smile. 'I'm DC Tony Bairstow, one of DCI Raven's colleagues. DCI Raven is currently out. May I be of assistance?'

Chandice looked him up and down. The detective appeared helpful and competent, but he wasn't exactly hero material. Right now, Chandice needed a hero, and that meant only one thing. 'Thanks, but I need to speak to Raven in person. Can you tell me where he is?'

CHAPTER 34

Raven sat on the edge of his seat, taking in the lined and wrinkled face of his companion sitting opposite him in the care home. Eric's skin was paper thin, stretched taut over the contours of his skull. His watery eyes were sunk in their sockets, lined with red flecks, and he looked close to death, separated from that other place by only the gauziest of veils. His breathing was slight and his chest rose and fell almost imperceptibly with an irregular pattern. Raven waited, afraid that the old man might take his final breath at any moment, and it would all be over. That Eric's secret would die with him. That it would all be for nothing.

Yet when the old man spoke, it was with surprising vigour. 'There's nowt wrong with me. I don't know why they took me to the hospital.'

'I took you to the hospital myself,' said Raven. 'Last night. Do you remember?'

Eric shook his head in annoyance. 'Why would you do a damn fool thing like that?'

'Because you went outside on your own. You walked all the way up to Oliver's Mount during a thunderstorm.'

251

Eric stared back, clearly sceptical. 'I did?'

'I found you at the cenotaph. You were scrabbling in the mud. Don't you remember anything?'

'The cenotaph…' The word seemed to stir something in Eric's mind. 'The lads, all gone. All those poor lads.'

'You remember them?'

'We have to,' said Eric. 'We have to remember the dead.'

'We do,' agreed Raven. 'We mustn't ever forget them.'

'Buried,' muttered Eric. 'Dead and buried.'

'But not forgotten. Tell me about the men who died.'

Eric turned mournful eyes to him. 'So many dead. Too many to count. I went to visit them, you know. After the war.'

'Was that in Italy? Where you served with the Green Howards?'

Eric nodded. 'At Cassino. They came from all over the world to fight and to die. From England, Canada, Poland, India… thousands upon thousands of graves.'

Raven fell silent. He had lost friends in combat himself. But not in such numbers, such unimaginable numbers. Somehow, men of Eric's generation had faced that horror and come back from it. They had returned to civilian life and carried on, almost as if it had never happened. But they had remembered their dead, year after year, never forgetting.

'We have to remember,' repeated Eric, mirroring Raven's thoughts.

Raven pulled out his much-thumbed black-and-white photograph and passed it to Eric. 'Do you remember this?'

Eric handled the photo as if he had never seen it before. Then he smiled and pointed out one of the faces. 'That's me. Look, I was just a lad.'

'Very good, Eric. Do you recognise the others?'

The old man's finger slid hesitantly across the image. His pale lips moved as he named each man.

Raven reached out and pointed to Jack. 'That's my grandfather. I'm Tom Raven, Alan's son.'

'Jack Raven. He was a right one.'

'I'm sure he was. He brought the gun home. That's right, isn't it, Eric? Do you remember the gun?'

'Gun?'

'Jack found it in the monastery at Monte Cassino. After the Germans fled. You were with him. Remember?'

Slow realisation dawned on Eric. 'He brought it home with him when the war ended. Kept it in his house.'

'That's right. He did. Did he ever show it to you?'

'Oh yes. He liked to show it.' Eric tapped his nose conspiratorially. 'But only to his friends.' He frowned. 'Are you Jack's friend?'

'I'm his grandson. Tell me about his friends. When did he show them the gun?'

Eric's mouth opened in a toothless grin. 'He brought it with him. That day in Scarborough.'

'The day of the photo?' Raven gently nudged Eric's attention back to the image in his hand.

'That's the one. He had it with him the whole time. Bold as brass! That was Jack all over.'

They were edging closer to the truth, but Raven knew that he was about to venture onto thin ice. He would have to tread slowly, one careful step after another. 'Do you remember Eileen? She was Vincent's sister.'

'Oh yes. I remember Eileen all right. She was a sweet lass, a couple of years younger than Vincent.'

'She met a German.'

Eric's brows knitted together. 'What was his name?'

'Heinrich. His name was Heinrich Meyer.'

'Ah yes. I remember now. He was a nice lad. He and Eileen were in love. But when Vincent came home he didn't like it.'

'Vincent didn't like Germans.'

'Not one bit. Then again, he had a difficult time of it. They didn't treat him well.'

'And so he wanted to get rid of Heinrich?'

'Aye, he did. He got a group of us together. Malton lads. Persuaded us to go along with his idea. And Jack came too.'

Raven knew that only a few steps remained now until the truth was finally out. He took them slowly, hardly daring to breathe in case he broke the spell. 'And Jack brought the gun with him.'

'That damn gun.' Eric's face fell. 'It was nothing but trouble. I wish Vincent had never found out about it. I wish Jack had never brought it home. Never found it in the first place.' His hands gripped the arms of his chair, the knuckles white as bone.

'Stay calm, Eric,' said Raven soothingly. 'There's no need to get upset. So you and Jack and the others, what did you do?'

Eric's eyes were fixed on a place somewhere behind Raven's head. He was staring directly into the past. Seventy-five years back in time, and he could see it clearly. 'Vincent had a plan. He managed to trick Heinrich into coming with us. Heinrich trusted us.' He shook his head in anger. 'He should never have trusted us! That was his mistake.'

'Go on.'

'We only meant to frighten him. That was what Vincent said. Frighten him and make him leave Eileen. It was all we planned to do.'

'Is that why Jack brought the gun?'

'It was to scare him off. That was all the gun was for. We never meant to use it.'

Raven opened his mouth to speak but held his tongue. The wrong word now could ruin everything. As long as Eric was speaking, the story would unfold.

'We went to Scarborough for a lads' day out. Five of us, plus Heinrich. There was a bus from Malton twice a day. Tuppence return, that was the fare. We got off at Ayton and met Jack there. As soon as we got off the bus, Heinrich began to suspect. But it was already too late. Jack showed him the gun and we took him into the woods.'

Eric's face was white now and his eyes were open wide as he watched the events he described unfold. 'We walked until we were well away from the main road, then Jack held the gun to Heinrich's chest. Vincent said, "We'll give you a choice. You can run away and go back to Germany, leave my sister behind and never see her again. Or we can end it now, here in the woods. No one will ever know or care. It's your choice." Well, what could Heinrich do? There was no choice. He swore he would go. Vincent made him agree to write a letter saying that he'd decided to leave England. The plan was working. I can't say I liked it, but Vincent was our friend.'

'What went wrong?' Raven didn't want to hear the truth, but he needed to. For his grandfather's sake, for Heinrich's sake, for his own sake.

'He shot him! That was never the plan. We never meant to hurt him.'

'Who shot him, Eric? Was it Jack?'

Eric turned his face to Raven. 'Jack? No! Jack would never have fired the gun. He wasn't a killer.'

Raven breathed a long sigh of relief. It felt like he'd been holding his breath ever since finding the gun in the attic. 'So it was Vincent then?'

But Eric shook his head emphatically at the suggestion. 'No, not Vincent. He never meant it to happen that way.'

Raven frowned. 'Then who?'

'Donald.'

'Donald Cartwright?' Now it was Raven's turn to shake his head. After everything that Eric had recalled, had he got this final detail wrong?

'Donald was sweet on Eileen, you see. When the war came and all the other men went off to fight, Donald had to stay behind because of his eyesight. He was angry about that. Couldn't accept it. But they set him to working on the farm, and so he thought he was in with a chance. With Eileen, I mean. More than that, he was set on marrying her. But then Heinrich came along…'

'And Eileen fell for him instead.'

'I told Donald to get over it and find another lass, but he wouldn't hear of it. So when he saw his chance to grab the gun, he took it.'

'And shot Heinrich. What did the rest of you do?'

Tears began to run down Eric's dry cheeks. 'What could we do? The war was over. You couldn't just go around shooting folk. We would have been hanged if anyone found out!' His chest convulsed as the crying took hold. 'We buried Heinrich in the woods. He was dead. Buried. Forgotten. But you should never forget the dead. You should always remember them.'

His shoulders shook as he gave himself over to grief.

CHAPTER 35

The care home was like something out of a kitsch horror movie. There was even a great gothic tower looming over the edifice. Chandice pushed open the entrance door, half expecting to be greeted by undead wraiths wandering the corridors for eternity, but instead she was met by a friendly nurse.

The place was hot, though. God, it was hot. Why didn't someone turn the heating down? Chandice quickly stripped off her parka and approached the desk. 'I'm here to see DCI Tom Raven.'

The nurse didn't appear to know who she was talking about. 'Is Mr Raven a resident here?'

'No, he's a police detective. He's here investigating a...' Chandice just managed to stop herself saying "murder". Perhaps she was starting to pick up some of Tom's habit of evasion. 'He's here on police work.'

'I'm sorry,' said the nurse. 'I don't know where he is. Have you tried phoning him?'

'About a hundred times!' Chandice was finding it hard to contain her exasperation.

A tiny elderly lady was making her way past the

reception desk. She stopped and came up to Chandice. 'I think I may be able to help you.'

'You can?' Chandice was grateful for assistance from whatever quarter it might come.

'Let me take you to Judith's office. If anyone knows where the chief inspector is, it will be her. She's the manager of the care home, you see.'

'Thank you very much.' Chandice signed her name in the visitors' book and followed the old lady down the corridor.

'My name is Violet. Are you a colleague of DCI Raven?' The old lady peered at her closely and Chandice guessed that she was being interrogated for information. Or gossip.

'I'm working with Raven on an investigation, yes. I'm a forensic anthropologist.'

'Hmm. That does sound important.'

Chandice laughed. 'Really, it's all about old bones.'

'Bones. I see. That would be the Forge Valley skeleton?'

'I can tell that you've been keeping up to date with the investigation.'

'Well,' said Violet, 'DCI Raven never reveals anything, but reading between the lines I'm pretty sure the remains found were those of someone I used to know.'

'Oh, gosh, I'm so sorry to hear that.' It hadn't occurred to Chandice that she might ever bump into someone who knew Heinrich. The idea that Violet may have been friends with the murdered man was horrifying. 'I understand what you mean about Raven though. He never tells me anything.'

Violet scrutinised her carefully and Chandice felt the back of her neck grow even hotter than it already was. She wondered how much Violet had guessed about the nature of her relationship with Raven, and if she might start to ask even more questions, but all she said was, 'Well, he is a police officer, I suppose.'

They had reached an oak door and Violet knocked once before entering. Chandice followed her in, grateful that her interview with Violet had been brought to a close.

Inside the office a middle-aged woman and an elderly man were sitting together on an L-shaped sofa in the corner. The man was about the same age as Violet. The woman, Chandice deduced, must be the care home manager.

'Oh, hello Judith,' said Violet. 'I'm sorry, I didn't know your father was here.'

The old man looked up, squinting through filmy eyes. 'Hello, Violet.'

'Hello Donald. What are you doing here?'

'My daughter's taking me out to lunch.'

'How nice.'

Judith appeared vexed by the interruption. 'Violet, was there something you wanted?'

Violet introduced Chandice. 'This young lady is looking for DCI Raven. You don't happen to know where he is, do you?'

Judith seemed surprised. 'I didn't even know he was here. But if you leave her with me, I'll see if I can track him down.'

Violet turned to Chandice and offered her a dainty handshake. 'It was very nice to meet you. I do hope you find what you're looking for.'

*

After leaving Eric in the hands of a carer, Raven set off down the corridor. He needed time to think through the implications of Eric's story.

If Eric could be relied upon, then it was Donald Cartwright who had shot Heinrich. So it must have been Donald who killed Raymond to prevent him from confessing, and then Natalia because she had seen him leaving Raymond's room.

But that didn't add up. As far as Raven could tell from his visit to Malton, Donald was largely incapacitated by poor eyesight. He couldn't drive. He wasn't even able to go shopping. He was dependent on his daughter for all kinds of tasks. How could he have engineered two murders? There was also no record of Donald having visited Larkmead on the day of Raymond's death.

Could the visitors' book be wrong?

Or was Raven still missing something?

Donald hadn't even been able to read the letter Raymond sent him. According to him, his daughter had read it to him. But if that was true, his daughter must know the truth about Heinrich's murder.

It didn't make sense.

He took the corridor in long strides, spotting a familiar face coming his way as he neared the exit. Violet Armitage.

He broke his stride, wondering if he ought to tell the old lady what Eric had said. The story of Heinrich's death concerned her as much as anyone. As Eileen's best friend she had a right to know the truth. But no, it was better to keep what he had learned to himself for now.

He nodded a brief greeting to her. 'Violet.'

'Chief Inspector, how nice to see you again. Have you been talking to Eric?'

'Yes, but I'm afraid I can't say anything about it now. I'm in rather a hurry, actually.'

'Too hurry to meet an attractive young lady?'

Raven stopped. 'I'm sorry?'

Violet gave him a wink. 'A forensic anthropologist has come looking for you. She seems very nice.'

'Chandice? She's here?' Raven tried to work out why Chandice might have come looking for him at the care home, but could think of no possible reason. They were due to meet that evening for dinner. 'Where is she?'

'I left her in the office with Judith and her father. Do you know Donald? He's another of the Malton crowd.'

'Donald?'

Donald from Malton.

Raven's brain shifted gear again, struggling to process this latest information. There was only one Donald from Malton that he had ever heard of. 'What's his surname?'

'Cartwright.'

Raven stared at Violet uncomprehendingly. 'But Judith's surname is Holden.'

'Well, that's her married name.'

Slowly, Raven's brain began to supply him with the answers he needed.

Judith Holden was Donald Cartwright's daughter. Donald's daughter had read the letter that Raymond sent after the discovery of the skeleton. She knew about Heinrich's murder.

Judith killed Raymond and Natalia to protect her father.

Violet gave Raven a puzzled look. 'I told Judith that your friend was looking for you. If you're quick, they should still be there.'

★

Chandice didn't understand what was happening. Violet had left the office but the manager, Judith, gave no sign that she intended looking for Raven as she had promised. Instead she seemed far more interested in what Chandice was doing at the care home.

'You're a forensic anthropologist? A bone specialist? Are you working with Raven on the Forge Valley murder?'

'Well, yes,' admitted Chandice. 'I work at the university, but sometimes I help the police to date and identify human remains.'

Judith regarded her intensely. 'And is that why you want to speak to Raven? You have news about the skeleton?'

'Not exactly.'

'What then?'

Chandice picked her words with care. She didn't need Raven standing over her to know that the news about Craig Clarkson and his grandfather wasn't something to be discussed openly. 'It's a confidential police matter.'

'Is it, indeed?' The question hung in the air like a threat.

The old man on the sofa cleared his throat. 'Judith,

perhaps it would be best to go and find DCI Raven and let him know that he has a visitor?'

But Judith didn't seem to think that was such a good idea at all. 'Let me handle this, Dad.'

Her words did nothing to reassure her father, and he began to knead his hands together in agitation.

Chandice wasn't the least bit reassured either. She knew she was in danger, but didn't understand precisely how or why. 'Judith, may I ask why you're interested in the Forge Valley case?'

As far as Chandice was concerned, the focus of the investigation was on the six men from Malton that Raven had identified as suspects – although why he'd picked out those six, he had never explained. He'd told her the names of five of the six, withholding the last for reasons of his own. Victor Hunter was the name she had picked up on as a key suspect, but there had also been a Donald on the list.

Violet had called Judith's father Donald.

Was the man sitting on the sofa just a few yards away Heinrich's killer? Despite the sweltering heat of the building a cold shiver ran down Chandice's spine. She began inching her way towards the door.

Judith spotted her movement and seized an object from her desk. Silver glinted as she gripped it in her palm.

A pair of scissors.

Chandice glanced at the door. It was only a few feet away. She could be free in seconds. She dashed towards it, but Judith beat her to it.

Chandice felt a spike in her arm. Looking down she saw that Judith had stabbed her with the tip of the scissors. Blood was running down her arm.

'Judith!' hissed Donald, but his daughter ignored his plea.

'Shut up, Dad. This is all your fault, remember?' Her voice was as cold and hard as the weapon she brandished. She raised it in front of her, directing her next words at Chandice. 'Get away from the door. Move over to the wall, and sit on the floor.'

Chandice did as she was told, stepping slowly away until she felt the solid wall behind her back. She slid slowly down its smooth surface until she was sitting with her legs stretched out in front of her. She held her wounded arm, staunching the bleeding.

Judith approached, the scissors held in front of her. Her father looked on in agitation, but there was nothing in Judith's expression to indicate that she had any doubts about what she was doing. 'Right,' she said to Chandice, 'start by telling me everything you know about the police investigation. And then tell me why you came here today. If you try to escape or if you call for help, I'll cut your throat.'

★

Raven turned from Violet and sprinted back up the corridor. A couple of old ladies tottered towards him on walking frames, but he dodged around them, leaving them tut-tutting behind him. The wound in his leg took the chance to remind him of its presence, flaring up with a jab of pain. He knew that if he didn't slow down it would get a lot worse. Soon it would be hurting like a bastard, but he didn't care about that.

He redoubled his efforts, pushing thoughts of his own suffering aside.

When he reached the oak-panelled door to Judith's office he twisted the handle, but the door held fast. He banged against it with his fist and called out the names of Chandice and Judith, but there was no reply.

He weighed up his options.

If he ran to reception he might be able to find someone who could unlock the door for him. But locating the keys and explaining his need for them would waste valuable seconds.

If Chandice was in the office with Judith and her father, those seconds might cost her life.

There was only one other option that Raven could

think of. He took it.

★

The banging on the door could only be Raven. Chandice wanted to call out his name, but Judith came a step closer, the scissors in one hand, the other pressing a finger to her sealed lips.

Silence!

Chandice clutched her knees with her hands, pressing herself back against the wall. It was an instinctive reaction, drawing herself into a ball.

It was fear.

She had never felt so frightened in all her life.

The pounding on the door ceased and a dreadful hush descended on the office, so quiet that Chandice could hear the thumping of her own heart.

Raven had gone away. The desire to scream and shout returned, more powerful than ever, but when she opened her mouth, her voice had fled.

Judith lowered her hand a fraction, seeming to relax just a little.

Then there was an almighty crash and the solid oak of a door panel cracked down the middle. A second crash followed, and the panel splintered in half and fell to the floor. A hand slipped inside and turned the lock.

Judith cried out, rushing forwards and jabbing with the scissors.

Chandice found her voice and screamed.

But the door flew open and Raven staggered through the opening, only a slight limp to show for his bravado.

Judith retreated to her desk, showing Raven the scissors. 'Come any closer and I'll kill her!' she yelled.

Raven didn't need telling twice. He stayed where he was, lifting his palms to show that he was unarmed. 'There's no need to kill anyone. Let's talk instead.'

★

Raven stood with his back to the door, surveying the scene in the office. Chandice was on the floor, curled up like a child, her eyes alive with fear. A red stain was spreading over her upper arm but she was otherwise unharmed.

Judith stood over her, the sharp blades of the scissors ready to strike.

And behind her sat Donald, looking almost as frightened as Chandice.

Raven could tell from the look of determination on Judith's face that she would carry out her threat if pressured. So his priority was to keep the situation calm.

There were two ways this could go. One in which Raven talked Judith into laying aside her weapon. She and her father would be arrested. Chandice would walk away.

He didn't want to think about the other one.

'Let's talk,' he said.

Judith shook her head. 'There's nothing to discuss.'

'I think there's plenty to discuss.' Raven caught Donald's filmy eye. 'Eric told me what happened with Heinrich. I know that you killed him.'

Donald didn't try to deny it. 'I only gave him what he deserved.'

'Really? Heinrich didn't deserve anything of the kind. You simply shot him in a jealous rage because Eileen chose him instead of you.'

The steel scissors flashed in Judith's hand. 'I can tell that you only know half the story. You're not such a great detective after all, Chief Inspector.'

'Perhaps you would care to enlighten me?' The scenario was playing out just the way Raven had hoped it would. With a little encouragement from him, Judith and Donald would make their confessions. Few people could resist the opportunity to tell their own stories, especially when they had a captive audience. As their words tumbled out, the tension would gradually leak away. A peaceful resolution would ensue.

Just as long as everyone stayed calm.

'That horrible man died because of what he did to the girl,' said Judith. 'Do you really think my father's a cold-blooded murderer? Do you think his friends would have gone along with killing an innocent man?'

Raven stared at her in puzzlement. 'What are you talking about? What girl? What did Heinrich do?'

'Eileen,' said Donald. 'That German bastard, he raped her.'

Judith nodded. 'He raped her and left her pregnant. It's hard enough for a woman to get justice now after being raped, let alone in 1946. But when my father found out what he'd done, he gathered together a group of friends. They decided to take matters into their own hands.'

'We gave him the punishment he deserved,' said Donald.

Raven replayed the story that Eric had told him. There had been no mention of rape. Eric had been very clear that Heinrich and Eileen had fallen in love. Violet had said exactly the same. 'That's not what happened,' Raven told Judith.

'But it was in the letter that Raymond wrote to my father. My father isn't able to read, so I read it for him aloud.'

'What did the letter say, exactly?'

Judith frowned. 'Raymond was troubled by the discovery of the skeleton in Forge Valley Woods. He referred to what he and my father and the others had done in 1946. He expressed the opinion that the police would discover the identity of the remains' – Judith flashed an angry glance in Chandice's direction – 'and start looking for the culprits. He suggested that the four surviving members of the group should go to the police and make a full confession.' Her voice filled with contempt at the notion. 'Can you imagine my father doing that? Can you imagine him – and Eric and the others – standing trial for a murder that took place seventy-five years ago? Not even a murder – an entirely justifiable killing!'

'And did Raymond's letter explain why he and the

others shot Heinrich? Did the letter mention a rape?'

'No. It was my father who explained that to me after I read the letter. He told me exactly what had happened and why he had done it.' For the first time the beginnings of doubt had entered Judith's eyes.

'And that's why you murdered Raymond,' said Raven. 'You smothered him and made it look like suicide to stop him going to the police. And then you killed Natalia too, because she saw you leaving Raymond's room. You pinned that murder on Troy Woods.'

From across the room, a fresh look of terror had entered Chandice's eyes. Of course, this was the first she had heard of the present-day murders. Raven had never mentioned them to her.

Judith didn't deny Raven's accusations. Instead she turned to address Donald. 'Dad, you told me about the rape. You said that's why you shot him. You told me the truth, didn't you?'

The slight hesitation in Donald's reply gave the game away. 'I... I would never lie to you, Judith. You know that, don't you?'

For a second nobody spoke or did anything.

Then Judith moved. With a scream of fury she crossed the room to her father's side. Her arm traced out an arc, a glint of metal in her outstretched hand.

'Judith!' The blade drew a line of red across Donald's arm.

Raven leapt towards her, biting back the pain in his thigh, reaching out to stop her. But he was too late. The blade made a second cut, this time across Donald's neck.

Raven seized hold of Judith's arm, braced for a struggle. But she put up no resistance. Her wrath was directed entirely at Donald. 'You lied to me! You told me a disgusting lie to save yourself. I killed to save you from going to prison. And all for nothing!'

Raven prised her fingers loose and plucked the scissors from her grasp. The metal dripped red with blood.

Donald clutched at his throat. His mouth opened, but

no words came out, only a gurgle. He coughed, spitting blood. But it was a pathetic sight. He had no strength.

Raven lowered him onto his back and applied pressure to the neck wound with his hands. Donald was haemorrhaging blood at an alarming rate. Raven knew that to save him he had to stem the flow. He had once seen army medics treat an injury like this in combat, but had never done it himself. Very quickly his hands were swimming in blood.

'Damn it!' he yelled. 'Someone phone for an ambulance!'

'I'll do it,' said Judith calmly. She picked up her phone and made the call, back in control after her moment of madness. 'Ambulance, please,' she told the emergency services. 'A man has been stabbed in the neck. A severed carotid artery, I believe. Yes, at Larkmead Nursing Home. Thank you.'

Always a manager, she was managing once more.

CHAPTER 36

Raven hated hospitals, yet here he was again. This time it was to see how Chandice was faring after her ordeal at Judith's hand. She had been treated for her stab wound while he had gone with Donald in the ambulance.

He found her sitting in the discharge lounge ready to leave. Despite her dishevelled appearance she still somehow managed to radiate a quiet beauty, even here among the noise and chaos of the emergency department.

He sidled up to her and sat on a plastic chair, acutely conscious that it was his fault she was here. Those missed phone calls... if he'd taken a moment to return them she would never have driven to Scarborough to come looking for him.

'Hi.'

'Hi.'

'So, how are you?'

'I'm fine,' she told him. 'My wound wasn't deep. The nurse cleaned it up and bandaged it, so I'm ready to go home.'

'Good. That's great news.'

'What about Donald?'

'Not so good.' After arresting Judith, Raven had sat in the back of the ambulance watching with alarm as the paramedics worked to keep the old man alive. Raven's prompt action to staunch his neck wound had saved his life, but the bleeding had been profuse. 'He lost a lot of blood, and the oxygen supply to his brain was disrupted. They took him straight into the operating theatre on arrival. He'll live, but the doctors say there'll be serious lasting damage. He'll probably lose the use of one or more of his limbs. He may not be able to speak. He may even end up completely paralysed.'

Chandice digested the news. 'So there's no chance he'll be able to go on trial for Heinrich's murder?'

Raven sighed. 'I don't think that will be possible. There are only three surviving witnesses to what happened – Donald, Eric and Vincent. Donald can't give evidence, Eric's dementia will make his evidence inadmissible, and I don't think Vincent would agree to talk.'

'Vincent. That's who I wanted to speak to you about today. I discovered that Craig Clarkson – the guy who came to visit me in York – is his grandson. So I thought that Vincent was the murderer.'

Raven told her what he had learned from Eric. 'Vincent wasn't a killer. He simply wanted to scare Heinrich away from his sister. He never intended to harm him. I expect that Craig was simply trying to find out what had happened. He is a historian, after all.'

Chandice fell silent, pondering his words. When she spoke again, she sounded downbeat. 'So after all this, there's still no justice for Heinrich.'

Raven tried to push the positives. 'There's justice of a kind. Donald's punishment at the hands of his own daughter was more cruel than any prison sentence. And Joseph will finally learn the truth about what happened to his father.'

'The truth,' mused Chandice. 'That was the first casualty. I should have turned and run at that point.'

'I don't understand what you mean.'

'Don't you?' She turned her dark eyes on him, boring into his and fixing him in place. 'You've never been able to tell me the truth, have you, Tom? Right from the beginning, you told me only what you thought I needed to know. There was always something you held back.'

He started to speak, but she placed a finger over his mouth, sealing his lips.

'I told myself that it was to be expected, because you were working on a police investigation. Of course you couldn't tell me everything. I tried to convince myself that I was okay with that. But I wasn't. I can't live with a man who only tells me part of what he's thinking.'

'If this is about what happened today–' Raven thought again about how he should have played things differently. It wasn't just the missed phone calls. He had put Chandice at risk because he hadn't told her about the present-day murders. She'd had no idea there was an active killer out there, doing their best to cover up the historic crime, leaving a trail of bodies in their wake. She hadn't understood the danger. If only he could have been more open...

'It's not just that, Tom, although I have to say that I've never been stabbed before while on my way to see a boyfriend. It's everything about you. You're unresponsive. You don't share your feelings. I don't know what you're thinking half the time.'

He didn't try to contradict her. He knew she was right. But he would do anything to avoid losing her.

'I could change,' he offered.

'No, Tom. You can't. You're too set in your ways.' She leaned across and kissed him once more on the lips.

He had no answer for her this time. Her words echoed exactly what Lisa had said when she left him.

'Goodbye, Tom.' Chandice rose to her feet and he watched her walk out of his life, powerless to stop her.

★

After the crime scene had been thoroughly inspected and documented by the CSI team, and all the exhibits bagged up and removed, Jess made a bee line for Scott.

He gave her a furtive look and tried to scurry away, but she intercepted him before he could escape. 'What's going on?' she demanded.

'With what?'

'With you and me. Why did you lie about your mother? Why did you tell me she was still alive?'

His shoulders slumped. 'I'm sorry. Really I am.'

She could see the anguish in his face, but she needed him to understand how hurt she'd been by what he'd done. 'It was a horrible trick to play. And stupid. You should have known better than to try and fool a detective. It wasn't exactly hard for me to find out the truth.'

'I'm sorry,' he repeated. 'I shouldn't have lied but I didn't know what else to do.'

'I don't understand. Come and walk with me. Explain what you mean.'

They set off together along the leafy street of Deepdale Avenue, away from the busy road that ran past the care home. One side of the avenue opened to the wide green playing fields of Scarborough College. The other side was lined with large detached houses, and behind them Oliver's Mount sloped steeply up to its flat top.

Scott walked quickly and Jess had to hurry to keep up with him. This wasn't the laid-back Scott she was used to. But after a minute he slowed his pace and began to speak. 'I panicked. It was all going too fast. You and me, I mean.'

'Scott, really? Going too fast?' She wondered if he was joking, but he seemed deadly serious. 'All we did was take a walk together across the sands.'

He took a deep breath in and out, as if trying to calm himself. He really did look like panic was about to take charge of him again.

'Take it easy, Scott. There's no hurry. Just chill.'

'Okay, yeah.' Her words seemed to have the desired

effect. 'The thing is, you remind me too much of my mum.'

'Caitlin.'

'Yeah. You look just like a younger version of her. I don't mean that to sound creepy, it's just the truth.'

'Okay.' Jess realised that Caitlin had been just thirty when she'd been murdered. Barely nine years older than Jess herself. All the same, she wasn't used to boyfriends telling her she looked like their mum.

'And after what happened to Mum... I didn't want anything bad to happen to you. You know, because of me. In case there's some kind of curse that follows me around. Does that sound silly?'

'Well, yeah, just a bit.' Despite everything, Jess couldn't stop a smile from spreading over her face. 'Actually, Scott, it sounds really silly.'

'I suppose it does.' He smiled along with her. A smile suited him so much better than a scowl. It lit up his face, making his eyes dance. 'But you haven't even heard the really silly part yet.'

'Go on,' said Jess tentatively, wondering what on earth could be coming next.

'The really silly part is that I've never had a girlfriend before.'

Now she wondered if she could really believe him. A good-looking guy like Scott? Girls must surely be queuing up to take him out. 'No. Seriously? Never?'

He shook his head. 'I'm a pretty shy kind of guy. I don't really know how to do relationships.'

'I can tell.'

Jess wondered what she was taking on with Scott. A guy in his twenties too timid ever to have had a girlfriend. With a murdered mother. Who looked exactly like her. How weird could it get? 'Is there anything else I should know?'

'Anything weird, you mean?'

'Weird, yeah. Or creepy.'

'I'm not sure. There might be. But if we take it slowly, I'll try to tell you everything. And I'll do my best not to break it off again.'

'You have to do better than that, Scott. You have to promise not to break it off.'

He nodded, timidly at first, then eagerly. 'Yeah. I promise.'

'Okay,' said Jess. She took his hand in hers. 'We'll take it slowly. We can be as chilled out as you like. Like I said, there's no hurry. But if you've never had a girlfriend before there's a lot I'm going to have to teach you.'

'Like what?'

'Like remembering Valentine's Day. Like always sending me flowers on my birthday. Like never telling me my bum looks big.'

He nodded again. 'I can do that. Yeah.'

She nudged him playfully in the ribs. 'I'm just kidding, Scott. I'm not that kind of girlfriend!'

'You're not?'

'Definitely not. But I can tell that you really do have a lot to learn.'

*

Back at the station, Raven was met by Gillian, her stern face moderated for once by a trace of sympathy. 'Are you all right, Tom?'

'I'm fine.'

'Donald Cartwright?'

'He'll live, although if the doctors are right about the extent of his injuries he may not consider that to be the best outcome.'

'And his daughter?'

'Judith? Safely in custody. Her lawyer says she'll plead guilty to two counts of murder and one of attempted murder.'

Gillian seemed to relax a little at the news. 'It's a good result, Tom. Well done.'

He shrugged. If this was a good result he ought to be feeling a lot better than he was. 'You were right about the murder of Heinrich Meyer. No one will ever stand trial for that.'

'Don't beat yourself up about it, Tom. It happened seventy-five years ago. It would have been a miracle if you'd been able to put together a case strong enough for the CPS to take to court.'

She was right of course. She'd been right all along. He guessed he'd just been trying to prove her wrong.

Because of all people, Raven knew that miracles never happened. The best you could hope for in this life was a flicker in the dark from time to time. A brief flicker of hope.

'Go home now, Tom. Take a few days off. Get some rest.'

Rest. No doubt Gillian was right about that too. He should go home and catch up on his sleep, if he could manage to fall asleep after all that had happened. But he didn't feel like resting just yet.

He headed out.

On the way to the exit he encountered Dinsdale. The DI tried to shuffle past unnoticed, but Raven wasn't willing to let him off the hook that easily. 'Got some paperwork to do, Dinsdale? And on a Friday evening too. I hope that having to drop charges for Troy Woods doesn't keep you from getting home for your tea.'

Dinsdale shot him a malevolent look. 'I'm still going to get that bastard on a string of other charges. I wasn't wrong about him. The lad's a villain.'

'Sure, but not a murderer.'

Raven wondered if Dinsdale would put up a protest, try to reclaim some of his dignity. But it seemed that this particular battle was over. Dinsdale put his head down and scuttled away along the corridor, a brown manila file pressed to his chest like a shield.

Raven let him go. He had more important things to do.

★

The smell of salt was strong by the harbourside. Raven

leaned against the railings, watching the fishing boats return at the end of the day. Gulls followed them, hoping to steal an evening meal for themselves. They swooped and soared and filled the darkening sky with their raucous cries.

A boat docked at the jetty beneath him. The crew of three set about their tasks, securing the boat with ropes, unloading the day's catch and hauling their crates ashore.

Raven had seen his father do the same jobs, standing with his hand in his mother's, watching with pride as a young Alan Raven went about his work. But that was before the drinking had begun, or before he had become aware of it. Before the black eyes and the bumps in the night. Before he had come to hate his father.

He had never known his grandfather. Jack Raven had died at sea long before he was born. But now he felt he knew him. A little, at least.

Jack had been a joker. A Jack the Lad. One who had been roped into playing a horrible trick on an unsuspecting German.

But it hadn't been Jack's finger on the trigger when Heinrich was shot. Only Donald could be blamed for that.

Raven set off along the eastern pier. His leg showed him no mercy, but he swallowed the pain and kept going all the way to the end, until the lighthouse on the inner pier was behind him.

He looked out.

The sea was boundless, stretching out beyond the curve of the bay, reaching all the way to the distant and unseen shores of Denmark. Raven pictured the first of his seafaring ancestors crossing those grey waters, coming to a strange land intending to reave and pillage, but deciding instead to stay and settle. An unbroken line of Ravens had followed, their names now lost to time. Alan and Jack were the only ones he knew, and once he had gone those names too would pass out of living memory.

He unbuttoned his black coat and reached into the inside pocket, feeling the cool touch of metal there. A quick glance behind confirmed that the fishermen were busy with their tasks and that no one was watching.

He drew out the gun.

Weighing the Walther one last time in his hand, he wondered how many lives it had claimed. Heinrich's for certain. Perhaps others too. After all, killing was what guns were made for, and this one was a trophy from battle.

If you want peace, prepare for war.

From a hillside far away in Italy it had found its way into his hands. A piece of living history. A link to the past, but not one that he wanted to keep. It had brought no peace, only death and destruction. It was good for nothing now and was best gone.

With all his strength he threw it as far as he could into the waiting arms of the sea. The gun broke the surface with a splash and sank from view. In an instant it was gone beneath the waves and he hoped it would never resurface.

He turned and left the harbour, making his slow, limping way along the foreshore. A walk of twenty minutes that took him forty, and by the end of it his thigh was burning. He reached the Rotunda museum and permitted himself a short rest against its curved stone wall.

The building was of classical design, something of a cross between a Greek temple and an astronomical observatory. In all the time he'd lived in Scarborough he had never been inside. Museums had never been his favourite places, although they were a lot better than hospitals, that was for sure.

He climbed the steps to the entrance and went inside. More steps faced him, spiralling upwards. Well, that was the trouble with rotundas, they were tall sons of bitches. With a wry grin to himself he began his ascent. Before long he found himself amid relics of another age – rocks, crystals and fossils. The teeth of mammoths were displayed in cabinets next to the bones of plesiosaurs. Eventually he reached a darkened room looking through glass at the museum's star attraction.

Gristhorpe Man. A Bronze Age chieftain. According to Raven's loose knowledge of history, that made the prehistoric warrior even older than the first Vikings. Thousands of years old.

Old bones.

Perhaps, Raven reflected, that was why Chandice had been attracted to him. Not despite the age gap but because of it. Maybe he had been less an object of desire, more a subject of scientific curiosity. He chuckled to himself, saluted the old soldier in his resting place and made his laborious way back to Quay Street.

Pushing open the front door, he was startled to discover an intruder in his home. A young lad stared back at him from the kitchen doorway, his eyes as wide as saucers.

'Fuck,' said Raven. 'Who the hell are you?'

The boy said nothing, his lips frozen in astonishment. Then a familiar figure appeared behind him.

'Raven, mate, how's it going?'

It was Barry. Perhaps miracles did happen.

'This is my assistant, Reggie. Reggie, say hello to Raven.'

The lad still seemed startled by his encounter and was unable to find his voice.

'He don't say much,' said Barry, giving the boy a slap on the back, 'and he's a bit skinny too. Not much good at lifting, but I'm training him up. He'll be champion by the time I'm done, won't you, Reg?'

Reg mumbled something and slipped away.

Barry beamed at Raven. 'So, I promised I'd get started, and I always keep my promises. You'll be glad you decided to get this work done, I can tell you. I dare say it'll be a right mess once we start ripping out walls and floors and so on, but when it's finished it'll be worth it. You can be sure of that.'

Raven nodded, relieved that work had begun at last, but uncertain about the destructive forces he had unleashed. If even Barry thought it would be a mess, he couldn't imagine how bad it might get.

Things definitely needed to change though, he was certain of that. The house was unfit for purpose, and so was he. Chandice had told him as much. But at least in Barry's hands the house could be fixed. He wasn't so sure about himself.

On the bright side, Hannah had replied to his email at last, promising to come and stay with him when the house was finished. So that was a prospect he could look forward to. A tangible reward that would hopefully mark a new beginning.

He knew that hope was just a flicker in the darkness. But right now it was all he had.

He eased himself into a chair, allowing his aching leg to rest at last.

★

It was time for the machines to be switched off.

Becca made one last attempt to persuade Greg and Denise to give Sam a little longer, but they were resolute in their decision.

'Do you think this isn't painful for us too?' Denise asked, her face ashen, her eyes red. 'We've been through so much as parents. We just need this to be over.'

Becca could understand their point of view – just. But if Sam had been her son, she would have clung to him forever.

Dr Kirtlington was in attendance, supervising the operation and making sure that everything went as planned.

That Sam dies, as decided.

Becca bit back her anger at the thought. There was no place for negative emotions now. She knew she couldn't change the outcome. The decision wasn't hers to make. These would be her last few minutes in Sam's company and she was determined to make them count.

Unlike Denise, her own eyes were dry. Tears would come later in an outpouring of grief like a rising flood. She couldn't imagine how she would begin to cope without Sam by her side.

'Everything ready?' Dr Kirtlington signalled to the nurse assisting him to step back from the bedside.

Greg threw an arm around Denise, as if in readiness to stop her throwing herself at her son. Yet there was no sign that Denise was about to do any such thing. She and Greg stood together, supporting each other as they braced themselves.

Becca had no one to lean on.

'I'm going to switch off the life support functions now.' Dr Kirtlington moved to Sam's side. First he removed the feeding and hydration tubes that had succoured Sam these past twelve months. Then he turned off the ventilator that had supported his breathing. In its wake, the room fell eerily silent.

'How long will...' Greg's voice tailed away, his question left unfinished.

'A matter of minutes, I expect,' said Dr Kirtlington gently. 'I'll wait outside and leave you alone with Sam. Call me if you need me.'

'Thank you, Doctor.'

Becca was left alone with Greg and Denise. And with Sam.

She moved to his side, pulling up her usual chair. Normally when she came to him she had lots of news to tell him. Today she had nothing. She sat in silence, the only sound the gentle beeping of the heart monitor, the only movement the continued rhythm of the monitor displays. So far none of Sam's vital signs had stopped. His heart, his breathing, his pulse rate were all still normal.

If she closed her eyes she could convince herself that he might live.

In the silence, a bar of music came to mind. It was the song the Larkmead residents had been singing when Becca and Raven had gone to see Eric.

We'll Meet Again.

The tune had taken firm root in her head.

Playing familiar music to Sam had done nothing to rouse him. Perhaps something new would have an effect.

She searched for it on her phone and set it to play.

'What's this?' asked Greg.

'One final song.'

Ed Sheeran had provided the opening music for her and Sam's relationship. Now Vera Lynn would supply their swansong.

Denise stood up. 'I can't bear this.'

Greg reached for her hand, but she dashed out of the room, her eyes swimming with tears.

'You should go with her,' said Becca.

Greg hesitated then followed his wife, leaving Becca alone with Sam.

She held onto his hand, determined not to let go until it was over. 'I'm not leaving you, Sam,' she promised. 'Don't worry. I'm not going anywhere.'

She let the song play until Vera Lynn's voice came to an end, leaving only a bittersweet echo behind.

'Do you remember that time we first met?' she asked him. It was one of her favourite stories, one she had recounted to him often during the past twelve months. 'It was a lovely hot day in July. I was sitting on the sand, down on the South Bay with Mum. We didn't usually go there. It gets far too crowded in the summer. Normally we stay on the North Bay if we ever get time to go to the beach at all, but it was hot, and Mum wanted to sit there and eat an ice cream, so we did.'

Talking about that day, Becca could taste the sweet vanilla on her tongue, smell the biscuity flavour of the cone, the tang of salt in the air, the scent of suncream on pale, red and bronzed skin. She could hear the cries of children, feel the heat of the sun on her face.

'The tide was coming in, pushing families further and further up the beach. People were packing up their deckchairs, rolling their towels, gathering together all their belongings and retreating into a smaller and smaller area of sand. The usual chaos of the holiday season. And there was one little boy, standing on top of his sandcastle as the sea came in. The waves came rushing past, cutting him off and leaving him stranded on top of his little castle. I waited for his mum or dad to come and rescue him, but they didn't. So I got up and hurried over to him, and as I was almost there, you came from out of nowhere and scooped him up in your arms just before a big wave came crashing in and washed right over his castle.'

Despite herself, Becca felt herself smiling. 'I said to you, "What are you thinking of, leaving a small child alone on the beach like that? You ought to take better care of your boy." And you just stood there, a perplexed smile on your face. "I thought you were his mum," you told me. "I was just about to hand him over to you." And then the little boy said, "I wish you were my mum and dad." But then his real mum arrived, all shouts and curses, and snatched him back, not a thank you or a smile or anything. And we just looked at each other and laughed, and I thought, this guy is so kind. He really would make a perfect dad.' Becca blushed. 'I never did tell you that last bit, did I? It was my secret.'

She looked down and could hardly believe what she saw.

Sam's chest was moving, calmly rising and falling just like the sea on that hot summer's day. How was that possible? The ventilator was off. He shouldn't be breathing at all.

The heart rate monitor continued to beep, sending out a steady rhythm.

Becca's own heart quickened. 'Sam?'

His eyelashes flickered. But that was impossible. It must be her imagination or a trick of the light.

But there it was again.

'Sam?'

His fingers moved, gripping hers. A steady increase in pressure against her skin.

'Sam!'

His eyelids fluttered and opened slowly like the unfurling of a flower. He blinked. Once, twice, three times. Then turned to look at her.

His voice was weak, barely more than a croak. 'Becca?'

'Oh my God, Sam!' She wrapped her arms around him, scared of damaging him if she held on too tightly. He was a butterfly emerging from a chrysalis, a chick leaving its egg to spread its wings for the first time. New life. The most fragile and precious of treasures.

Tears began to trickle down her cheeks. 'I thought I'd never see you again,' she sobbed. 'After the accident, I thought I'd never hear your voice.'

A shadow passed across his face at mention of the accident. He shook his head very gently from side to side. 'Accident?'

'What about it, Sam?'

'It wasn't an accident. Someone tried to kill me.'

THE DYING OF THE YEAR
(TOM RAVEN #3)

A hit and run. A suspicious death. A vendetta.

Sam Earnshaw's recovery from a year-long coma should be an occasion for celebration. Instead, he reveals that the hit and run incident that left him close to death was no accident. Someone deliberately pushed him into the path of a speeding vehicle.

As DCI Tom Raven leads the investigation into the attempted murder, he soon uncovers a web of dark secrets and lies. The attempt on Sam's life is not the first time a killer has struck.

And it won't be the last.

As the bodies mount up, Raven is forced into a race against time, whilst facing serious questions about his own life and future.

Set on the North Yorkshire coast, the Tom Raven series is perfect for fans of LJ Ross, JD Kirk, Simon McCleave, and British crime fiction.

THANK YOU FOR READING

We hope you enjoyed this book. If you did, then we would be very grateful if you would please take a moment to leave a review online. Thank you.

TOM RAVEN SERIES

Tom Raven® is a registered trademark of Landmark Internet Ltd.
The Landscape of Death (Tom Raven #1)
Beneath Cold Earth (Tom Raven #2)
The Dying of the Year (Tom Raven #3)
Deep into that Darkness (Tom Raven #4)

BRIDGET HART SERIES

Bridget Hart® is a registered trademark of Landmark Internet Ltd.
Aspire to Die (Bridget Hart #1)
Killing by Numbers (Bridget Hart #2)
Do No Evil (Bridget Hart #3)
In Love and Murder (Bridget Hart #4)
A Darkly Shining Star (Bridget Hart #5)
Preface to Murder (Bridget Hart #6)
Toll for the Dead (Bridget Hart #7)

PSYCHOLOGICAL THRILLERS

The Red Room

ABOUT THE AUTHOR

M S Morris is the pseudonym for the writing partnership of Margarita and Steve Morris. They are married and live in Oxfordshire. They have two grown-up children.

Find out more at msmorrisbooks.com where you can join our mailing list, or follow us on Facebook at facebook.com/msmorrisbooks.

Made in United States
North Haven, CT
12 October 2023

42648319R00178